PLANNING

Perfect

Also by Haley Neil

Once More with Chutzpah

PLANNING

Perfect

HALEY NEIL

BLOOMSBURY

NEW YORK   LONDON   OXFORD   NEW DELHI   SYDNEY

BLOOMSBURY YA
Bloomsbury Publishing Inc., part of Bloomsbury Publishing Plc
1385 Broadway, New York, NY 10018

BLOOMSBURY and the Diana logo are trademarks of Bloomsbury Publishing Plc

First published in the United States of America in February 2023 by Bloomsbury YA

Text copyright © 2023 by Haley Neil

Bloomsbury books may be purchased for business or promotional use.
For information on bulk purchases please contact Macmillan Corporate and
Premium Sales Department at specialmarkets@macmillan.com

Library of Congress Cataloging-in-Publication Data
Names: Neil, Haley, author.
Title: Planning perfect / by Haley Neil.
Description: New York: Bloomsbury Children's Books, 2023.
Summary: Summer vacation quickly becomes complicated for Felicity Becker as she
tries to plan a perfect wedding for her mom, figure out her feelings for her friend Nancy,
and wonder what dating will look like for her as an asexual person.
Identifiers: LCCN 2022024693 (print) | LCCN 2022024694 (e-book)
ISBN 978-1-5476-0749-5 (hardcover) • ISBN 978-1-5476-0874-4 (e-book)
Subjects: CYAC: Asexual people—Fiction. | LGBTQ+ people—Fiction. | Mothers and
daughters—Fiction. | Dating—Fiction. | Jews—Fiction. | LCGFT: Novels.
Classification: LCC PZ7.1.N3965 Pl 2023 (print) | LCC PZ7.1.N3965 (e-book) |
DDC [Fic]—dc23
LC record available at https://lccn.loc.gov/2022024693

Book design by Jeanette Levy
Typeset by Westchester Publishing Services
Printed and bound in the U.S.A.
2 4 6 8 10 9 7 5 3 1

To find out more about our authors and books
visit www.bloomsbury.com and sign up for our newsletters.

To Courtney,

Who would have been the first combination forensic paleontologist/astrophysicist/neuroscientist (if she didn't love dancing and writing so darn much).

Happy Birthday! Pretty cool present, right?

PLANNING

Perfect

SEVEN HOURS AND FORTY-SIX MINUTES UNTIL THE ELECTION

At any given point, I have a to-do list running through my mind. Brush my teeth? Check. Finish my homework? No problem. Most of the time, there aren't serious consequences if I miss an item on the list; I could theoretically ask for an extension on a project. Except my brain doesn't work like that. If it's on my list, I *have* to get it done.

Item number two on today's list: get through the school day. Right now, I should be in my Irish Literature class, diligently taking color-coded notes on James Joyce. Instead I'm stuck in the front office. Arguing with the school secretary was decidedly not on my agenda.

Mrs. Abrams sits back in her swivel chair. "You can't refuse a detention."

"Yes, I can," I say indignantly. "Because it's not my fault."

She sighs and looks at her computer screen. "This is the fifth time this year, Miss Becker. You've already gotten a warning."

"Those weren't my fault either."

She ignores this. "We talked about this last time. I can't go making exceptions to the school tardiness policy just because—" She waves her hand like I already know the answer.

Just because my mom doesn't know how to be an adult, I finish in my head.

This time is different though. Being a little late for some classes doesn't make a big difference. Having *detention* does. Especially with the election today.

My mind runs through the worst-case scenario. I get a detention, which tarnishes my school record and makes me miss the election. I look awful to colleges and don't get in anywhere. I have no real prospects for my future. Then I probably die in some secluded cabin under mysterious, murder-related circumstances.

Fine, the last one is a stretch. I need to stop falling asleep to true crime podcasts. Though, in my defense, there was a new episode of *Murder She Solved*, and I was fairly positive we were going to find out the killer this week (we did not).

"I'm not going," I say in a matter-of-fact tone. I won't. It's the principle of the thing. I'm not going to take the blame for this.

"I haven't done anything wrong," I continue. "I was ready a full thirty minutes early this morning. I *ironed*, Mrs. Abrams."

She takes a deep breath. "The bus is always an—"

I cut her off. "It's not an option. My mom is . . ." I feel ridiculous even saying this. ". . . *morally opposed* to the bus. She believes pickup and drop-off time is some sort of formative mother-daughter bonding experience."

"No one is morally opposed to buses," she says.

I give her a pointed look.

"I don't know what to say, Felicity. Rules are rules," she continues.

This is especially frustrating because I agree with her.

I love rules. I love the structure of knowing that there's a *right* thing to do and a *right* time to do it. Bonnie, my therapist, says that I should "Examine opportunities where I can practice flexibility," but I don't think that applies to school start times.

"Tell that to my mom, then," I say. "It's her fault; put her in detention." I take out my phone and type. I'm not getting anywhere with Mrs. Abrams alone.

Felicity: you better be close, front office stat you're in trouble they're trying to give me a DETENTION

if i miss the election because of you, i'm getting emancipated

She responds almost immediately.

Mom: Still in the parking lot! Be right there!

I can practically hear her cheery tone through the screen. Which is even more annoying. It would be a lot easier to stay angry at my mom if she wasn't so likeable.

She struts into the school office moments later, wearing an oversize Disney T-shirt and shorts, both of which I know she slept in last night. The sleeves aren't long enough to hide the floral tattoo that takes up most of her left upper arm. She has her faded teal hair pulled up in a messy bun with a pen sticking out of it.

It's because of things like this that people often think she's my older, rebellious sister. That and the fact that she's so young.

My mom has never done things in the right order. Like with work, she designed and sold this tech software when she was still in college that basically just tells companies what other software to buy (though, she says it's more complicated than that). Then, when I was four, she created a deeply addictive phone game that

3

became a brief but very real cultural sensation. I mean there's a movie franchise around *Sleepy Dog* now. It's wild.

She took her weird turn of financial fortune and her old love of fan fiction and now spends her days ghostwriting the book adaptations of big-deal movies.

So, she had the serious adult job when she was in college, and now her work sounds like the kind of thing a six-year-old would make up if their kindergarten teacher asked them what they wanted to be when they were older. Untraditional to a fault.

Especially when it comes to me.

She was in her early twenties, fresh off the success of selling her software-selling software, when she decided to head to the sperm bank. Basically killed my bubbe, if I'm to trust the way my grandma tells the story.

"You're supposed to struggle a little with your career, build character, work your way up, find a nice Jewish boy to settle down with, and *then* have kids," Bubbe said when she was over to break fast last Yom Kippur. They got in a huge fight after that one.

"Hi," Mom starts, looking at the desk in front of her. There's a nameplate next to the computer. "Mrs. Abrams," she reads.

"Oh, Mrs. Becker," Mrs. Abrams says.

"*Ms.* Becker," Mom corrects. "Felicity tells me I'm in trouble."

Mrs. Abrams makes a face like she can't figure out how Mom knows this, even though I fully used my phone right in front of her. What, does she not realize texting is a thing?

"Oh, no, you're not in—"

"Because," Mom continues, "this morning was entirely my fault. Lissy keeps yelling at me to wake up earlier, and I've been so good lately, really, you can probably see that in your records, it's been over a month since I was running late." She pauses, like maybe Mrs. Abrams is going to fact-check her apparent lack of tardiness. "I'm on deadline with a work project," Mom adds, "and stayed up too late, so yes, I did turn off my alarm, but that was a mistake, and even then, Felicity tried waking me up. I sincerely apologize. Tried apologizing to her in the car, but she wouldn't take it. I hope at least you can forgive me."

Mrs. Abrams looks even more confused.

"Now," Mom goes on, "I assume you have these policies in place so that students don't disrupt classes or miss any learning opportunities. My daughter has not once disrupted a lesson, even though I've told her it could be fun." She looks over at me and winks. "I guess my biggest concern here is why she isn't in class yet. It seems like you're keeping my daughter from learning." Her voice is full of concern.

"She *should* be in class already," Mrs. Abrams says, taken aback. I don't think she was remotely prepared for the whirlwind that is Hannah Ruth Becker.

"Exactly," my mom says. "So, she can go?"

I think at this point Mrs. Abrams just wants both of us out of the office. "Yes, she can go. This won't be tolerated further, Ms. Becker. Felicity, I expect you to arrive on time the rest of the year." She fills out a note for my teacher and hands it to me.

"Thank goodness the school year is almost over," Mom jokes. She takes me by the arm and steers me out of the office.

"I'm not talking to you," I say once we're in the hall.

"Those sound like words, child of mine."

I frown.

"That was kind of thrilling," she adds. "Have any teachers you want me to talk to next?"

"No," I say seriously. There's roughly a 60 percent chance she isn't joking.

"Ah, well." She shrugs. "Good luck with the election. Break all your limbs."

"Definitely not a saying," I point out.

"Seems like it should be." She kisses the top of my head. "Have a good day. Love you, Lissy."

"Love you," I grumble back before heading to class.

The thing is, I do love her. It would just be a lot easier if she was a normal mom.

FOUR MINUTES UNTIL THE ELECTION

I'm going to murder Brody Wells.

He's standing right outside the classroom where we're supposed to have our election, blocking the door with his lacrosse stick. It's slung over his shoulder like this is something normal and not an inconvenience to those of us trying to get inside. Not that anyone else seems to mind. He has an entire group around him, probably hanging on his every jock word and showering him with praise.

"Move," I say sharply, my arms folded against my chest. "You're in the way."

"Oh, shoot, my bad," he says in a faux apologetic voice. He flashes one of those grins that everyone thinks is really charming. "I barely even notice when I'm holding this thing."

Ah, yes, because the giant lacrosse stick is something unnoticeable.

I don't even know why he has it out. What, does he think he'll need sporting equipment for an event committee election? It's probably some convoluted power move, a reminder to all of his adoring fans that he's an athlete and they should love him for that.

I would like to make it clear that my hatred for Brody Wells is entirely justified. We've known each other since kindergarten.

He tripped me in the playground during a round of tag, and it's only gone downhill from there. Especially when it comes to this club. All he does in our meetings is distract people. Nothing is ever serious with him. This group is simply the butt of one of his ridiculous jock jokes. I have no clue why he even shows up in the first place.

He steps aside and then waves the lacrosse stick like he's directing traffic. "After you."

At the very least, I should be allowed to hit him with his own lacrosse stick for condescending nonsense like that.

I glare at him. He has on his jersey like he's coming from practice, even though classes just ended. His hair is in its typical cornrows, a look he's been sporting for the last few years. There's this glint in his dark brown eyes like he's daring me to follow his lead.

I don't move.

"After me, then," he says with a shrug. He starts walking, but then pauses and turns back toward me. "Good luck with the election," he adds.

What a jerk.

I wait a moment before following him inside, checking my phone like that's what I was meant to be doing all along. I won't give him the satisfaction of winning. After what I deem an appropriate amount of time, I head into the classroom and sit in my usual seat. I take a deep breath. Not even a rude lacrosse player can take away that feeling of belonging I always get during these meetings.

My high school does a lot of things that might seem unusual. We don't have class rankings or a dress code. We barely even have AP classes because they don't want to simply "teach to a test." As an American public school, there's one normal thing that we're required to have for fear of inciting a nationwide riot: school events.

Enter the Social Friends Committee, the time-consuming club that I love with my whole heart.

It started with a booth. The club fair freshman year had all kinds of offerings, but the Social Friends Committee table was clearly the best, with its carefully organized brochures and event posters that looked like someone had created life-size Pinterest boards.

"Senior Committee President, Molly Matsuda," the girl behind the table introduced herself. "You look like someone who likes to be in charge."

I took it as a compliment; I'm always very careful with how I present myself. Mom likes to joke that I look like a fifties house-wife. She blames Bubbe, who used to buy me all these old-fashioned dresses when I was little. "They're too pristine; she needs something she can play in," Mom would say, holding up whatever smocked or pleated dress Bubbe had just given me. I loved them though.

Now that I'm the one in charge of my wardrobe, it's all neat dresses and skirts and blouses and sweaters, styles that are simple and sophisticated and give me the air of having traveled through time. There's something so satisfying about being intentional and put together. Part of it is the sense of control: I have the power to make sure everything matches, from my stockings all the way to the shade of my eye shadow. Plus, it doesn't hurt that I can find vintage-style options online that look flattering and fit my curves.

Molly Matsuda walked me through all the responsibilities of

the Social Friends Committee. She told me how the club is behind all the major school events, the most notable being prom. "If you join our group, you get to be in charge of making memories," she told me. I signed up on the spot.

Since then, I've dedicated more time than I should probably admit on getting the right color schemes for the Valentine's Day Bake Sale or picking fonts for our flyers. It's more than just that feeling of control; I'm good at putting all the pieces together. Plus, I get to craft perfect experiences that other people will remember for the rest of their lives.

Each grade is in charge of different events, but the freshman and sophomore ones are basically a joke. I mean who comes to an Arbor Day Dance or gets excited about writing secret thank-you letters for Teacher Appreciation Week? The serious stuff is reserved for the upperclassmen, a point made clear by the fact the leadership positions aren't even available until junior year.

With voting happening in . . . three minutes, according to my phone.

Today's number one item on my to-do list: win this election.

If I get a leadership position this year, I'll basically be guaranteed one as a senior. I'll look great when I apply to schools and probably land a design internship in college. From there I'll get a job at an event firm and plan events professionally. I'll be able to make memories for a living and do this thing I love for the rest of my life.

I run a hand through my tamed-straight, auburn hair. Two years of buying streamers and decorating posters and printing out flyers has led to this. I'm prepared for any outcome . . . as long as it's the one I want.

I've got this. I don't need to worry.

Felicity: i'm worried

Nancy's response comes almost immediately.

Nancy: You shouldn't be

I try to remember her schedule. When you have a long-distance friendship, you get used to wait times with their responses. Even though Nancy is only in Vermont and I live outside of Boston, we haven't been able to see each other in person for a whole year. We've both been so busy with school, communication tends to be of the texting variety.

She should be in the middle of a soccer field right now, that's it. Nancy was temporarily benched because she hurt her knee a few months ago, but her doctor just gave her the go-ahead to go back for practices, with what Nancy referred to as "slight but annoying" modifications because she's still not entirely back to full strength. I've never been much of a sports person, but from what I've gathered, they expect you to be phoneless for practice.

Felicity: go kick a ball, you're not making any sense

Nancy: I'm right and also warming up

I can see that she's typing something else as the Social Friends teacher advisor, Mr. Lu, walks into the classroom. The tables are usually arranged in rows, but today they're pushed together to form a big rectangle. When Mr. Lu sits at the teacher's desk by the SMART Board, it looks like he's presiding over a war room. I put away my phone.

"Hey, Friends!" Mr. Lu says, overly enthusiastic. "Who's ready for some election fun?!"

Election fun? *Sure* . . .

Mr. Lu is the sort of teacher who could be cast as a high school student in a teen drama. He's young enough to be "relatable" despite being old enough to have a teaching degree. He teaches things like Literary Justice, an entire course dedicated to understanding social movements through literature, so he's solidified his position as *the* cool English teacher.

He hands out the election survey.

I run my hand over the paper, smoothing out the creased fold in the middle of the sheet. There are enough positions that every upperclassman will have a role, which doesn't really seem fair to me. I've only seen about half of these people here for regular meetings. Some of the positions seem like a real stretch; Chief of Moral Support and Executive Snack Finder aren't exactly titles you can put on a college resume. Not that it matters, because I *am* going to get the Junior Committee President position.

I've worked so hard for this, I have to.

I straighten in my seat and instinctively smooth out my lucky dress: a checkered green-and-white find from ModCloth with a Peter Pan collar and pockets hidden in the skirt. It was hot today when I got dressed, but I forgot to account for the arctic air-conditioning in the school that kicks in near the end of the academic year. The goose bumps on my arms are so prominent they might start honking.

Voting at the beginning of June might seem early, but it's a tradition for the Social Friends Committee. This way the seniors can pass down their leadership wisdom before they're done with school next week. At least for those jobs that require said wisdom. I have to doubt there's much skill to executively finding snacks.

As soon as we're given the go-ahead, I write down my responses.

I pause when I get to the words "Junior Committee President," taking my time writing my name like it's some fancy meant-to-be-framed autograph. "Junior Committee President: Felicity Becker" just looks *right* on the page.

I earned that title, I know I did. I always meet my project deadlines, I volunteer for every event, I even stay late to help everyone else finish their tasks. I've put in the time, way more time than anyone else. No one deserves the leadership position more than I do.

After I vote for myself, I watch Mr. Lu intently like that will make the process go faster. It doesn't. The Social Friends Committee isn't a large group, but it still takes roughly a million years for everyone to fill out their forms and somehow even longer for those votes to be tallied.

Mr. Lu claps his hands together. "Who's ready for some results?!"

I tense. As he reads off names and titles, all I can think is that this is it, it's happening, I'm going to be—

"Felicity Becker: Chief of Moral Support!"

What?

I blink a few times like that will help this whole thing make sense.

It doesn't.

Mr. Lu keeps reading off the list, but I'm barely even functioning enough to comprehend what's going on. Chief of Moral Support? When have I even offered anyone here *moral support*? I've volunteered at every event I could, dedicated weekends to planning, and now I'm CHIEF OF MORAL SUPPORT?!

Who could possibly do a better job at running the junior year events? I mean, that includes the Halloween Haunted Hallway. I've had a Pinterest board ready for that since fall.

". . . and introducing our Junior Committee President: Brody Wells!"

Of course. I should have known this would happen. Hard work means nothing if you're up against a friend-to-all lacrosse player. *Nothing*.

Brody dramatically bows and mimes placing a crown over his neat cornrows, looking around to see if he got a reaction. People who are not me probably find that nonsense charming.

Though I would prefer to immediately storm out of the room in a huge, dramatic fit, I manage to sit through the rest of the meeting. I even get work done, finalizing some details for the upcoming senior week, our last event with the seniors before they graduate, because I'm a professional.

I don't check my phone until I'm out of the meeting.

The first message I see is from Mom.

Mom: Running late!

Of course. It's like this morning didn't mean anything. I text her quickly and tell her not to bother, which I'll admit is a little childish. I can usually get a ride from Anesha Patel (our new Senior Poster Coordinator, who also happens to live on my street).

The other message is from Nancy.

Nancy: It will all work out

Well, Nancy, it didn't work out.

I failed.

ONE HOUR AND TWENTY-ONE MINUTES
AFTER THE ELECTION

I can tell that Eric is cooking empanadas the moment I walk into the house. Our Everything Empanada tradition started as a fun way to deal with loose ingredients in the fridge, right around the time my mom started dating Eric Flores. After three and a half years, it's transformed into the challenge to rival all challenges. Each week we try to make at least one new filling combination. From the mess I can see when I get to the kitchen, it looks like this week's new creation is a leftover fried rice empanada paired with a duck sauce salsa.

I take a deep breath. The biggest reason I could tell what he's making so quickly was the smell, the distinct scent of my favorite combination already baking: a traditional dough mixed with cinnamon and vanilla, filled with dulce de leche, cream cheese frosting, and strawberries. Because of the election, probably.

"We're not celebrating," I say before he can ask.

He looks over his shoulder, hands still sealing the dough on his new batch. "We hate them," he says. "No one can appreciate true genius." He pauses and turns around to look at me properly, squinting like he might just be able to read how I feel.

"I'm fine," I supply. "Cross my heart, et cetera." Then I add, "I was actually named Chief of Moral Support, so there's that."

Eric lets out an actual snort. "Oh, you're serious?"

"So dead serious they could feature my demise on the next season of *Murder She Solved*," I say.

"Wanna talk?"

Eric *always* wants to talk. If he could, he'd probably spend every day like he was living in the wrap-up of some family-friendly sitcom where two of the characters have a heart-to-heart and hug it all out.

I shake my head. "All good, really." I smooth out my dress like that will make me feel more put together. "Roo is coming over," I add.

"Ah, good Sir Rupert Basra," Eric says, in a voice like he's narrating a special on Arthurian legends. "Tell him he's welcome to join us for Shabbat."

My mom and I aren't *exactly* traditionally observant when it comes to our Judaism, but we still try to have a family dinner on Fridays, a habit dating back to her childhood. When I was little, that meant it was mother-daughter bonding time, featuring takeout, store-bought challah, and more junk food than we reasonably should have consumed. It's never just the two of us now; it's an odd night when Eric isn't in our house to begin with, and Roo, my longtime partner in crime, makes any excuse to come over and eat Eric's homemade food.

I nod. "I'm just going to . . ." I point to the stairs leading to the second floor and, more importantly, my bedroom.

"Um, Felicity, actually," Eric starts, "there's something I wanted to ask."

I raise an eyebrow. "Yes?"

"You know how much I care about you and your mother, right?"

Ah, this again.

Eric is almost constantly concerned about boundaries and making sure he isn't breaking them. He loves to bring up how he feels about our family almost as much as he loves offering to talk. We've been due for another one of these check-ins; it's been almost two weeks.

"We care about you too," I say like I'm following a script.

He takes in a breath before continuing. "I'm glad to hear that. Over these last three and a half years—exactly, today's our half-year anniversary—I've come to see you two as a part of my family. And you can always tell me if you feel differently, I know I'm the outsider here, but I just wanted to . . . check in, because I'd never want you to feel left out or—"

This could go on forever.

I sigh and walk over to Eric. "We see you as family too," I say, placing a hand on his shoulder. "Now buck up, Flores. Don't want you to get so mushy you forget about those empanadas."

He laughs, like he's truly relieved that I didn't change my mind about him in the last twelve days. "All right, go to your room, kid."

Another successful, heartwarming moment wrapped up. With that, I walk to my room so I can wallow in my misery.

―――― ⚊ ――――――― ⚊ ――――

"Brody Wells," I say, pacing the space between my bed and my dresser. "Brody. Wells."

Roo yawns from his spot lounging on my bed. We've been friends since second grade when his parents moved to the suburbs from Boston. He's become such a permanent fixture in my home that it would look weird without him taking up half of my bed or helping himself to the entire contents of the fridge.

"Do you know how many events he missed last year? He didn't even help set up prom! And whenever he did show up, he just spent the whole time chatting with anyone who would listen. You know who should have been voted Chief of Moral Support? Brody Wells, that's who."

This time Roo stretches and fluffs the pillow behind his back.

"He's just . . . he's so . . . he's a *lacrosse* player, you know?"

"I'm a lacrosse player," Roo says.

I stop pacing long enough to make a pointed look at Roo. "In practice only. You know what I mean." Roo is the last person you'd think of if you were trying to conjure up an image of a lax bro. He looks more like a young Tan France, but with black hair and a somehow even sharper sense of style.

I start pacing again. "He's just such a self-obsessed jock," I continue. "I mean 'bro' is even in his name, Roo. It's in his name. There's no possible way this works out well with him in charge. He's going to have ridiculous lacrosse player ideas and then do nothing and just make my life—"

Roo cuts me off. "Felicity, this isn't the end of the world."

I substitute my pointed look for a glare.

Roo sits up, moving his legs to the side of the bed. "Working with Brody might not be as bad as you think. You'd be working with other people if you were president anyway."

"No," I say. "I'd be doing all the work. I'm still going to be doing all the work probably, if I want to make sure everything runs smoothly, just without the credit and a bunch of added obstacles."

"And what happens if things don't run smoothly?" he asks. I can tell that he's annoyed with me from his voice; it's peak judgey.

I don't even take time to think of my response. "Our entire school is at jeopardy of having the worst high school experience ever, and they'll all go mad and become zombies or, worse, men's rights activists."

"Oh boy," Roo says under his breath. "What did your girlfriend say when you told her about this?"

I hate when he says that.

Roo has been calling Nancy my girlfriend since we met her at the BE YOURSELF retreat last year, a Northeast symposium for LGBTQIA+ teens. Even though that is obviously ridiculous because we're just two really good friends. I might even venture to say best friends (with Roo acting like this, he doesn't deserve the title). Just because we text all the time and spend hours together on FaceTime and sometimes even schedule nights to stream movies together doesn't mean Nancy and I are dating. Friendship does not automatically equate romance.

"She's a friend, Roo," I say, annoyed.

Roo shrugs. "I just don't think you should gal pal yourself, is all."

I let out a little huff of breath. "She's busy now, anyway."

For a second I think about what she texted me before the meeting. *It will all work out.*

It didn't though; nothing has worked out. Slacker lacrosse player Brody has my job.

"Well," Roo continues, "I really think it's going to be fine. I mean, the surprise is . . . a lot, but you have to step back and think of what will happen in the long run. Unexpected doesn't have to mean terrible."

He doesn't get it. I love Roo, I really do, but there's always been this block with us when it comes to things like this. Everything he does is *effortless*. He gets the right grades and knows exactly how to dress. Hell, he's even good at sports! All of that combined is just rude. For me, everything is *work*. If I want the grades, I have to study for them. If I want a leadership position on my resume, I bust my butt, and even then it isn't good enough.

This isn't about a surprise; this isn't about some little unexpected turn. It's as though all of my hard work was deemed useless.

But I don't know how to verbalize it clearly to him.

Because to Roo, this really is a small twist. In the long run, he'd probably take the loss and turn it into something even better, like a job or an internship to fill the time he would have spent running school events. For me, this could cost me my whole future.

I don't have a leadership position, so no schools accept me, so no one ever hires me, and then I'll likely morph into a useless blob of unproductivity and wasted potential.

I sigh. Bonnie, my therapist, would probably tell me I should make the choice to take my mind along a different path of thought. She might even tell me to listen to Roo.

I walk over and sit next to him on the bed. "Are you going to make T-shirts with that? Write a self-help book and tour the world giving motivational speeches?"

"I hate you sometimes," he says.

"Back at you." I pause. "Unexpected doesn't have to mean terrible?"

He nods.

I rest my head on his shoulder. "Fine, I guess we'll see who's right."

We sit there for a moment, staying close. I think one of the reasons we've been friends for so long is that Roo fits. His pressed slacks and tailored shirt look like they belong in my organized room; my head feels right against his shoulder.

"All right," I finally say, since I've had to deal with one too many mushy heart-to-hearts today. "I think it's about time to eat."

We head downstairs and are immediately put to work setting the table, which is a welcome distraction. We've done this enough times together that Roo even knows to set my favorite fork in front of my seat.

Mom comes down from her attic home office right before it's time to eat. She's changed her hair again; it's now a deep purple that she let dry in messy waves. "Both of my children are here!" she says, walking up behind Roo and ruffling his hair. I think she's the only person who could ever get away with that.

"Hello, Second Mother," Roo says, his too-formal response to years of my mom telling him not to call her Ms. Becker. "How's the writing?"

Mom lets out an exaggerated sigh. "The big green dude got angry at the most inconvenient time," she says. She's technically allowed to use the real names of characters with us, but she never does.

"Ah, doesn't he always," Roo says.

"When'd you do this?" I ask as my greeting, pointing to her head.

"You like? The teal was fading," Mom says.

I shrug. "Kind of boring by your standards."

She tsks. "Never happy, this one." She walks over to Eric and kisses his cheek.

"She was raised wrong," Eric says lightly, playing along.

Mom's actually dressed now, though her outfit isn't much better than the pajama look she rocked for her little school office performance this morning. She has on jeans and a hoodie, like she's ready to go undercover in one of my classes.

We sit down to a table crowded with challah and the savory selection of empanadas. Eric always keeps the sweet ones in the kitchen until dessert.

"You went to the kosher market?" Mom asks, looking down at the table. I didn't even notice the insignia on the bag.

"I am getting over the pain of the homemade challah debacle," Eric says. "I've admitted defeat."

"It was like a rock," I helpfully point out.

There's nothing that beats a proper fresh challah, but the ones delivered to our local grocery store are usually stale by Friday. The kosher market though—so fresh the bag fogs up from the heat. It's a half-hour drive into Brookline, and you have to get there early before they sell out, but it's a thousand percent worth it in my expert opinion. Eric is not an expert and therefore thought he could get out of the early drive by baking his own. He was very wrong.

"That second attempt was vaguely food-like," Roo offers as half-hearted support.

Eric does one of those "thanks, bro" head nods.

We don't do anything traditional for Shabbat, we don't even light candles, but we do have our own Shabbat rule: Friday night dinner is reserved for positive bonding time, with an emphasis on the positive. This is usually fine, except for when everything I've diligently worked for over the past two years comes crashing down around me and I can't even yell about it as I stuff my face.

It's fine, I'll wait until after dinner.

The good thing here is that no one is policing my mind as we eat, because boy oh boy are my thoughts anything but positive. I keep imagining all the ways I can explain the horror of earlier today to Mom to properly paint the proverbial picture. Should I literally paint a picture?

No, I'm not skilled enough to execute the Renaissance-style masterpiece this atrocity deserves.

I focus on eating and crafting the perfect rant. It'll have all of the important rant-like features: the passion, the rage, the hand motions. I'm so focused that I'm not really paying much attention to the conversation as I polish off my fried rice empanadas, until I notice Eric get up and walk to the kitchen. He's already getting dessert, bless him.

Mom's finishing up an animated explanation of her latest project. She's almost done writing her first draft, and since she's a verbal processor, I feel like I've already read the book five times.

"What about you, child of mine?" she asks. "How's your day been?"

Ah, it's my turn. This would be the perfect time to pull out that Renaissance-style painting.

Instead, I give her a thumbs-up.

"Felicity is having an amazing day, *I'm* here," Roo answers. "You know, I was actually a little down earlier, but Felicity is just so great at offering *moral support*. Turned it all around."

I can't murder Roo at the dinner table, as that wouldn't be considered positive. Even if I really want to.

"Well, I'm happy things are looking up," Mom says. Then she glances back at me. "And the election?"

"Worked out just the way it was meant to," Roo says before I can talk.

Maybe I should make a dark vision board to explain my many frustrations. It can feature images of fire and Roo's face with the eyes crossed out, which is probably less dramatic than an actual murder.

I'm still thinking of my dark vision board when Eric walks in from the kitchen with the plate of sweet empanadas.

"Who's ready for the good stuff?" he asks.

Mom looks over at the dessert with the same expression she reserves for the penguins at the aquarium: pure, unadulterated joy. "Have I mentioned that I love you yet today?" she asks. I assume she's talking to Eric, but her eyes *are* still trained on the food.

Eric lets out this little nervous laugh, just like when I reassured him that he's part of the family earlier today. It's kind of weird, but, then again, Eric can be kind of weird. I mean, anyone who wants to talk about feelings as much as he does is automatically pretty strange.

Then he does something else that's a little odd: he places the plate directly in front of my mom. I know she was just gushing about the dessert, but come on, we all want some.

"Eric?" Mom's voice is a few notches higher, like she's just been surprised.

That's when I see it, the words written in chocolate on the empanada at the center of the plate: *Will you . . .*

Eric gets down on one knee, right next to Mom's chair.

Wait, what?

"Hannah, ever since I met you and Felicity, I've felt . . . more complete, I guess. I've felt like I've found my home, my family. I talked to Lissy earlier today, and she said that you both feel that way too. So tonight, with our little family"—he pauses—"plus Roo," Eric adds, quickly smiling in his direction, "I wanted to make it official. You can pick up the empanada."

Mom lifts the "will you" pastry, revealing a ring underneath. It's an oval emerald encased in tiny diamonds, all set in gold. An engagement ring, my mind registers.

"Will you marry me, Hannah Ruth Becker?"

What follows is a frankly disgusting display of laughter and kisses and crying that would be adorable if my mother was not one of the participants. "Yes! Yes, of course!" she finally gets out between kisses.

WHAT IS HAPPENING?

I must have fallen asleep or been hit in the head very, very hard, because this can't be real. It doesn't make any sense. We were just having a normal, boring, family night in. Engagements don't happen during family nights in. They happen at fancy restaurants or in the middle of a garden with a photographer carefully hidden away so as to not ruin the moment but also capture the memory-worthy big proposal. There should've been signs before something like this happened. Mom should've gotten a manicure, at least.

I should have known this was coming.

There were many ways I had seen tonight going, most involving a celebration of my big victory. I'm still processing the loss of my rightful position, but, whatever, I adjusted the plans to fit a nice mother-daughter post-school/work rant.

In none of these plans did Eric Flores propose to my mom over Shabbat dinner.

Well, I guess Mom and I are going to have something very different to talk about now.

TWO HOURS AND SIX MINUTES
AFTER THE ENGAGEMENT

Roo asked me five times if I was okay before he left. The last time, he made a point to say that he knew I was not actually okay, but his sister was waiting outside to drive him home. They've been sharing a car ever since she got back from college for the summer.

"You're making matzo toffee; we're at DEFCON zero levels on the Felicity disaster scale. Text me," he said as a goodbye.

Matzo toffee is the one thing I know how to make by myself. I'd argue that this does not necessarily indicate that there is a disaster, as it could also mean that it's Passover, I'm PMS-ing, or Bubbe is coming over for a visit.

I mean, in this case, yes, obviously it's because of a disaster.

The thing about making matzo toffee is that it's half comfort, half time to sit and wallow while you wait for everything to set. This is the perfect time to really hate the world and all things in it.

For example, I hate the fact that after Eric proposed to my mom, the two of them just went back to their everyday routines. They did the *dishes* together, and then Eric put in a load of *laundry*. How can they be acting so casual on a night like this?

I start to formulate a mental list of everything that is terrible:

(1) Brody Wells, in general. (2) The specific fact that Brody Wells took my job. (3) Chocolate and toffee take at least two hours to cool and properly set on matzah. (4) Eric proposed to my mom, thus forever changing my life as I know it, and (5) I basically gave him permission to do so.

Eric isn't the problem, really. He already feels like one of us. I guess the biggest issue here is that I shouldn't have to deal with their engagement in the first place. If Mom was normal, she would've done the whole wedding thing before I was born. I mean, even with kids who have parents who get remarried, second weddings are less of a production. Right?

I want her to have a special day; she deserves it. I just know it's all going to fall on me.

This Shabbat engagement is the perfect example. No photographer, no party planned around the big ask, no decorations. If there wasn't a ring, it barely would've been clear that anything happened in the first place. They need me or the wedding is going to end up happening in our living room on a random Tuesday with no guests.

I'm near the end of hour one in my waiting-for-the-toffee-to-cool journey when Mom walks into the kitchen.

"Hey, child of mine," she says. She's already in her pajamas, soft, heather-gray sweatpants that I also have a pair of and the same oversize Disney T-shirt she wore to bed last night. She glances at the counter, where I've left out the box of matzah. "Big day," she adds.

I look up from my phone, pausing the YouTube video I was watching to kill time. "Yep."

"I didn't even really get to congratulate you on—"

"I didn't get it," I cut her off. "Roo was just being a jerk."

"Oh," Mom says. "What did they give you?"

"Chief of Moral Support."

Mom scrunches up her face. "Kinda insulting."

"Tell me about it."

I'm standing by the counter, since only winners are allowed the comfort of sitting. Mom walks over and pulls me into a hug.

"I'll make us tea."

She doesn't just make any tea; she throws together chamomile with cinnamon, honey, and vanilla: comfort in a cup. Then she guides me into the living room and forcibly puts a throw blanket over my shoulders.

"Talk."

So I tell her about the election as I cradle my mug of tea, giving her a play-by-play, starting with my expectations and ending with the death of my hopes and dreams.

When she finally talks, she asks something I never would have considered. "Are you going to quit?"

I hadn't even thought about that as an option; I just jumped to misery and the assumption that I would have to work twice as hard next year to do what I want. *Am I going to quit?* After all of my hard work, I was rewarded with a massive failure. Does that mean I should give up completely?

"I don't know," I say, because now that Mom has introduced that as a possibility, I'm not sure.

"I'm not saying you should," she clarifies. "I know what this all means to you."

A lot, it means a lot. There's something special about planning and organizing an event so carefully that you start to see it all come together. Then, when it's finally time, you get to watch as other people enjoy your carefully crafted experience.

For junior and senior year, that means prom and graduation. Those are events people remember for the rest of their lives.

Is it worth it though? I won't even really have any control now. I'll have to deal with the major obstacle that is Jock Charming Brody. Maybe I *should* step down.

"You don't have to decide right away," she adds. "I just want you to know that I'll support you, whatever you decide."

She will, too. No matter what I do, she'll support me. Meanwhile, I'm here talking up all of her attention on the night she got engaged to the love of her life.

I was so worried about how she didn't have the right kind of engagement, and here I am making it worse.

I cuddle up to her. "Okay, show me the ring," I say.

She cracks a smile. "Oh, it's my turn, huh?" She holds out her left hand in front of us. Eric hit it out of the park with this one; different, delicate, and stunning, it's so entirely right for my mom.

There are a lot of thoughts running rampant in my mind right now: When is the wedding going to happen? How much will change? What do we need to do to prepare, and when should we start?

Instead I ask, "Are you happy?"

"The happiest," she says.

I nod, like I knew she was going to say that all along.

I guess I did.

"You know this wasn't the biggest surprise," she says. "Eric and I have been talking about this for months." She says it casually like I really should have known by now.

Have they been talking about getting married for months? I mean, it makes sense. They're both relatively competent adults, and springing an unwanted engagement on someone is pretty unreasonable. Should I have been less surprised? Did I somehow tune out these conversations they were having?

"We don't want to drag this out," Mom continues. "I was thinking we might have the wedding somewhere fun, make a little family vacation out of it. Maybe Niagara Falls? Or that town in Maine we used to go to for day trips?"

I try to picture the wedding: Mom in a long gown, A-line with some sleeves to cover the tattoo on her left arm, Eric in a nice suit, not a tux; that'd be too formal for them. I can practically see a Pinterest board version of the reception coming together with fairy lights and mismatched vintage china settings and a simple white cake with berries dotted along one side for a pop of color.

It's like Mom can read my mind because the next thing she says is, "I really want you to be involved in all of this."

Involved. This is classic Mom. She's great at so many things, but then others . . . Like groceries or school paperwork or very basic scheduling when we're running errands; if I'm not in charge, she'd probably get lost on her way to Target before dying of scurvy.

Not that I have a problem planning her wedding; I knew this was coming, and I'll definitely be able to organize something better than what she could manage alone.

"I'll have to look at my schedule; I'm in high demand."

"Attagirl," Mom says.

"But you have to be the one to tell Bubbe," I continue. "This isn't the kind of thing you can put off."

Mom groans. "She's so much nicer to you though."

"You're engaged; she'll be excited."

"Oh, no, she won't," Mom says. "First, she's going to berate me for the lack of pictures. She'll sprinkle in a disparaging comment or two about Eric. Then, to top it off, she's going to try to take control of the whole thing."

"She can't, you already put me in charge," I say.

Mom lets out a soft laugh. "I'm pretty positive that's not what I said, interesting jump you've made." She gets up from the couch. "You okay if I head to bed?"

"I object to sleep."

Mom gives me a serious look.

"I know, bed by eleven," I say.

She nods before gathering our now-empty mugs. "Don't eat all of the matzo toffee, I'm going to want some tomorrow."

I might be feeling marginally better now, but that doesn't mean I'm going to cut back on my matzo toffee consumption.

Still, I'll save her a piece.

ONE DAY AFTER THE ENGAGEMENT

I decided to send Nancy the equivalent to a trash heap of an info dump before going to bed.

When I wake up, I see that her response is a simple What?

Felicity: yep. position wrongfully misallocated, mother betrothed, world slowly dying due to human greed

She responds quickly.

Nancy: Tad extreme. Are you okay?

Felicity: *shrug*

That's not even remotely close to an adequate explanation, but I don't know exactly how to follow that up. In my defense, I'm still probably going through a sugar crash from my nighttime culinary adventure.

Nancy doesn't send anything back in the fifteen minutes it takes me to work up the will to get out of bed and brush my teeth. Ugh, she wants more. Fine.

Felicity: the weird thing is i'm happy for them? it's just a lot. mom was all i don't want to wait and let's have the ceremony in niagara falls or this cute little town in maine or somewhere like that and then she said she wants me involved and just gahhh

I hit Send and then add, i'm okay

I place my phone on the nightstand and make my bed. Despite the fact that yesterday was the last day of academic classes for seniors, the rest of us poor suckers have another three and a half weeks to go. On top of my metric ton of schoolwork, I volunteered to help set up the senior week events and prep for graduation, all adding up to the tragic fact that I don't get a real weekend. This morning it's just me and James Joyce.

And the occasional text from Nancy.

My phone lights up after I change into my homework pajamas: a matching set that I pretend is a very comfy power suit.

Nancy: Niagara Falls is too touristy. Have it here

If only.

As I flip through *A Portrait of the Artist as a Young Man*, my mind wanders and not just because the writing is virtually unreadable. It *would* be amazing if we had it in Vermont.

When we went to the BE YOURSELF retreat, most of the time was spent on the UVM campus, but there were a couple of excursions out and about to nearby towns. There was a hike up this mountain with an absurdly beautiful view of seasonally still ski lifts and greenery that went on seemingly forever. It was all so serene, like a nature escape from the strip malls and near-identical houses of suburbia.

This isn't exactly the same as my mom's Maine wedding idea but . . .

Felicity: i wish

I trudge through another few pages before I deem it acceptable to check my phone again. There's already a message from Nancy.

Nancy: We do have a pretty picturesque apple orchard . . .

I know that she's just saying that to play along, but still, how amazing would that be? I mean, her family owns an apple orchard. That's basically the perfect place to host a wedding. Plus, I'd be able to spend time with Nancy again. I picture it, the next few months panning out with wedding errands, surrounded by all that nature. Nancy by my side as I write out place cards and string fairy lights and watch a few episodes of *She-Ra* before bed. I can see it all so clearly.

I want it to be real.

I don't give it any more thought before sending off my next message.

Felicity: tell me more

$$\equiv \text{———} \equiv$$

When I walk downstairs for breakfast, Eric is already in the kitchen. The counter is cluttered: cinnamon, the small container of vanilla extract, a carton of eggs, a bowl, a whisk. The entire room smells like a diner mid-brunch.

"Is that challah French toast?" I ask.

"Best way to finish off the leftover bread," Eric confirms.

I pull out a chair at the kitchen table and take a seat. "How's Sleeping Beauty?"

"Told me last night if either of us even thinks of waking her up before noon, we're at risk of a gruesome murder."

I let out an involuntary yawn. "She shouldn't make threats she can't follow through on."

"I don't know, she sounded pretty serious," Eric jokes. "Plus, you two keep watching all those murder shows and listening to that true crime podcast. Might've worn off on her."

It's usually just the two of us this early on weekends. I guess Saturday breakfast has become a tradition now. I remember the first time I found Eric in the kitchen without my mom; I got so weirded out that I turned right back up the stairs and hid in my room until I could hear Mom stomping around, thus signaling she was awake. Even then, it wasn't necessarily unexpected. Mom and Eric dated for a full year before he was even allowed to stay past dinner. It wasn't like he was a stranger.

I'm not sure when these breakfasts became a thing, or even when Eric went from Mom's boyfriend to just Eric in my head. I guess he's spent so much time here, he became a fact, something permanent and normal in our lives.

While Eric finishes making the challah French toast, I run through my list for the day. One lab report, a reading analysis, and ten questions from my Algebra textbook. It's fine, I can wait a little before I absolutely need to get work started. It won't hurt me to waste some time with breakfast.

Eric walks over with the food and slides my plate to me across the table. "Your mom says you're our new wedding planner. Is there a Pinterest board?"

I tsk. "I haven't even consulted my new clients yet." I grab the bottle of syrup and pour enough on my plate to drench my two slices. "I have to make sure this is *your* dream wedding."

"You know, I *did* dream about my wedding when I was little," he says, using his fork to point for emphasis.

No, actually. I had no idea.

"My dad, real tough guy," Eric continues, "would say all of these things about what boys were supposed to do and supposed to think about and all that, but my older sisters—they had me looking at bridal magazines since I was this big." He lowers his fork, like that will help me determine how old he was at the time of his story.

I start to rearrange my image for the wedding. Something picture-perfect, just like Eric would have seen growing up. What's in a bridal magazine? I should get one of those to check.

"And?" I ask. "What did it look like?"

"Oh, cake, tons of food, I'd look real nice in a tailored suit. The traditional stuff. Except it was at Fenway," he adds.

I let out a little snort. "Ah, yes, the *full* traditional checklist," I joke. "I'll look and see if any Red Sox players can make it to the reception."

"See, you get it." He smiles and takes a bite of his French toast. "I think it'll be fun. Doing this all together."

"You think Mom's going to help?" I ask.

Eric doesn't miss a beat. "Of course! I'm telling you, she's excited. It's like this big, fun group project."

I give him a skeptical look. "When's the last time you did a group project? I'm not sure I'd classify them as 'fun.'"

"It'll be like a big, fun, group bonding . . . um . . . party?" Eric tries again.

"Marginally better," I concede.

So now I have something new to think about: Eric's perfect traditional wedding (which apparently includes some homages to baseball). I go back to the list in my head: lab report, reading analysis, ten questions for Algebra, and, surprise, start a Pinterest board for Eric. I'm sure there's a tasteful way to include his childhood dream . . . maybe literal red socks as a part of his day-of outfit? I'll figure it out.

There's something reassuring about knowing that he cares. I'm not just making sure that my mom gets this special day done right; I'm also helping Eric fulfill a childhood dream.

And, just maybe, I'll get to see Nancy in the process.

It'll take a lot of work, but I'm pretty sure I can pull it all off.

TWO DAYS AFTER THE ENGAGEMENT

"You're going to have to go in eventually," I tell my mom.

"We don't know that for sure," she says stubbornly.

We've been standing outside my grandparents' house for a good two minutes. It's getting weird at this point.

"She was nice on the phone. I mean, she even said we could celebrate over brunch," I remind her.

"Ha!" Mom says, like she's a detective from an old-timey movie who just figured out the big plot twist. "Oh, she has you fooled. Do you notice how she chose our weekly brunch for this celebration, even though she knows Eric works on Sundays? Not a coincidence."

"You talk about her like she's the evil stepmom from a fairy tale. How would you feel if I treated you like that?"

"Ugh, if I become as bad as her, banish me. Send me through a portal and move on with your life."

I roll my eyes. "I'm knocking."

"Five more minutes," Mom whines.

I don't listen.

She's like this every Sunday, even though we've been having weekly brunches with Bubbe every weekend since I was twelve.

It started when Bubbe had open-heart surgery. We didn't know if she was going to make it at first, which was pretty scary. She said that the only thing she wanted was to spend more time with her girls, requesting that we come over for a weekly Sunday brunch if she made it home. It was such an emotional moment that Mom promised right there in the hospital room.

Before that we saw Bubbe for major Jewish holidays and birthdays, but that was about it. She lives so close by that we could have easily seen her more, but Mom just never wanted to. Now we're locked into the family obligation. Whenever Mom tries to get out of it, Bubbe goes full Jewish guilt trip on the situation. *I could die, you know? How would you feel if I died and the last thing you said to me was that you didn't care about our time together?*

It's easier to just show up and eat.

I would like our brunches a lot more if the two of them ever took a break from bickering. I've always gotten along with Bubbe; we understand each other. Mom is the odd one out—everything from her purple hair down to her ethically sourced sneakers seeming out of place in this house. It's so weird to think that she grew up here.

Bubbe answers the door almost immediately. I wonder if she could see us standing outside from the window. "My girls," she greets.

I can see my mom tense. "Mom," she says curtly.

It's always so strange seeing my mom near Bubbe. I guess the two of them could look marginally alike, if they made different life choices. Like I've seen pictures from when Mom was growing up; they used to have the same color hair, a deep auburn just like mine. Except Bubbe's is gray now and Mom's hair changes all the time. Then there's the fact that Mom is soft compared to Bubbe's hard body and stiff posture, but there's something about their faces that tells you they're related. I think it's the eyes—they're both a particular shade of blue that reminds me of the ocean.

Mine are brown.

"Hey, Bubbe," I say, giving her a quick hug.

"Come in, come in, you could catch a cold out there," Bubbe says, waving us into the house.

"Ah yes, the freezing June cold," Mom mutters.

"What was that, Hannah dear? You're always mumbling."

"Nothing, Mom."

Bubbe purses her lips like she knows it wasn't nothing, but moves on. "Well, I already set out the food. I got it catered," she brags.

"Takeout is different from catering," Mom says.

Bubbe frowns. "So contrary."

We go right into the formal dining room. Bubbe always has us eat in here when we're over, even though it feels too fancy for regular meals. At least today we have a good excuse: we're celebrating an engagement. That's got to warrant some formality.

Bubbe already laid out the food, unpackaged and served on her own platters. She took out the nice china too, the ones she usually only has out for Passover or the High Holidays. The first thing I notice is that she ordered sausages (probably chicken ones since she doesn't eat pork). Mom and I haven't eaten meat in years, something Bubbe definitely knows. The second thing is that there are only three place settings on the table.

"Dad's not coming?" Mom asks.

"Oh, you know your father. Such a hard worker," Bubbe says.

It's not unusual for Zayde to work through our weekly brunches, but I thought he'd at least take time off to celebrate his only child's engagement. I can't tell from Mom's expression if she's disappointed or not.

We take our seats.

Bubbe is always at the head of the table, meaning that the two of us are flanking her on either side. It feels like she's about to run a business meeting.

We haven't even finished serving ourselves when Bubbe jumps into interrogation mode.

"So, have you set a date?"

"I don't know, Mom. Soon."

"Soon? What does soon mean? Soon isn't a date, Hannah."

Mom focuses on serving herself a couple of pancakes.

"There's so much that goes into a wedding," Bubbe continues. "You know, if you need any help . . ."

Mom gives me a quick look, as if to say, *I told you so.*

"Don't worry, she's already put me in charge," I say.

"My perfect little bubbeleh. Of course you'll take care of it." She passes me the orange juice. "How's school?"

Ah, my turn for questioning.

"Right now it's mostly finals prep," I say.

"A lot of work. You know, those tests can make or break your grades," Bubbe says.

"Mom!" There's warning in my mom's voice.

"What? Is this about that little snafu over winter?" Bubbe asks.

I can practically feel the blood drain from my face. I really don't want to talk about that.

"It's like I can't say anything in my own house," Bubbe continues.

Luckily my mom cuts in. "Mom, stop," she says.

"So now I can't even talk to my granddaughter. Fine, I see how it is." Bubbe takes a pointed bite of her fruit salad before she continues questioning me. "What about your extracurriculars? Wasn't there something coming up with that dance committee you're on, the one with the silly name?"

I straighten the napkin in my lap. I hate disappointing Bubbe. "I was elected Chief of Moral Support," I attempt to say in a serious voice.

Bubbe laughs. "Can you imagine that on a resume? What would college admissions think?" She turns to look at my mom. "Hannah, this is why I've been saying we should transfer Felicity to a private school. None of that hippie nonsense. Chief of Moral Support," she repeats. "Have you ever heard of anything so ridiculous?"

I take a sip of my orange juice. Bubbe's right; it *is* ridiculous.

"What is that club even called again? The Social Friends Gathering?" Bubbe continues.

"The Social Friends Committee," Mom corrects.

"Exactly. Utterly ridiculous." She takes a sip of her drink before looking back at me. "It's fine, we'll get you an internship."

"Mom, that's not—"

"Oh, no," Bubbe keeps going, "it's a perfect idea. I know just who to connect her with. You remember Deborah Segal, right? Oh, our families go back ages. She used to teach your mother's Hebrew school class, Felicity. She's at an event firm in Boston now. Oh, gosh, what is it? Hartman and Co.? I'll add her to my list," Bubbe says.

This seems to throw Mom. "What list?" she asks, hesitantly.

43

"Of people I'm inviting to the wedding," Bubbe says like it's obvious.

"No, that's not—"

But not even Mom can stop Bubbe when she's on a roll. "It's settled. I'll connect you two at the wedding, Felicity dear. An internship will look so much better on your applications."

She's not wrong.

I start to imagine it all, a new year ahead of me with an internship doing the thing I love most. Then my resume will look amazing and I'll get into a great school, and then I'm basically guaranteed a career.

She just offered to introduce you to someone, calm down, I tell myself. I'm jumping ahead too quickly.

Mom doesn't seem to notice the importance of Bubbe's offer. She's stuck on the wedding list comment. "We want something small," she says.

"Don't be ridiculous. This is your only wedding," Bubbe says. "We hope," she adds after a beat. "You have to let me invite people."

"We hope? What's that supposed to mean?"

Which leads to a very long argument in which Bubbe somehow gets ten people, absolute max, that she can invite.

Never underestimate the power of a Jewish grandmother.

———————————

When I get home, I google Hartman and Co.

Their website is seriously impressive. Professional photographs that artfully display images of their past work, a list of accolades.

I keep reading the site, and then I do a separate review search to fact-check.

Um, okay. It's not just *an* event firm in Boston; it's *the* top event management agency in New England. I only find one negative review, and it's someone complaining that they couldn't hire Hartman and Co. because they were already booked.

I switch back to the tab with the official website and find Deborah Segal on the staff page. She's the *Senior Director of Event Operations.*

Bubbe coming in for the win. A school club is nothing compared to an internship at Hartman and Co. This isn't just something that might look nice for colleges; this could help my entire future.

For the first time, I wonder if it's a good thing that I lost the election. Maybe I was meant for something much better.

What did Roo say? I need to think about the long run and that surprises aren't bad?

Maybe he's right and unexpected doesn't have to be that terrible after all.

SIX DAYS AFTER THE ENGAGEMENT

I'm not athletic. I find the fact that I have surrounded myself with sporty friends, Roo and Nancy, that is, mildly hilarious. I tried tennis at one point—Bubbe thought it would be good for me—but that never worked out. Sometimes I go on the elliptical, since Mom has one in the basement from a short-lived workout phase, but that's about as far as I'm willing to go.

I *am* on a sports team. Golf, to be specific.

In my defense, it's the team at our school with the least commitment. It's barely even a team, if I'm being honest. More like a gathering of students hitting balls around with clubs. I'm sure other schools take this more seriously and have real practices and participate in like . . . high-stakes tournaments, but not us.

It's the last official team meeting. Really, it's just an excuse to celebrate the end of the school year, which feels awfully premature to me since we haven't even started exams yet.

There's an assortment of homemade baked goods arranged on a plastic folding table that has seen better days. I pick at a dry brownie. I'm not great in the kitchen, but even I could've done better than this. I wonder if I should ask Eric to make brownies when I get home.

I give up on the food and dump my plate in a trash bag that's been taped to one of the table's legs. Roo promised to pick me up because his lacrosse practice is nearby and, unlike me, the concept of driving without strict adult supervision doesn't terrify him. Cocky license-haver.

My phone buzzes with a text from Roo that he's here. I wave goodbye to my fellow golf members. People started leaving already, so it's a sparse group left.

I'm grateful that Roo is taking pity on me and driving . . . until I see the car.

The first problem is that Roo is in a strange car, a minivan instead of the simple sedan he shares with his sister. The second very major issue is the person in the driver's seat.

This has to be some very mean prank.

"Hope you don't mind," Roo says as I open the back door. "Amira took the car today, so Brody said he'd give us a ride."

Brody Wells waves from the front seat. He's holding his phone, so it looks like he's just trying to show off his screen. "Hey, Felicity!" he says. The tone of voice is too nice for my personal horror movie villain.

"Brody," I say cautiously. "What a surprise." If he can sound nice, so can I.

He turns his attention back to his phone. That's when I hear it, the familiar *beep-bop-bop-beepity* sound that filled my childhood. He's playing *Sleepy Dog*.

I bet Roo put him up to it.

It's not like it's a secret that my mom created the game. It's more that no one really cares anymore. *Sleepy Dog* was this cultural phenomenon of the past; we've moved on to new obsessions.

Except for Brody Wells, right now, trying to torment me.

"It'll be like I'm not even here," he promises, turning off the game and putting his phone in one of the cup holders. "You two can do whatever friend things you had planned."

I didn't set an agenda for the car ride, but sure.

Which maybe isn't the complete truth, because I did want to talk about wedding stuff. My biggest source of panic currently is the wedding venue, largely because I can't get the idea of an apple orchard wedding out of my head. Plus, we'll need the venue to finalize a date before I can work on invitations.

Roo's the one who speaks. "If you give Felicity free rein, she'll probably force you to listen to wedding stuff. Her mom's getting married," he explains.

I mean, yes that's exactly what I was just thinking about, but that doesn't mean I want to discuss it with freaking Bro-y Brody.

"Oh, I love that," Brody says, starting the car. "Don't you just love love?" He glances back at me from his seat in the front, then turns to look at his backup camera.

He's making fun of me, isn't he? He'll never get Sleepy Dog to her bed with that kind of attitude.

"Love's fine," I say, voice flat. "It's the venue that's more of the issue."

"She has a plan, but she's too scared to follow through with it," Roo says.

I glare at the back of his head, then take out my phone.

Felicity: it's bad enough you've forced me into the enemy's car
if you keep going i will retaliate

"What's the plan?" Brody asks.

I don't have to tell him if I don't want to. I could just make up some alternative or say something generic. A temple, a garden, a museum . . . There are a ton of options.

"I'm thinking about this apple orchard," I say.

"She's not going to do it," Roo cuts in. "Won't ever pursue the things that make her happy."

First of all, that's a total lie; I pursue matzo toffee all the time. And second, if he makes a girlfriend joke right now in front of Brody Wells of all people, I'm going to have to file friendship divorce papers.

"I might," I say stubbornly.

"She won't," he counters.

My phone buzzes.

Roo: And how exactly are you going to do that?

I jab my knee into the back of his seat.

Roo winces, then lets out an audible sigh.

Roo: Manners

Brody is doing us a favor by taking us home

Don't break his car

I want to have the last word. I'll text him that Brody is actually awful and this is all a part of his scheme to seem like a nice guy. Enemies deserve knee-shaped indents in their cars. Then I'll deliver a perfectly eloquent retort about how capable I am, how no matter what, I'll do what's best for this wedding. How the apple orchard was never a real option and even if it was, I'm not scared of talking to Nancy. Or the prospect of spending time this summer with her . . . in person. Because why would I be? We're friends. We talk all the time. Nothing would be different in the slightest. My hesitation is purely logistical; it would be too difficult to plan a wedding out of state.

But Roo puts his phone in his bag, then turns up the music on the car radio, effectively silencing me.

I guess Harry Styles gets the last word on this one.

To-do list: find a venue, start study guides for Irish Literature, Algebra I, and Biology.

Finals are important, because none of this will matter if I flunk out of school, but that admittedly is less of a risk this week. It's the academic lull before study panic sets in; best to take advantage of the down time to stress about something else.

I grab my phone off the nightstand and pull up my favorite contacts. My finger hovers over Nancy's name on the screen. This is silly. She didn't actually mean it when she said we should have it at her family's place. There's no way she was being serious.

I FaceTime her.

She picks up after the second ring. She must have just gotten out of practice, because her black hair is still in the messy bun she reserves for soccer. "Hey, Fe!"

Nancy is the only one who calls me Fe. Sometimes Mom and Eric call me Lissy, but everyone else usually sticks to Felicity. I like that the nickname is just something special between the two of us.

I jump right to the point. "Did you mean it?" I ask.

"The 'hey'? Or . . . ?" She raises an eyebrow.

"No, the wedding thing," I clarify. "Because it's like . . . a ridiculously big ask. I mean, a wedding involves all this planning, and it would intrude on your family's space, and my mom wants to do it pretty soon. I'd probably have to come up to visit before the ceremony and everything so I could get things ready."

"See, I think all that sounds fun." Nancy pauses to take a big sip from the water bottle in her other hand. "I have zero summer plans now that I'm not going to soccer camp; you'd practically be doing me a favor." She gestures to her knee, the robber of said camp dreams. It must be a bad recovery day since she has on her brace. "Hell, you all could come up as soon as school is over," she adds. "Plan it here, have the wedding at the end of the summer."

I laugh. "Right, like that's a possibility."

She shrugs. "Why not? What, don't you want to spend time with me?" She has this sly look on her face, like she's tempting me to say yes.

I smile. It's such a Nancy look, playful and daring and cute. Of course I want to spend time with her. It just doesn't make sense to have the wedding in Vermont.

"We can't intrude for the *entire* summer," I point out. "Where would we even stay?"

"Easy, you'd stay in the cottage. Next question," Nancy says.

"The cottage?" I ask.

"I'm going to be with my aunt Gwendoline; there's an entire unoccupied guesthouse on the orchard grounds. You're practically doing me a favor by making this summer less boring. Oh!" she gasps. "We could do sleepovers!"

"Nancy, this wouldn't work," I say.

"It might," she says. There's some noise in the background, too

51

muffled to make out what's going on. Nancy looks at something off-screen. "Gotta go, my dad's here. But seriously, just give it some thought. I think this might be my best idea yet."

With that, she ends the call.

I keep thinking about Nancy's idea all evening. While I work on my Biology study guide and grab some leftovers for dinner. While I take a study break to research local venues.

It doesn't help that she keeps sending me pictures of the orchard with notes like "stunning view" and "can't you see this as the ceremony space?"

I want to commit to this, I really do. I can already picture how I'd decorate the space and a few options for color schemes that would work for the orchard. I think I could get Mom and Eric on board.

There's just this part of me that feels like it's too good to be true. I run through everything that could go wrong: we'd be a burden to Nancy's family, she'll change her mind, all the wedding stress will ruin our friendship, Mom and Eric will hate the idea. This won't work.

I hear Roo's voice, taunting me, saying I'm not going to do it. *Won't ever pursue the things that make her happy.*

This would make me happy. The venue is a total dream, plus Nancy is the one who brought it up in the first place. I start to picture how much fun we'd have together, working on the wedding and hanging out in person.

Can I pull this off? Can I get a whole summer with Nancy *and* secure the perfect venue?

The more I think about it, the more it feels right.

TWO SPRINGS AGO

I joined Queer Club a month into freshman year. It's technically called the Genders and Sexualities Alliance, but everyone calls it Queer Club. At my first meeting, I felt like this small confused baby surrounded by self-actualized students—the juniors and seniors who solidly knew who they were. I was mostly just confused.

Because, the thing was, I knew I wasn't normal. I didn't think about sex and intimacy in the way my friends did, and I was pretty sure that was a problem. I wanted romance, someday, but the whole attraction thing? I was sure something was wrong.

Queer Club was the first place where I heard terms like "asexual spectrum" and "biromantic." It was the first time I realized other people felt the same way I do.

The retreat was Roo's idea. One of the benefits of our weird high school is that they offer a number of trips and retreats, including a Habitat for Humanity bus trip to Maryland, a tour of Italy for the Latin students, and, last year, the BE YOURSELF Northeast LGBTQIA+ symposium in Vermont. I was helping organize a fundraising auction through the Queer Club to raise money for trip scholarships when Roo practically demanded we sign up.

There were all these team-building and growth exercises, which were the right amount of cheesy, and we even got to go out on these Vermont-based excursions. And, of course, it's where I met Nancy Lim.

It happened in the middle of a small group share. We were discussing representation and identity, which everyone had *strong* opinions on, and I was up. Time to talk about *She-Ra and the Princesses of Power.*

"... it's a fact. They're just wives and it's no big deal. And from the very beginning, they have part of each other's costumes, which, yeah, was because the creative team wasn't sure if the higher-up exec people would let them have queer wives in a kids show, but still. Seeing them, seeing queer love as fact, well, it was the first time that I saw a romance on-screen and thought, 'I want that.'"

I probably would have continued my rambling explanation for longer if Nancy hadn't spoken.

"Spinnerella and Netossa? Obscure. I love it," she said in a whisper by my ear.

I turned my head. There she was, in a different group, seated a few feet behind me. She was looking away, as if nothing had happened, but I knew it was her.

Then, as if she could sense my gaze, she pushed back her long black hair behind one ear and glanced quickly back at me.

My first thought was that there was no way the two of us could be friends. She looked too sporty to put up with my penchant for dresses or compulsion to style my hair every morning. Nancy gave off serious "roll-out-of-bed-and-go-with-the-flow" vibes. She was wearing a plain T-shirt, unremarkable shorts, and scuffed-up sneakers. She probably wouldn't like me; those kinds of girls never do because I'm too high maintenance and prissy and annoyingly fascinated with stationery. I'm always too much.

My second thought was that since we both liked the same show, we might be soulmates.

I waited to respond until the next person started speaking to our group. "Let me guess, you're more of a Catra and Adora girl," I said quietly.

"What can I say, Catra's hot," she admitted.

We watched five episodes that night after the scheduled symposium activities and spent the rest of the trip by each other's sides.

—

On the last night of the retreat, Nancy invited me up to the roof. My first instinct was to panic. Was this supposed to be romantic? Sneaking out onto a roof at night seems like peak romance. I stopped myself from reading into things. After all, we barely knew each other and I was pretty sure friends could platonically invite friends on stargazing trips.

Even right at the beginning, Nancy made me feel like I could just be myself with her. There was something so fun and exciting about being with her, the easy flow of conversation, the way we always seemed to be on the same page. I didn't need to worry.

We were staying in the same dorm, but on different floors. "I saw one of the college students head this way yesterday," she said, leading the way up the stairs. "Told me all you have to do is prop the door open." She had a book under her arm, the sleeve of her sweatshirt blocking the title. Our apparent doorstop for the night.

"Hm," I said, holding the hand railing as we walked up, "would be funnier if we got ourselves locked outside."

"When we tell the story later, let's say we were stranded for hours. Saved by a plucky grad student who, in a stroke of luck, heard our cries from below."

I laughed. The building was only four stories tall. I doubted it would be that difficult to hear us if we were actually locked outside.

Nancy propped the door open and headed out.

It was a clear night. I had been worried that the light from the other buildings would ruin the view, but that was definitely a misguided fear. The stars seemed to pop against the deep night sky.

"So, what brought you here?" Nancy asked after a moment of silence. She wasn't even looking up at the stars. Instead her eyes were trained on the ground as she attempted to walk in a straight line across the roof, one foot after the other like she was on some imaginary tightrope.

"I accidentally killed my stepsister and made it look like the owner of the local ice cream shop was to blame," I said.

She stopped her progression across the roof for a moment to look back toward me.

"It's a podcast reference," I explained.

"Never got into those," she said, returning to her pretend tightrope. "I'm more of a listen to music or play a video game kind of girl."

"You're missing out on great content."

"Like stepsister slaying," she said.

"Well, on season three of *Murder She Solved*, sure." I watched her move, so gracefully. If I tried to walk like that, I'd trip. "I'm actually an only child," I added.

"Oh, me too!" she said, voice excited like she just found out we were both members of the same exclusive club.

"I think that makes us both selfish and spoiled."

She shook her head. "Speak for yourself; I'm a very well-rounded individual." Her voice had this light twinge to it, playful.

After a beat, she continued, "I meant to the retreat. I've known I'm queer for a while, but I know everyone's journey is so different." She walked back over to me and took a seat right there on the ground. "Do you ever stop and think about the words? If I had to choose a label, I'd probably go with queer. Or lesbian. But I don't know how I feel about needing to slap a label on a person, you know? Why do we need to have words for it? Just to make other people feel more comfortable?"

I nodded. "It helped me, though," I say. "Knowing that there were words for how I feel. I'm somewhere under the ace umbrella," I clarify. "And biromantic. Which are not exactly mainstream terms. So just hearing that other people identified that way, that I wasn't weird for everything in my head . . . well, it meant a lot to me."

"How'd you know?" Nancy asked. "Is that too pushy to ask? You don't have to answer," she added quickly.

"No, it's fine," I said, sitting down beside her. But I wasn't really sure how to answer in a way that she'd understand. Because it wasn't a single moment that had flipped the switch in my head, that made it all clear to me. I think part of that was this expectation I had. I thought I was supposed to feel attraction, that eventually it would happen. I kept waiting for it, too. Roo started to have crushes, though at first those were strictly limited to actors in action films. There were people at school who were objectively cute and had nice personalities; maybe someday I'd wake up and understand. All of a sudden those people would transform from cute to hot and then I'd feel normal.

So, when that kind of attraction kept not happening for me, I was sure there was something off inside my head. And, because of who I am as a person, I started to do research.

Said research might not have been the most technical. It was the summer after eighth grade. I was about to become a full-fledged high schooler, so I was pretty sure that I needed to figure all of this out before freshman year. I started with rom-coms, then moved on to romance novels. The novels were more informative because you actually got to see into the character's thoughts, hear an explanation of why they liked their love interest and how that love felt. I read about all different kinds of relationships: straight ones, queer ones, books about men and women and nonbinary folks. I consumed story after story of two people falling in love, reading about the intricacies of how different relationships developed. I even took notes, writing down when the couples hit each predetermined milestone, like maybe if I understood the formula all the real-life feelings would make sense. By the end of the summer, I knew two things: I loved love in all forms, and I still didn't understand attraction.

Roo joined Queer Club first. He would talk about the meetings, say how helpful they were and how nice it was to have that kind of community. But it still took me a month to get up the courage to go too. I kept thinking that there wasn't a place for someone like me, for someone who didn't fit neatly into a category like lesbian or bisexual.

Which was why it was such a relief when I learned that there were words for how I felt. Even then, it took me a while to settle on which of those words felt like a good fit. Was I asexual? No, I didn't think so, because sometimes when I read those romance novels, I did like the sex scenes. Sometimes I thought I might want that too, under whatever specific conditions were set up in the book. So then maybe I was demisexual, meaning I'd need an emotional attachment before I felt attraction. Except how would I know for sure, if all of this was based on hypotheticals and fictional characters? I eventually decided I liked the terms ace-spectrum and biromantic, meaning I could like anyone romantically, no matter their gender identity, but that attraction was something separate. I might not feel attraction, it might be fleeting, it might depend on having an emotional connection first. I liked that the term spectrum included all of those options.

I don't know why, but I told Nancy everything. We sat on the roof under the stars, and I explained it all, from my fears of not feeling like I was normal to the romance research. She shared too, explaining what it was like to have her first crush on a girl to her experience coming out to her family.

". . . and I walked in and there was a banner that said 'Love Is Love' hanging up in the living room. My great-aunt even baked me a rainbow cake; it was kind of epic," she said.

"That sounds wonderful," I said.

My own experience was much smaller than that, just my mom

and I hanging out on the couch. I said it mid-movie, and my mom had to hit Pause so she could offer her overly mushy support.

Maybe I should have told Nancy about that movie or the way my mom reached out to hug me, no hesitation, before I had even finished speaking. Instead, I said, "I came out wrong."

She raised an eyebrow. "I don't think there's a wrong way to do it."

"Oh, no, there is," I said. "I told my mom I was bisexual, even though I already knew I was on the ace-spectrum."

Nancy didn't say anything, like she was waiting for me to continue.

I sighed. "I think I was just convinced she wouldn't get it. Like maybe it would be easier to use words she definitely already knew. And I guess 'bisexual' felt close enough. I did eventually tell her, and she was awesome both times." I paused. "So, yeah, there is a wrong way."

"Wrong way, right way, normal," Nancy said. "You use those kinds of qualifiers a lot."

"And . . . ?" I asked.

"Just something I've noticed," she said.

We were quiet after that. The two of us sitting on that dorm roof underneath the stars.

I'm not sure how long it was before she broke the silence. "Hey," she started. "Let's be friends."

"Aren't we already?" I asked.

She laughed. "No, I mean real ones. Like after this is all over, let's keep being friends. I know I'm in Vermont and you're going back to Massachusetts, but why does that have to stop this?" She waved between the two of us like that captured our entire friendship.

I paused like this was something I really had to consider. "I might be able to make that work."

"Good," she said, taking out her phone.

We exchanged numbers on that clear, starlit night, and we've texted every day since.

NINE DAYS AFTER THE ENGAGEMENT

Technically, I invited Roo over to do research and help me set up a plan to convince Mom and Eric to go along with my Vermont idea. Watching trashy reality TV isn't exactly unrelated.

"I can definitely plan a better wedding than Jessica K.," I say, waving to the TV.

"Jessica K., your tropical theme is not fooling anyone; it's February in Michigan," Roo yells at the misguided bride on the screen.

"To be fair, it's still better than the Barbies and Beer one last episode," I say.

I open my designated wedding ideas notebook and pick up the pen I put on the coffee table.

"You better not be writing 'tropical theme' in there," Roo says.

"Psh, that's Jessica K.'s thing."

What I actually write down is: "Late night reception snacks? Mac and cheese bar? Cliché?"

I'm a much better event planner than these people. I mean, even the Arbor Day Dance was better than this mess we're watching now.

We're at the part of the show where, after all of the planning, you finally get to the ceremony. This is usually a huge feat and involves overcoming at least one major disaster, like rain or a bridesmaid getting sick. Jessica K. gets out of the old-fashioned convertible she tragically couldn't fit a surfboard into earlier in the episode. Her dress has so much bling on it she could interview to work as a disco ball. Not that her future groom seems to mind. When the camera pans to him, he's visibly crying, like his bejeweled soon-to-be wife is the most beautiful person he has ever seen.

I think about that sometimes, what my future spouse will look like when I walk down the aisle. I don't think I want them to cry, not anything too dramatic, at least. A couple of episodes ago, the groom bawled so hard his face got red. What I picture is something better, more personal. A moment where our eyes lock and all we can think about is our love. The person at the end of the aisle is always sort of blurry and out of focus. I mean, I'm biromantic; my soulmate could be anyone.

Except sometimes I get scared that the whole wedding thing isn't in the cards for me. I'm at the point where I feel good about being on the ace-spectrum. I just don't know if other people will be okay with it, people of the potential future partner variety.

There are expectations that come with relationships, all of those formulaic steps you're supposed to take. Like in the romance books I read, each couple followed a path of predetermined emotional beats. They'd catch feelings, kiss, face obstacles, and eventually overcome them, usually with a sex scene or two thrown in for good measure. All of that involves a level of intimacy I might never be comfortable with. The problem is the uncertainty. I just don't know if those regular relationship steps are things I'll ever take.

That doesn't mean marriage isn't something I still want. It's just something I might not get to have.

Will potential future partners be okay with how I feel? Will they understand? Will anyone even want to date me since I'm like this?

I try to picture it again, as though it's a guarantee. Manifesting and whatnot.

I meet the right person, and they're fine taking things at my pace. They listen to my needs, and I feel comfortable with them. We walk hand in hand across a beach at sunset. Then, if I'm to trust all my research, we end up in a situation where there's only one bed. Eventually, after a respectful amount of time, we get engaged and plan a tasteful ceremony at an estate house. I wear a beautiful gown with lace and a dramatic, low-cut back. The music starts and—

"Who walks down the aisle if there are two brides?" I wonder aloud.

"What?" Roo asks.

I turn from the screen to face him. "Okay, like last season, remember? There was that one episode where there were two brides. And one of them wore that fancy wedding jumpsuit, and the other walked down the aisle in a ball gown and had the big bride entrance. How does that happen? The decision there, I mean."

"You've been watching too much of this straight nonsense," Roo mutters. "Is this about Nancy? Are you picturing marrying Nancy?" He's full-on mocking me right now with his tone.

Jerk.

I'm not the lead in a CW show, so hard no on that one. "Stop," I say.

"Can't, I'm already picturing you and Nancy in the middle of some competitive tic-tac-toe game to decide who gets the . . . what did you call it? Big bride entrance?"

I groan.

"Lottery system, perhaps? No, I've got it! The bridal parties get together and vote."

"This isn't about Nancy; I was just curious," I say, annoyed. I turn my attention back to the screen.

"I think it's a little about Nancy," Roo says, but then he goes back to watching too.

Except now I can't pay attention. I'm distracted all the way through the vows and even into the reception, which is my favorite part because it's really where the whole event comes together.

I wasn't thinking about Nancy, just some hypothetical future soulmate. I really wasn't . . . before Roo mentioned her. Now that blurry figure has a face. It's Nancy holding my hand as we walk down a beach and accidentally have to share one bed. It's Nancy wearing an equally gorgeous gown, standing next to me, leaning in for a kiss.

Why is my brain like this?

Because Nancy and I are purely platonic. Like last summer, she told me all about when she got her first official girlfriend and everything that happened with the rise and fall of their relationship. Someone who likes you romantically wouldn't go telling you about how nice it is to make out with another girl. They would hide their summer fling, at the very least.

So there's obviously no way she sees me in any kind of romantic light. I don't see her like that either . . . except for a moment ago when I was picturing our wedding. Which was Roo's fault, so I can't be blamed.

The problem is, once I go down a thought path, it's really hard to stop. Now I'm not worrying about any of Roo's made-up claims of romance because I'm too busy figuring out all of the realistic ways that having the wedding in Vermont could destroy our friendship. Nancy and I haven't spent that much time together in person, so I'll annoy her. She won't like the way I talk, she'll judge how I dress, I'll get on her nerves so much that she's going to say we have to leave the state, thus obliterating one of the most important friendships in my life and destroying my mom's perfect wedding.

I pause the show.

"Okay, serious time, and if I hear you say the word 'girlfriend' I'm legally allowed to punch you in the nose."

Roo protectively covers his face. "Yes?"

"Do you think it will be . . . normal with Nancy? If I pull this off, I mean."

Roo sighs. "As someone who had to be a third wheel for a week and a half, I'd say you're fine. You had more inside jokes in three days than you and I had in three years."

"Awfully close to nose-punching territory, Basra," I warn. Last names are for serious business and threats.

"It's just," I continue, "well, it's just that it's been so long. What if she sees me and is like, 'Wow I forgot what you're like in person; leave, you monster'?"

"Seems unlikely," Roo says.

"But not entirely out of the realm of possibility," I counter.

Roo shakes his head. "She's your friend; it'll be fine."

She *is* my friend, a close friend who would never run and hide because I'm annoying and overthink everything and dress like a fifties housewife. Let's say she does hate the real-life Felicity; it's not like the world is going to end. What's the likelihood of that happening again so soon after the Social Friends Committee disaster?

"All right, let's see if Jessica K. can pull off her definitely offensive hula routine," I say, reaching for the remote.

"You know she can't," Roo says.

I turn the show back on.

TEN DAYS AFTER THE ENGAGEMENT

I summon Mom and Eric to the living room the next evening.

"What's under the sheet?" Mom asks.

I shush her. I didn't drag up my old toddler art easel from the basement and cover it with the sheet from the guest room just to give everything away before my reveal. "I'll get to that," I say.

"Is this the project you were working on last night?" Eric asks from his spot on the couch.

Well, this and my study guides, so sort of. I don't respond to Eric because that would distract from my totally professional nighttime presentation.

"Guys, focus," I say, clapping my hands together. I take a deep and deliberate breath. I'm ready.

"All right, as you're probably aware, you two are engaged." *Great start.*

Mom doesn't make a joke about what I just said like I was pretty sure she would. Instead she holds up her left hand and wiggles her fingers. The emerald glints in the overhead light.

"Exactly," I continue. "And, as you're engaged, that means that you'll be getting married." *Oy vey.*

I straighten my shoulders. *Pull it together, Becker,* I tell myself.

"Mom mentioned that you were thinking of making a trip out of the wedding and having the ceremony kind of soon, so . . ." With that I pull the sheet off the easel.

"What am I looking at?" Eric asks.

"A vision board," my mom answers.

I nod. They are, in fact, looking at a vision board. Specifically, one that's decorated with pictures of Vermont and rustic weddings I found online. There's one picture where the bride and groom are posing in between two rows of apple trees and another of an outdoor ceremony space shaded by all of the surrounding greenery and three different possible arrangements for the reception space. Then there are the pictures of Vermont: streets lined with cute little shops and lush mountains. I added a small cutout of a bottle of maple syrup for good measure.

"Imagine, if you will, a quaint, adorable, all-around lovely village. In Vermont. Now picture how amazing it would be to have your wedding there."

I pause, as if to allow them the time to imagine as directed, before continuing, "Well, it turns out you're both in luck, because I have the perfect place!"

Mom lets out a laugh, which isn't exactly encouraging.

"Did you create a vision board so we'd take you to Vermont?" she asks.

"I created a vision board for your perfect wedding," I correct. "I also found a venue and a place to stay and called Eric's boss to see if he could get the time off."

This time Eric laughs. His "boss" is his younger brother who owns and operates the tattoo shop a couple of towns over. It's actually where my mom and Eric met, back when she got her second tattoo, a diamond landscape on her rib cage that Eric designed. She claims she was obsessed with his use of colors when she found his work on Instagram, but fell for the artist the moment she walked into the shop. It was love at first tattoo consultation.

"How much time off did you ask for?"

"The summer," I answer.

Eric stops laughing.

"Felicity, you want us to go away for the whole summer?" Mom asks.

"Well, yeah. It'll be so much easier to get everything planned if we're actually there. Obviously, it will have to be pretty low-key, and we'll do a lot of the prep work ourselves." She has to know this part already; she's the one who said she didn't want to drag it out. I mean, to throw a proper wedding, you really need about a year. We've watched enough TLC wedding content together to know that.

"Plus, Nancy's great-aunt has this apple orchard, which is seriously the ideal venue, and there's an entire cottage that Nancy said we could stay in," I add. "You can write anywhere; Eric's been saying he wants to take some time away to focus on his art, plus he already got the okay to leave—"

"How exactly did you pull that off?" Eric asks.

"Oh, Matty said he was already planning on forcing you to cover for him a lot when the baby arrives," I explain. Matty's wife, Tia, is four months pregnant with their first child, and I've heard babies are a lot of work, so I get the desire to force someone else to help out more when you are a sleep-deprived newborn guardian.

"He said you might have to come back for a couple of appointments you already booked, but other than that . . ."

Eric whistles. "Summer vacation . . . Haven't had one of those in a while."

"Plus, it's a pretty great excuse to get me out of our brunch obligation. I wouldn't mind a break," Mom says.

"See," I say, "it's perfect."

Mom looks at Eric. "I just want to have the wedding somewhere fun with our family. I'm in if you are."

Eric puts his hand on his chin like he's thinking about this so deeply he might turn into a statue. "I guess we're going on vacation!" he finally says.

I can't help but smile.

Successful presentation: check.

Mom and Eric's approval: check.

Now all I have to do is pull off an entire wedding in a couple of months. How hard can that be?

I think I'm going to fail therapy today.

When Mom and Eric agreed to my whole Vermont wedding scheme, they didn't realize that meant a therapy hiatus. I mean, the office I go to has virtual sessions as an option. Except there are apparently very specific rules about where licensed therapists in Massachusetts can practice, meaning virtual visits are out while I'm away. This is my last session before we leave.

I wonder if Bonnie will be angry about that. Maybe she'll accuse me of coordinating the trip just to get out of seeing her. She'll probably say this is some sort of sign that I'm doing terribly, worse than before.

Instead she asks, "How are you feeling about the wedding?"

"Good to neutral," I say. "Is that bad? I should probably be all joy; there's just so much to do."

"We don't need to characterize our emotions as good or bad; we just need to feel them," Bonnie says.

I nod. She's always saying things like that.

"Why are you worried that there's so much to do?" she continues.

"Because weddings are a lot to put together," I say. "You have to book vendors and decorate and send out invitations and coordinate with guests, and from the looks of it with Eric's big family and Mom's friends from college and the people Bubbe wants to invite, there'll be at least fifty people. And that's if my grandma doesn't go over her guest limit. So . . . yeah. It's a lot."

"A lot for . . ." She trails off.

"Me," I answer. "All the things I'll have to do."

"But it's your mother's wedding," Bonnie presses. "Isn't this a lot for her? For Eric?"

I practically snort at that. "I'll be in charge," I say.

"Why?" Bonnie asks. "You're sixteen; this isn't your wedding."

"Well, out of the three of us, I think I could do the best job," I say, like this proves my point.

Bonnie has this look on her face like she's carefully examining my soul. It makes me uneasy. "Be proud of everything you can accomplish, but remember, this isn't your burden alone," she finally says. There's something about it that feels very Jedi master to me.

"I want to go over some coping techniques," she adds. I like this part. I'm much better at the clear activities than I am with the *openly communicate what's going on in your head* part of seeing Bonnie.

We spend more time than we usually do on this. I wonder if my mom sent her an email to ask for that, like some sort of going-away tool kit so I'm not a mess in Vermont.

Before we wrap up, Bonnie says, "Remember, Felicity. I'm still around. If you need anything, you can email or even text if it's urgent. And I'll see you again when you're back."

I nod. I've never texted or emailed Bonnie before. The likelihood that I will now is slim.

"You're in a good place," she adds. "I really do believe that."

She's right. I *am* in a good place.

"Thanks, Bonnie," I say, getting up from my seat.

Maybe I didn't fail therapy today after all.

FORTY-FIVE DAYS UNTIL THE WEDDING

Now that we have the venue, everything is kicked into superspeed. We have to send out invitations pretty much immediately. Then there's the catering and the cake, and I need to figure out if we're going for a band or DJ.

With finals over, at least I can focus on this. I run through my to-do list, trying to figure out what I can work on now. I picked out the style for the invitations; I just need to get the guest list finalized. I've already started booking appointments and making calls for local vendors, but it's tough figuring everything out from Massachusetts. We're leaving for Vermont in a few days; it'll be easier once we're actually there.

My phone dings from its spot on my bed. I turn it over and see a notification for a new email from Bubbe. I swipe to read it.

Dear Felicity,

I've attached my list of guests to invite to the wedding. Just ten, though of course a few will need plus-ones.

Talked to Deborah at temple and told her all about you. Apparently, Hartman and Co. does have a fall internship.

I knew we could find something good for you! She's so
excited for the wedding, joked that it would be like a little
pre-interview for the internship. Better make sure this is
the best event you've ever planned!

All my love,
Your Bubbe

Oh, wow, okay. Not only is the senior director for freaking
Hartman and Co. coming to my mom's wedding, but she also sees
the event as a pre-interview. If this goes well, does that mean she'll
just give me the fall internship? It's basically like I'm auditioning
for the position.

I walk through it in my head. I plan the perfect wedding, the
senior director for Hartman and Co. attends, she loves it, I get my
dream internship, which helps me get into a ton of schools, and
then I never have to worry again because my whole life is set.

Maybe that part is an exaggeration, but I can't help it. I'm too
excited.

I have to go tell Mom.

I rush out of my room and head down to the first floor.

"Hey, Mom, Bubbe sent her list and—" I stop mid-stairs when
I hear their voices. I think someone just said my name.

I creep closer until I can make out what they're saying.

". . . don't want this to be another stressor," my mom says.

"Or, you could look at it this way: it might be exactly what she
needs. Get her away from here. Fresh air, family time. She gets to
be with her friend," Eric says.

Yep, they're definitely talking about me. I shouldn't listen . . . but, then again, they shouldn't be talking so loudly in the kitchen if they don't want me to eavesdrop.

"Yeah, I . . . You're right, it'll be good to get away."

"Plus," Eric continues, "it's a productive project. Something good to focus on."

"That's why I'm worried. Weddings can be . . . a lot. Plus, she won't be able to see her therapist while we're gone. I just don't want her taking on too much and this turning into a repeat of everything that happened over winter."

No. I can't believe she'd bring that up now.

"We won't let that happen. She's doing so well. I mean look how she did with finals."

"I caught her sneaking caffeine," Mom says, voice serious. "And I had to send her to bed three nights in a row."

In any other house, for any other teenager, those wouldn't be big concerns.

Except I'm not normal. What did I expect would happen? Of course she was paying close attention during finals. *You're the one who put herself in the hospital during midterms*, I think. *All your fault.*

"Han, come on. Cut her some slack."

"I'm allowed to worry," Mom says. There's a pause before she speaks again. "I don't have to worry about this? Do I?"

"Not at all," Eric says.

They're quiet now, but my head feels very loud. I hate this. Mom shouldn't be concerned about me; I won't let it get that bad again. I've been working so hard with Bonnie during our sessions. Mom has to see that.

She's the one who's irresponsible. I have everything together now. There's no need for any of this.

I turn around and walk back up the stairs. If she's already worried about me going overboard with this wedding, I'm not about to tell her what Bubbe said in her email. She'd probably call off the whole wedding out of pure concern.

What's the worst that could happen? She gets a beautiful wedding? I'll tell her after I get the internship.

LAST WINTER

The official diagnosis: dehydration and exhaustion, with a bonus concern of "alarmingly high" blood pressure.

According to the doctor, I was at risk of a heart attack.

The reason: three days without sleep and overconsumption of caffeine, from a combination of coffee and energy drinks. There was also the very large bruise on my forehead from when I fainted, which is technically what sent me to the hospital in the first place.

It wasn't the first time I alternated between coffee and Four Hour Energy Boost. It definitely wasn't the first time that I studied through the night.

Collapsing during breakfast was new.

It was my last midterm exam. If I had just gotten through it, I could have gone home and slept it all off. That felt like the worst part, missing the test. No one wants to postpone an Algebra midterm.

When I got home, there were all kinds of new rules. No more caffeine, not even tea, a strict 11:00 p.m. bedtime, checks to make sure I actually followed said bedtime, and therapy.

Part of it felt hypocritical. Mom stays up all the time. She's jokingly asked for coffee in an IV more than once.

Except none of that ever sent her to the ER.

So, I followed the rules. I went to therapy, went to bed when I was supposed to, switched over to non-caffeinated chamomile, and stopped buying cases of Four Hour Energy Boost. I've only slipped up on coffee a few times.

I handled it.

When I took the exam a week after I left the hospital, I got a 96 percent.

FORTY-TWO DAYS UNTIL THE WEDDING

It's pouring rain the night we arrive in Vermont. Yes, *night*. It's 10:21 p.m. by the time we pull up in front of the main house at the orchard.

Nothing is going as planned. We were supposed to arrive around four. Nancy was going to give us this beautiful tour of the orchard so Mom and Eric could see the wedding venue, and then we were going to have a picnic at the top of one of the hills so we could see the sun setting over the apple trees. This, obviously, would provide the perfect backdrop to illustrate how right I am about the venue as we discussed specifics for the ceremony and reception.

Except Eric forgot he rescheduled an appointment with one of his clients so it wouldn't conflict with the wedding and had to go in to work for a few hours, and then Mom was "in the groove" writing, and since she's back on deadline that means she absolutely can't be disturbed when she's finally being productive, and don't even get me started on the last-minute packing, which was decidedly not my fault since I've had all my stuff ready since school got out last week. If this is any indication of what it's going to be like trying to herd these two around for wedding prep, things aren't looking great for my summer.

"We made it," Mom says as she turns off the ignition, as though she accomplished a big goal.

I don't say anything back. Late people don't get credit.

"We're staying here?" Eric asks, pointing to the house.

The main house at the orchard is huge. It's three stories of fresh white paint and crisp green shutters. It looks more like a destination bed-and-breakfast than a home. I can see that there's one light on through a first-floor window, but the rest of the house seems dark.

"No, that's Nancy's great-aunt's house," I say. I've seen it before in pictures and a few times when I FaceTimed Nancy. "We're staying in the cottage."

I actually haven't seen the cottage. Nancy outright refused to show me beforehand because she swore the surprise would be worth it. Not that it really matters; it's just the place we're going to be sleeping in for the summer. The important stuff is where we'll set up the chairs and the dining tables and dance floor. Years from now, that's what we'll remember.

I mean, fine, I'm curious.

I look over at the main house. Could Nancy hear our car pull up with all the rain? Am I supposed to call her? I was texting updates at first when it became increasingly clear that we weren't going to arrive in time, but the last one I sent was when we finally left. It's been hours. She could be watching something, rendering a timely text useless, so I should obviously call. Though her great-aunt could be asleep and calling would wake her up, and then she'd tell us we had to get off her property immediately, and then Mom doesn't get the perfect wedding and Nancy never talks to me again and—

The door to the house opens, and Nancy runs out to our car. She knocks on the window opposite of mine. "Can I come in?" she yells over the downpour.

Mom unlocks the car, and Nancy slides onto the seat next to me.

She's soaked from her short time in the rain. Her simple blue T-shirt looks like it's right out of the washer, and her long black hair is so wet she could trick someone into thinking that she just got out of the shower.

"Hey, Fe," she says.

"Hey," I say back.

She moves in for a hug and then pulls back. "Sorry, you probably don't want to hug me like this," she says.

"I do," I say too quickly. "I mean, um, I don't mind."

She smiles.

Hugging Nancy is so comfortable. Even though we're in the back of my mom's car, which I've been sitting in for hours, and Nancy's soaked from the rain, it feels *right*.

She pulls back and greets Mom and Eric. She's met them via phone before, but this is her first time seeing the nonscreen versions. "Hi, Ms. Becker, Mr. Flores," she starts. "So excited to welcome you to Belmont Orchards!" She waves toward the window like we can see the whole place through the rain and darkness.

"So formal. It's totally fine to call us Hannah and Eric," Mom says.

Nancy gives her a thumbs-up.

"Thanks for welcoming us in for the summer. Lissy's been so excited," Eric adds. "Wouldn't stop talking about coming here."

He hasn't even officially joined the family and he's already coming in with peak dad embarrassment.

"No, no, we're so happy to have you," Nancy insists. "Aunt Gwendoline's already up in her room, but she's been really excited for the company. You all can meet tomorrow when we do a proper tour." She looks out the car window. "Ugh, it's miserable out there. We have to walk to get to the cottage." Her tone is apologetic.

"I packed umbrellas," I offer.

"This is why I love you," Nancy says casually.

I'm fairly positive I'm blushing now. Good thing Roo wasn't able to hear that.

There's a whole scramble to get the stuff we need for the night (we'll come back for the rest when it's less miserable outside), and then I hand out umbrellas. There are only three, so I tell Nancy that we can share.

"Ready?" she asks.

I nod.

She opens the door.

Nancy and I take the lead. After we dash out of the car, we head around the side of the main house, through a very muddy field, and past a row of trees. "We're almost there," she promises as we race along. "You'll love it, I swear."

Nancy stops abruptly. I'm the one holding the umbrella since I'm taller, so she's temporarily subjected to the elements at full force. "Sorry," I say, taking a step back.

Which is when I see the "cottage."

We're standing in front of a massive red barn. This has to be some kind of joke. What does Nancy expect us to do, sleep with animals? Before I can say anything, Nancy lets go of my arm and pulls a key out of her pocket. Then she goes over to a beige-painted door on the side of the barn and unlocks it. "Come on," she says, already walking in.

I follow, but stop as soon as I get inside. Well, that's not what I expected.

The inside of the barn looks like a luxury cabin had a baby with an HGTV "after" montage. It's absolutely stunning. We're standing in a large open concept living area, with a kitchen in front of us that looks like it was renovated *right* before we arrived, leading to a rustic chic dining area and matching living room. The ceiling is high and vaulted, and the entire back wall of the building is made of glass. Nancy turns on the lights so I can see out. It overlooks a pond. You've got to be kidding me; this place is too idyllic to be real.

"Bedrooms are down those stairs." Nancy points to a spot near the glass wall. "Don't worry, the landscape slopes, so you still get windows in the rooms. There are three full bathrooms, one up here and two downstairs. I did a grocery run earlier, so there are some basics in the kitchen. I think that's everything."

I'm still adjusting to the surroundings, but Mom is already in creative expletive mode. Bubbe always scolds her for "talking like a sailor." She moves on to compliments. "This place is stunning! How? Who did this? Can I become their best friend?"

Nancy laughs. "My parents," she explains. "It's what they do for a living. My mom handles construction, and Dad's on interior design. This was originally supposed to be a guesthouse, but really it's their showpiece. They're actually going to be away for most of the summer because they have a few projects out of state, so I'm staying with Aunt Gwendoline."

I already knew this part. Her parents tend to work in the area, but they had scheduled out-of-state work when they thought Nancy was going to be away at soccer camp. After the knee injury destroyed that particular plan, Nancy opted to stay home instead of tagging along with her mom and dad.

"I'm going to befriend your parents," Mom says like it's a challenge.

Mom and Eric go downstairs to check out their summer room, and Nancy walks me through a few more specifics, like how to adjust the air-conditioning and connect to the Wi-Fi and work the massive TV in the living room.

"All right, one last thing," she says, heading to the stairs.

I follow.

She stops in front of one of the bedrooms. "This is technically the smallest, but I think you'll like it," she says. The wooden door is on a slider, which is something I've seen on home renovation shows before but never inside a real-life house.

"Oh," I manage.

The bed is set on a metal frame, painted in a distressed white. The bedding is white too, with accents of cream and tan on the decorative pillows and throw blanket artfully draped near the end. There's a chandelier over the bed. *A chandelier.* Except that isn't even what Nancy's excited about.

"Since you're going to be so busy planning . . ." she explains, walking over to the giant shabby chic desk.

"It's perfect," I say. Because it is. The whole room, from desk to chandelier, is better than I could have ever imagined when Nancy said she had a place where we could stay for the summer. Part of it's the aesthetic—I feel like I'm staying in my own perfectly designed and organized dream. Mostly, though, it's Nancy. She considered *everything*, from basic supplies to work spaces.

Her smile is so big and genuine it reaches her eyes.

"I'll leave you to settle in. We're still on for the tour tomorrow?"

I nod.

"I have an idea for after," she says. "Trust me, you'll like it."

After her "trust me" with this "cottage," I feel like I can definitively conclude that I'll love anything Nancy has planned.

Maybe . . . possibly . . . probably, I'll remember more from this summer than *just* the wedding prep.

FORTY-ONE DAYS UNTIL THE WEDDING

When we first meet Aunt Gwendoline, she's wearing an evening gown. *Gardening.*

Nancy asked us to come over to the main house around noon so she could give us our tour. Even with the late start time, I had to rush Mom through her breakfast. She didn't even wake up until 11:30.

Aunt Gwendoline is by the side of the house, bent over a flower bed, tending to a patch of peonies. She has on a large straw hat, the wide brim shading her face, bright green gardening gloves on her hands . . . and an evergreen, floor-length gown that is currently resting on the dirt.

"What are you wearing?" Nancy practically sighs as she walks closer to her great-aunt.

"I do believe you know the answer," Aunt Gwendoline responds simply. She has a smooth English accent like she just walked off the set of a period drama about Korean-British high society. "You told me to look presentable for our company," she adds.

"That's not what I meant."

Aunt Gwendoline ignores this. She puts down her shears and claps her gardening-glove-clad hands together. "Felicity! We've been eagerly awaiting your arrival, darling. This feels like meeting the hero of a great epic, the way Nancy talks about you."

"Aunt Gwendoline," Nancy says as if she's scolding a child.

"Nancy," Gwendoline says in the same tone. Then she turns her attention to Mom and Eric. "Our bride and groom! So lovely to meet you. I haven't been to a wedding since . . . well, my last one, I suppose. Fourth time wasn't the charm," she adds casually.

There are a lot of thanks and so-happy-to-meet-yous exchanged. As Eric enthusiastically shakes Aunt Gwendoline's hand, Mom leans over and whispers in my ear, "I want to *be* her."

"Plan on having three more weddings after this?" I ask quietly.

She lightly hits my arm. "You know what I mean."

Aunt Gwendoline has a little knowing smile on her face. "Now, kids, be safe. Have a splendid time. And, adults," she adds, looking at Mom and Eric, "I'll put together a bit of a sampling for when you get back."

"Cider," Nancy explains. "She's saying she wants to drink with you."

"Love that," Mom says.

Nancy tells Aunt Gwendoline to behave, and we head off on our tour.

The apple orchard is huge; we only ran through a small section of it to get to the converted barn last night. I feel like I need a map. There are paths, some dirt and some grass, running all along the grounds. Nancy shows us some of her favorite spots, including her top three ponds and the overgrown hedge maze. It isn't apple season yet, but we can see the growing fruit, not quite ripe, spotted along the branches.

Nancy stops in front of a small building with red-painted walls and a faded sign over the door that reads "The Belmont Orchards Store."

"The orchard used to be open to the public when I was little," Nancy says. "Aunt Gwendoline would fill that place with all kinds of baked goods: cider donuts, pies, tarts, scones. We'd get huge crowds, but it was a lot of hard work for her, and my mom and dad started getting so busy with their business. Mom converted the store into her workshop a couple of years ago." There's this wistful way to how she's talking. I wonder if I should say anything or if that would make it worse.

She continues before I make up my mind. "Then Aunt Gwendoline got bored with retirement, so she started Belmont Ciders. Turns out she likes alcohol just as much as she likes baked goods."

I don't like how excited my mom looks; she needs better role models as it is.

"It's a lot more manageable, at least," Nancy adds. "We supply a few local stores, and Aunt Gwendoline gets out her creativity coming up with specialty flavors. It works."

She pauses, looking over at the old store. I try to imagine how it used to be, with a line of customers out that door and the smell of fresh-baked goods filling the air. I feel nostalgic for it, and I wasn't even there.

Nancy turns away from the building. "Let's move on," she says. "We've got a lot more to see."

I don't know about moving on, but we do keep walking.

———

It turns out that trekking through an apple orchard the day after a storm can be a little messy.

My cute flats have seen better days. Most of our walk was dry, since the summer sun is both hot and relentless, but I still manage to step in enough mud to coat the faux suede on my shoes. I wore a yellow-and-white-striped sundress and forgot to put anything on my legs, so my thighs are angry. Mistakes were made when I got dressed this morning.

Nancy slips off her sneakers by the front door. "You can put yours here," she says.

I look down at my muddied flats. I should probably just put them in the trash with how much I've destroyed them. I take them off carefully and leave them by Nancy's shoes.

We already lost Mom and Eric to an outdoor cider tasting with Aunt Gwendoline. She had a whole picnic table set up and everything. Which means it's just the two of us in this absurdly large house.

Inside, there's a weird meeting of styles. Parts of it look like the converted barn while other aspects clash in an eclectic mix, a rustic chic décor meeting the inside of a peculiar antique shop.

"Aunt Gwendoline's a *collector*," Nancy explains. From the way she says it, it sounds like she's really calling her great-aunt a hoarder, but I don't think it's that extreme. "My parents keep trying to help her organize, but . . ." She trails off.

She keeps moving, heading right to the kitchen. "All right, big reveal time," she says. "Close your eyes."

I do what she says. "Do you have a very cute animal to show me?" I guess.

"I wish," Nancy says. "Swiftie's being elusive."

Nancy has a Burmese cat named Swift Wind, Swiftie for short, who I have not seen once even though Nancy and I FaceTime so much. I think he might be imaginary.

I can hear something crash in the background. "It's fine, I'm fine, keep your eyes closed."

I hear a cabinet door shut.

"Okay," she says. "Ready."

I open my eyes. She's standing in front of me holding a big jar of maple syrup in one hand and a plastic mold with three rows of maple leaves in the other. "We're making maple candy!" she says, like I know what that is.

"Yay?" I respond, hesitantly.

"It's basically just a sugar candy made of pure maple syrup. I thought it could be a fun, Vermont-themed wedding favor. You'll love it."

Candy *and* wedding planning? This girl knows me too well.

We get to work making the candy. The whole process is a lot like what I have to do to make the toffee part of matzo toffee: there's a candy thermometer and wait time and stirring. Working with any kind of sugar is a pain because it can be so temperamental. You have to get it to just the right temperature and then stir it in an exact way; it can all go wrong so quickly.

I fill the time talking. I tell Nancy about which parts of the orchard I think could work for the ceremony and then somehow devolve into a full breakdown of finals week. Nancy chimes in from time to time to add an idea or grumble about a test, but I'm doing most of the talking. It's not usually that way; she tends to match me in the chatter department. I think she's just hyper-focused.

I bring up the internship by accident. I haven't said a word to anyone about it, except for Bubbe, but she doesn't really count. She's the one who sent me the email in the first place. I can't tell Mom, because she's already worried that the wedding stuff will be too much for me. I can't even imagine how she'll react if she found out the senior director for Hartman and Co. will be using the event to essentially decide my future.

I probably should've told Roo. I was going to; I even had a text all typed out. Except I kept thinking about the way Mom's voice sounded when she said she was worried. Roo was there for everything that happened over the winter. Maybe he'd tell her, and then she'd call the whole thing off anyway. Maybe he'd be nonchalant and dismissive about it because everything just comes so easy for him, so it must be the same for me. Trying to impress a potential boss for an internship? No biggie.

I don't know which hypothetical is worse.

But with Nancy, there's not even really any thought to it. Part of that *might* be that she knows significantly less about the winter debacle. It's not that I hid the hospital trip from her; I just kept the details . . . sparse. Even if she did know, I can't see her being weird about this internship. She understands what it means to work hard and struggle for what she wants. After everything that happened with her knee, she's made that more than clear.

"My grandma invited the senior director from this big-deal event management company in Boston to the wedding. She's trying to connect us so I can get an internship with them next year."

Nancy, mid-pouring the sugar into the mold, looks up at me. "Fe, that's amazing!" she says. Some of the maple sugar flows out of the mold onto the counter. She curses under her breath and looks back at where she's pouring. "Can you imagine that on your resume?"

"I know," I say, grabbing a paper towel to clean up the spill. "I mean, it's not a guarantee," I add.

"Oh, yeah, of course," Nancy says, putting down the pot. "I mean, I'm sure it's going to be an insane amount of work to put something together that will impress the freaking senior director."

"Just some extra work on top of the normal wedding planning. No big deal," I joke.

Nancy waves this off. "It'll be the best wedding anyway, with you in charge. Plus, I'm here to help."

I give her a skeptical look. "You want to help? This isn't going to be fun."

"Yeah, trying the food and the desserts and looking at pretty flowers and finding fancy dresses"—she dramatically fake yawns—"what a bore."

"It'll be a lot of tedious stuff too. And, since we're having it so soon, a lot of DIY projects," I warn. "You are fully allowed to change your mind."

"Accept the help," she says.

I should leave it at that, but my blabbering mouth knows no bounds. "I'm a little nervous," I say quickly.

"Why?" she asks. "This is exciting, right?"

"Yeah," I start. "I know, it's just . . . I don't know. You don't think it's too much added pressure?"

"Well, what did Roo say?" Nancy asks.

I swear, the two of them love to bring each other up. Do I really need to consult him on this, anyway?

I mean, yes, normally. I'm just purposefully avoiding the topic with him right now.

"You're the only one I told," I admit.

"No, no, unacceptable. I think you broke the best-friend code."

"You would've told Diya?" I ask. Diya has been her other half for almost as long as I've known Roo.

"If she weren't in Ohio for the summer, we'd be throwing a massive pre-party party," she says. "If I was the one about to secure her dream internship, obviously," she clarifies.

She's right; I should have told Roo immediately. We could've celebrated before I left and discussed ideas and generally freaked out that Bubbe was able to pull this whole internship connection thing off. "I'll tell him," I say.

"Good." Nancy turns her attention to the candy. "We unfortunately have to wait for these to set now."

"Guess we'll just sit here in silence, then," I say.

"Only option," she deadpans. Then, practically in the same breath, she asks, "You want to tell me all about the wedding, right?"

"I have a detailed schedule of everything I still need to do memorized, if that's what you're asking," I say.

She laughs and walks over to the kitchen table. "I've got time, hit me."

We talk about the wedding until the candy is cooled.

If I have to see that Roo is unavailable to FaceTime again, I'm going to break my phone.

Doesn't he realize I have something important to tell him? I clearly sent a text that said, "URGENT!" I answer all of his "URGENT!" messages right away.

It's been a full day of this. If I hadn't seen him in an Instagram post from his sister's account, I would've thought he was in danger. Maybe in a coma or kidnapped, because that's the only reason for not answering your best friend's texts.

I shouldn't be nervous about telling him. I mean, it went so well with Nancy. He'll be excited for me.

If he ever answers his freaking phone, that is.

It's fine, I have stuff to do anyway. Ha, Rupert, I can be busy too.

There's a local French restaurant that offers wedding catering, and the food looks seriously delicious. I booked a tasting last week.

"Yay, lunch out!" Mom says when I remind her.

"No," I scold. "Not lunch out. We're going to a tasting; this is serious business."

"We're going to a serious business lunch," Mom yells to Eric, who's downstairs.

How exactly she survived to adulthood is unclear.

As we head out the door, I look at my phone one more time. Nope, nothing.

I open up my texts as though there's a chance that he did send me a message but it's just hiding. And a no to that absurd idea; the last message was from me.

I send Nancy a quick text.

Felicity: hey, do you want to come to a wedding tasting?

She responds right away.

Nancy: Um OBVIOUSLY

I smile. At least I have one supportive friend.

Nancy comes over to the cottage around noon, and we all head to the village for the tasting. This is pretty exciting because (1) food, and (2) it's our first time in town. Eric gets excited by the art store, and we almost lose Mom in a shop that sells Vermont-themed tchotchkes.

"Guys, come on." I wave toward the restaurant. "We're supposed to be there already."

Mom walks over and ruffles my hair, which she knows I don't like. "Lighten up, child of mine. It's summer vacation." She gives my shoulder a little squeeze, like that makes what she said better. At least she leaves the store and heads toward the tasting.

When we sit down, they give us the specialty catering menu so we can see if there's anything we're immediately drawn to.

"Oh, I like the sound of the pommes frites," Mom says, looking at the menu.

"Those are just fries," I point out.

"I know," she says.

I end up ordering for all of us. I select the cheese plate, mini-French onion soup appetizers, savory crepe trio, and macaron platter.

Nancy is a big fan of the cheese plate, but I think things really start to shine with the soup. I love a good French onion soup. This one is smothered in cheese with bits of bread that still have some crunch to them mixed in with the perfectly sweet onions. I open my wedding notebook and write, "delicious but think of the logistics . . . passed apps or sit down?"

"You know," Nancy starts, "this could work really well as a passed app. My cousin got married last year, and they had these soup shooters. Everyone loved them."

I add "soup shooters?" to the notebook.

"We could just fill water guns with soup and spray appetizers into our guests' mouths," my mom says.

Eric snickers.

"Not funny," I warn.

Nancy ends up being way more helpful than Mom and Eric combined. She tells me which of the crepes she thinks will be more universally liked and talks about options for different dietary restrictions. So much more thoughtful than *let's spray our guests with soup.*

Still, it's stress-inducing when Eric says, "Let's walk this off. I read about a ton of great hiking paths nearby."

He has to know that I'm not interested. I mean, a *hike*?

"We haven't even gotten to the macaron platter," I point out. "I can't leave yet."

"I could use a break," Mom says. She rubs her stomach for emphasis. "Maybe we can get them to go?"

Nancy looks over at me. I think she knows I want to finish this right. "We're so close to being done. We can ask for a to-go box and the check when the platter arrives."

Mom and Eric do this quick look exchange, like they're having an entire conversation via glance.

Mom talks first. "Yeah, okay, but we're walking after."

"Get some of that good Vermont fresh air," Eric adds.

I don't respond.

So that's what this is about. I think about their conversation before we left, how they said this whole trip will be good for me, as though everything back home was bad. They're trying to manage me like I can't take care of myself. What do they think? One tasting will send me back to the hospital? I'm clearly in control now.

I hate feeling like this; they're so condescending.

I won't let it get that bad again.

Nancy breaks the silence. "Actually, I was hoping to steal Felicity for some girl time. I don't want to spoil anything, but it does involve authentic Korean skin care straight from a care package my grandma sent me. Can't say anything more or I'll ruin it."

Mom smiles. "We can go for a family walk another time; that sounds like fun."

Saved from physical exertion. Nancy is a true hero.

The macarons arrive, and we all agree that we have to have them at the wedding. In addition to the cake, of course. We're not monsters.

Mom and Eric both have to go to the bathroom before we head out, leaving me and Nancy alone at the table. She took her sketchbook out around the time we got dessert and has been doo-dling ever since.

I lean over and glance at her work. "Watcha doin'?" I ask in a singsong voice.

She doesn't look up from the page. "Planning world domina-tion," she says flatly, but she's smirking.

"Lots of macarons involved in taking over the world," I say.

She moves the sketchbook off her lap and puts it on the table so I can see better. "Okay, this is rough, but I was thinking I could make something like this to display them. For the dessert table."

Her drawing looks like it should be framed. Delicate lines swoop around platters covered in tiny little macarons, with such impressive detail I find it hard to believe this is "rough." She added a pattern of tiny leaves around the framework that are drawn so perfectly they look like she invented a shrink ray, zapped some nearby vines, and traced.

"How are you so good at this?" I ask, looking at her design.

She shakes her head a little, like she doesn't believe me. "It's just a hobby."

I look at her sketch. It's too detailed to just be a hobby. "No, but all of this. I mean, you've been really helpful already. You don't have to be. I maintain you can back out at any time. I don't want to put the internship pressure on you."

"What pressure? I'm pretty sure I just roped you into an eve-ning of self-care."

"About that," I start, lowering my voice like maybe Mom and Eric could hear me from the bathrooms. "We're not just doing skin care, right? Because I have to look up local antique shops for the place settings, and I'm still researching photographers . . ."

"A face mask has never stopped anyone from researching," Nancy says. "We can do it over at my house."

Will the heroics ever stop . . . ?

Our server comes over and leaves us a printed-out version of the menu to take home. I slide it into my wedding notebook. I wonder if I'm going to get more wedding-related papers. It would be a lot easier if I had a binder or a folder. I don't want to lose anything.

I take a bite of my last macaron. Thank goodness I have Nancy to help me out.

Wedding Survey

Put a check mark next to your choices. Return as soon as possible.

Wedding Dress Color:

☐ White

☐ Ivory

☐ Champagne

☐ Cream

Color Scheme Options:
(Please pick 2+)

☐ Blush Pink

☐ Dusty Blue

☐ Lavender

☐ Sage

☐ Navy

☐ Burgundy

☐ Emerald

☐ Peach

☐ Gold

Ceremony Time:

☐ Morning

☐ Noon

☐ Evening

Cake Flavor:

☐ Strawberries and Cream

☐ Lemon and Raspberry

☐ Warm Vanilla with Fresh Mixed Berries

☐ Caramel Apple

Food:

☐ Sit-Down Meal

☐ Buffet

☐ Passed Appetizers

Favorite Flowers:

☐ Roses

☐ Peonies

☐ Tulips

☐ Orchids

☐ Hydrangeas

Music:

☐ DJ

☐ Band

THIRTY-NINE DAYS UNTIL THE WEDDING

"It's not the *right* shade of blue," I say, putting down a dinner plate.

"I was just thinking how wrong it looks," Nancy teases.

I ignore her tone. "It would be so much easier if my mom and Eric just picked their colors already," I complain. "It would take out a lot of the guesswork."

We're standing by a display of discount china, which is mostly on sale because they're parts of incomplete sets. This is exactly what I'm looking for. The sale in general, not the incorrectly blue plate. My vision for the reception is to use mismatched but complementary place settings. Except Mom and Eric still haven't given me their wedding surveys or indicated whether they like or dislike any of my ideas, which doesn't help when it comes to picking place settings.

"What about this?" Nancy holds up the tackiest plate I have ever laid my eyes on. It's painted with fluorescent cartoon flowers that have little humanoid faces.

I practically snort. "Only if it's your plate."

She makes this quizzical look like she's actually contemplating the idea before putting the plate back down.

"Oh, wait, this one. For real," she says, voice more serious. She points to one that has a muted sage toile design.

"Add it to the pile."

We manage to find ten different plates that feel appropriate for a summer apple orchard wedding. It's a good start. We'll need more, but at least this way I can focus on finding ones in specific colors as soon as we finalize the whole look for the event.

The discount china is at the very back of the store, so we carefully transport the plates to the checkout register. Nancy has six of them and I have four, since she is marginally more coordinated, being an athlete and all.

The woman behind the desk is the sort of suburban white lady who looks like she might ask us if she can talk to *our* manager. I think it's the hair. Something about it just looks like she walked into her salon and asked the stylist for the Rude to Waiters cut.

"Lovely choices," she says, ringing up our china selection. She carefully wraps each plate after she scans it. "Did you have any trouble finding these?" she asks as she scans the fifth one.

"No, it's exactly what we were looking for," I answer.

"You have a great selection," Nancy adds.

The woman smiles in this *of course I do* kind of way.

She finishes ringing up our purchase, and I pay with my *just for emergencies and also wedding stuff* debit card.

"Here you go," she says.

Nancy takes the bag for me since I'm still fumbling with my purse, trying to put away my card. My wallet is currently hiding in the one-too-many pockets that are supposed to be there for convenience.

"I just have to say," the woman adds, staring at Nancy. "You have the most interesting coloring. What are you?"

I look up from my purse. What did that lady just say?

"She's a Gemini," I blurt out. "Okay, 'bye." I take Nancy's hand and walk out of the store.

I'm not sure why my brain is like that. Was it even the right thing to do? I probably should have just told the woman to mind her own business. Or waited and taken Nancy's lead. Because blurting out a star sign and abruptly leaving seems like the wrong way to go.

I glance at Nancy, thinking maybe she's about to tell me that. She probably doesn't want to be my friend anymore because I panic and say ridiculous things.

Except when I finally stop moving and let go of Nancy's hand at the corner of the street, I notice that she's doubled over, laughing. "Did you really just tell that woman I'm a Gemini and bolt? You know I'm not even a Gemini; my birthday's in February."

"Yes, well, *she* doesn't know that," I say.

Nancy straightens and wipes her eyes. "Listen, I've been asked that kind of question way more often than anyone reasonably should have to deal with, and I've never seen someone be like, 'Okay, time to exit.'"

Now that Nancy isn't laughing hysterically, we resume walking. Luckily in my mad bolt out of the store, I did point us in the direction of the car. We have to cross the street to get to the town's designated free parking area, where Nancy found a spot.

"I just hate that question," I say.

"Because it's a sucky question," Nancy agrees. "I can't tell you how many people feel entitled to know my racial identity. Or think it's okay to call me exotic. Blagh." She makes an exaggerated face.

"Vermont is *very* white. People at school are usually okay, but older people . . . Let's just say that things like that back there are not uncommon. Like just because my mom's family is from Sweden and my dad's is originally from Korea, doesn't mean you get the thumbs-up to ask." She pauses before adding, "Wait, why do *you* hate that question?"

My cheeks warm up a little. This is definitely a smaller thing than what Nancy is talking about. I should probably feel embarrassed for even caring. "Oh, well. I never really know how to answer," I admit. "My mom, her whole family is Jewish. But because of the diaspora, it's just hard to pin down where they came from. I think they were Russian and Polish and German and maybe Dutch? Except it's not clear because they were forced to leave so many places. I usually just say Jewish," I explain.

There's more though. I tend not to talk about the whole *people being weird around me because my mom decided to have me alone* thing. It was never a secret. I mean, I've heard Bubbe complain about Mom's choice more than once, usually followed by something like, "You're such a blessing; this isn't about you." Except it *is* about me, basically by definition. And now there's this whole part of my genetic makeup that I don't know. I don't even know if I'll want to know someday.

So I don't talk about it, even with Roo. Bonnie keeps trying to open up a dialogue about it. I usually just pretend I don't care when, the truth is, I have no clue how I really feel.

I'm not sure why I continue, but I do.

"There's this other reason," I say. "People always end up asking about my dad or saying *parents*, plural. I don't know. I guess it's the assumption there." I shrug, as though it isn't a big deal.

Nancy nods, like this isn't a weird thing to say at all. "People suck," she practically sighs.

"Across the board," I agree.

We're at the car. Nancy gets into the driver's side since I am only permitted to drive with a licensed adult and am also vaguely afraid of things like parking and intersections.

"Hey, I have an idea," she says as she starts the car. "Let's go somewhere fun. We can't just go back home and end on *that*."

Which is how we end up at the bookstore.

The exterior looks like a big house, but inside is a whole other story. There's a maze of books and assorted knickknacks that stretch on so far I think I could probably get lost in here. Everything is spread out over two floors and scattered with seating. There's even a section that opens up into a café, offering sandwiches, pastries, and drinks. It's like they really do want you to come in and stay.

We end up in front of their stationery section, hidden behind the big staircase up to the second floor. There are cute little notebooks and pens and Post-it notes and enough greeting cards to cover every gift-giving need a person could possibly have.

"I've been thinking of getting a new binder," I tell Nancy as I browse the journals. "Something to keep all the wedding stuff together."

"What's your dream binder?" she asks.

"I don't have a *dream* binder," I say.

Nancy gives me a skeptical look. "Yeah, you do."

I pick up a notebook with a pretty floral design. She knows me too well. "I was thinking maybe sage or evergreen. Color block could work, if the shades complement each other. Not too big, so

I can actually carry it around. Maybe a one-inch ring size? And there has to be a pocket inside for my wedding notebook."

"Naturally," Nancy says.

"In an ideal world," I continue, putting back the floral notebook, "it would be personalized. Something simple, in case I want to repurpose it for other events. Maybe 'Down to the Last Detail' or 'Planning Perfect.' Not in any fancy script or anything, just neat lettering. And it can't be glossy," I add.

"That would render the whole thing useless," Nancy says with mock seriousness.

I pick up a leather planner. "Glad you understand."

We end up spending the afternoon in the bookstore. I pick up a couple of books that I think Eric might like and buy a mug for Roo, even though he is a terrible person who doesn't understand the importance of answering texts. Then we spend a couple of hours in the café. We each get a sandwich and share a slice of pie.

I'm sitting in my chair with one leg up on the seat and leaning back a little. Totally relaxed. "Not bad for a non-productive activity," I say.

"Non-productive activity? Fe, it's summer vacation. You know, breaks aren't a bad thing," Nancy points out.

"Get out of here with your self-care agenda," I joke. I take another bite of pie.

Nancy squints at me. "*This* is your self-care baseline?"

"Well, I did a great sheet mask yesterday," I offer.

Nancy shakes her head. "Unacceptable. Your summer can't be all about work. Thank goodness you have me."

"How exactly are you related to my apparently poor self-care habits and too-busy summer schedule?" I ask.

Nancy looks off in the distance, like she's an investigator who knows they're on the right track to solving a crime but hasn't put all the pieces together just yet. "I'm working on it."

"Good luck," I say. If Bonnie hasn't been able to help with self-care yet, I have my doubts.

Nancy cuts the last bit of pie in half, even though it was small enough to count as one bite. She pushes the plate in front of me. "I'll figure you out, Becker," she says.

There's this weird feeling in my chest, like the air just got thinner in the café. *I hope you do*, I think.

THIRTY-EIGHT DAYS UNTIL THE WEDDING

I walk into the barn-cottage holding a big cardboard package. When I found a website that would ship bridesmaid dress samples, I wasn't sure what to expect. I hope the dresses aren't crumpled up in there.

"Mom," I call out. "Guess what I got!"

"Is there a prize if I'm right?" she asks. She's sitting at the kitchen island with a cup of coffee in front of her.

I roll my eyes. "Dresses," I say. "For me. I got three different styles. All long, of course, but two have a little sleeve, and one just has straps." I set the box down on the counter, then carefully open it and take out the dresses, draping them over the back of the high-top chairs lined up by the kitchen island.

"Why don't we do that for wedding dresses?" Mom asks. "Just order something online."

I give her a disapproving look. "You have to go to a proper place for that. This is just a bridesmaid dress; it barely matters," I say.

"Not sure I believe you," she says. She takes a sip of her coffee. "Plus, I don't remember asking you to be a bridesmaid."

"Oh, yeah? Who else is going to do it?" I ask. I hold up one of the dresses to examine it. I knew these would get wrinkled packaged like that.

"I have friends, Lissy. I'm not some sad loner parent."

"And yet here you are, alone," I say.

"Actually, I have plans later with Gwendoline. She's going to teach me how to play bridge," Mom says like this proves some point.

"Great, I'll let her try these on."

She puts down her coffee cup and walks closer to me. Then she puts her hands on my face. "Will you be my bridesmaid?"

I swat her hands away. "Only if the dresses look good," I respond.

I try them on. I'm surprised I like the one with the straps. It's sleek with a low back that ends in a bow, which I was worried would come off childish but ultimately feels elegant. I was also worried my arms would look huge without any sleeves, but it's not bad.

"What color is that even?" Mom asks.

"Eucalyptus green," I say, looking at the tag. "This one's it, right?"

"It's so formal," she says. "You look like you should be getting ready for prom."

"Or a wedding," I point out.

"No," she says slowly, like she's giving it some thought. "I'm sticking with prom."

Oy vey, it's like she's incapable of taking things seriously.

"Mom," I say, trying to snap her back to our current situation. "What do you think?"

"You look marvelous, darling," she says in a dramatic, old-timey voice. "Who knew eucalyptus green was your color? I hope they vote you prom queen."

I walk over to the bathroom so I can examine myself in the mirror. I thought the color would work with my auburn hair, but worried it might be too light and make me look pale. Luckily, the shade is deep enough that it works. I picture the day of the wedding, standing there in this dress in front of everyone waiting for my mom to walk down the aisle. This fits with my whole vision.

"I'm sending the other ones back," I announce, walking out of the bathroom. "I'm going with this one." I pose, so as to properly display the look.

"I hope the chaperones are cool," she says.

It's fine, her jokes don't matter now. I have a dress for the wedding. Now we just need to find her something to wear.

⎯⎯⎯⎯⎯⎯⎯⎯

When I finally hear back from Roo, it's a pathetic sorry busy u ok?

Yes, I am. No thanks to you and your inability to type out simple words or respond in a timely fashion, Rupert.

I should ignore him.

I text back after five minutes.

Felicity: facetime tonight? 9?

He sends me a thumbs-up.

I should give him the benefit of the doubt. Maybe he *was* busy. Even if I did send him multiple messages and then saw the freaking proof that he was just hanging out with his family, which means he wasn't actually busy. Maybe his phone died and he got a concussion immediately after Amira took that picture of him, but everyone was so worried they forgot to tell me and now he isn't allowed to look at screens (because of said concussion), but he still risked it just in case I need him.

Yeah, that's it.

I walk over to the main house so I can meet Nancy for our flower shop outing. I didn't set up any appointments for this one, so we're just going to go and look at a couple of places. She's already waiting in the car, the air conditioner turned way up.

"So, I was thinking about our conversation at the bookstore, and I have an idea," she says as I buckle my seat belt.

"If it's that we should see some flowers, boy do I have good news for you," I say. "Bonus, I hear nature is great for self-care."

She smirks and puts the car into reverse. "Yeah, yeah, we'll see your flowers," she starts. "More importantly though, I've figured out the problem."

"Problem?" I repeat.

"Yep," Nancy confirms. "The problem is that you're ruining your summer."

Well, that's not what I expected her to say. I thought this was supposed to be about self-care. Shouldn't she recommend a yoga YouTube channel and move on?

"I am?" I ask. I can't tell whether this is a joke or if she really thinks I'm some sort of summer ruin-er.

"Yep," she says lightly. "Really messing it up, Fe. You're lucky though, because I know exactly how to fix everything." She's turned onto the main road, her eyes focused on the minimal traffic ahead.

"How?" I ask hesitantly.

"I've decided to take it upon myself to make sure you have some fun," she says. "You can't just spend your whole summer focused on the wedding stuff. *But*," she emphasizes the word, drawing it out, "I know you. And I'm not backing out of helping you get that internship," she adds. "Which brings me to my proposition." She pauses. I wonder if she wants me to guess. "For every day that I help with the planning, we have to do one totally unrelated, purely fun thing."

Her eyes flash to me as I make a face.

"Just one," she continues, looking back at the road. "And I get to pick."

This summer isn't supposed to be about having fun. If I get distracted, then Eric will be disappointed because I've ruined all of his childhood dreams and I won't have a chance with Hartman and Co. and I'll probably destroy my entire future.

I realize these thoughts are a bit dramatic, but I can't stop my brain from going there.

"But—" I start.

Nancy cuts me off. "One thing and you get a real summer. Plus, access to a really cool buddy with a really awesome driver's license."

"Did you just call yourself a 'cool buddy'?" I ask.

She nods. "That's how serious I am about this."

Isn't that what I wanted anyway when I suggested we come here for the summer? When I pictured it before, I was helping with the wedding *and* spending time with Nancy. Except most of that was about being productive and maybe watching something after, which I doubt counts as a full-fledged activity. So why am I worried about this? Is it because Nancy is going to pick what we do?

It feels safer, more comfortable, when I'm in charge, but I trust

Nancy. I can give up a little control if that means I'm saving my summer.

At least Bonnie will be happy I'm working on my flexibility.

"Only one thing?" I ask.

"For each day that I help out, yes," she answers.

I fidget with my sundress, a purple floral pattern that's supposed to look vintage even though I bought it new right before we left for this trip. "If it doesn't get in the way," I concede.

"I can work with that," she says.

I start to imagine this summer in a new way, like my vision for it is expanding and becoming more complete. I come up with pretend ideas for our adventures: driving to a beach and sitting by the water, seeing a movie in a local theater, packing a picnic. All with Nancy by my side.

I'm not even really paying attention when Nancy stops the car.

I look out the window. "No," I say.

Nancy tilts her head a little. "GPS says we're here."

"No," I repeat. "There is *no way* we're getting flowers from a grocery store for my mom's wedding."

We're parked in the middle of a giant parking lot. The supermarket takes up most of the strip mall, alongside a small clothing store and a Chinese restaurant that boasts an all-you-can-eat buffet. Not exactly the place you'd find fresh flowers in elegantly designed arrangements.

"We haven't gone in to check," Nancy says. "These might be the best grocery store flowers in the entire state, in the entire world even." She's having too much fun with this.

"It'll be too small," I say. "They won't be able to handle a wedding. Plus, and I need to make this very clear, this is a *grocery store*."

"Yes, but in its defense, it is the nicest grocery store in miles. We could pop in and see if they could make the cake too," Nancy jokes.

"No," I say, voice stubborn.

"You know, there are some nice flowers at the local hardware store; we could head over there next," she continues.

"You are a mean, terrible person," I say, voice flat.

Nancy laughs as she plugs in the next address. "How did you miss that this was a grocery store?" she asks.

I frown. "Google betrayed me," I say.

"Um-hum."

Our next stop isn't any better. Nancy at least gets me inside for this one before I turn it down, which is impressive, since I could tell it wouldn't work out from the car.

We're standing in a massive gardening center, in the middle of one of their greenhouses, right between a display of squash and their collection of peppers. This is the kind of place you go to when you're looking for herbs for your garden, not florals for your mom's wedding.

"It's too big," I say.

"Too small, too big . . . Who are you, Goldilocks?"

"Hey!" I say, realizing what she just said. "I'm not tasting porridge or trying out chairs. This place is basically a gardening warehouse, and I can't get in trouble for turning down a *grocery store*."

"Sure," she says. "Hopefully the next one is *just right*. Goldilocks."

It better be. There weren't a lot of options when I did my very serious Google research.

Our final stop of the day is in the middle of a proper town, which seems promising. Nancy finds a parking spot a block away.

When we walk up in front of the store, I sigh. It's an actual flower shop, complete with perfectly arranged bouquets in the window display.

The scent hits me when we walk in, distinctly fresh, all the florals coming together to create a single perfume that clings to the air. It's like we've walked into a candle.

"Hi, there," comes a voice from behind the counter. The florist is wearing an apron that matches her hijab, both a deep maroon. "How can I help?" she asks.

"Do you do weddings?" I ask. I'm fairly positive I know the answer, but what if I'm wrong? What if this is a flower store that only specializes in gifts? What if they do every kind of event except weddings?

The florist smiles. "All the time," she says. "They're kind of my favorite part of the job."

Thank goodness.

The florist, who introduces herself as Fatima, shows us the designs in the store and some pictures of past weddings organized in a binder. A few of the photos even depict chuppahs, which I wasn't expecting.

"We have a pricing guide and some of our packages, along with a brochure on our favorite arrangements," Fatima says, handing me the papers. I slip them into my wedding notebook, next to the sample menu from the caterer. I really am going to need something to keep track of this wedding stuff.

"I have to talk to my mom, I mean, you know, the bride, but wow. Your store is perfect."

She laughs. "We try."

"No, really," I continue. "I was beginning to think there'd be no flowers at this wedding. Can you imagine?"

"We nearly had to get them from a grocery store," Nancy adds in mock horror.

She's lucky I need her to drive with the way she's teasing me right now.

We thank Fatima the florist and head out of the store.

"Come on, Goldilocks, say it," Nancy bugs me once the door closes behind us.

"I'm not going to."

"You know you wanna though," she nudges.

I sigh. "It was *just right*."

Nancy's One Fun Thing today turns out to be getting maple creemees on our way home.

"It's like ice cream, but even better," she insists. "Like cold delicious syrup."

"Are there other flavors in Vermont?" I ask.

"Oh, I love maple syrup!" she says like she's thinking back to a particularly fond memory while simultaneously defending its right to exist.

I put up my hands. "I agree, absolutely delicious. I just think you're being a Vermont stereotype."

She raises an eyebrow. "Yeah?"

"Definitely," I continue. "Like, if I was going to show off Massachusetts, I wouldn't just force-feed you clam chowder."

"What about Boston cream pies?" she asks.

"I don't even like Boston cream pies."

She fake gasps. "I don't think you're allowed to return to the state now."

I shrug.

"This is a Vermont staple. I'd get kicked out if you didn't try it," she insists. She goes up to the counter and orders two cones.

She hands me the first one that's ready. It's a lot like soft serve, but even better. Airy yet creamy with that distinct maple taste.

"Good, right?"

I manage a little appreciative hum.

"You like it. You like my plan. My plan is perfect. You like ittttt," she practically sings.

I do. This stop was on our way home and involved ice cream; what's not to like?

If all of her plans are like this, her little self-care breaks won't be a problem at all.

THIRTY-SEVEN DAYS AND ONE NIGHT UNTIL THE WEDDING

I check how I look on my phone screen. I touched up my makeup and restraightened my hair for this, even though I logically know that I'm stressing over nothing. It's just Roo.

I call him at exactly nine.

"Hey!" I say, too cheery "There you are."

"Where I always am," he says. He's lying on his bed; I can tell from the angle of his face and the dark gray duvet cover under his head.

"You're never going to believe what happened," I start. "This might even redeem the Brody Wells election disaster."

"Speaking of Brody Wells," he cuts in.

I frown. *Speaking of Brody Wells?* What the hell does that mean?

"So you remember how I'm working this summer," Roo continues.

"At the purse place."

"Totes Adorbs," he corrects. "And we sell bags of all varieties."

"And Brody Wells really loves buying bags?" I ask.

"Well." Roo lingers on the word. "Remember when I said someone on the team helped me get the job? There's a chance I left out that Brody's mom is the owner and he's actually working there too." He says the final part all rushed together, like he's hoping maybe I'll miss out on the meaning if he speaks fast enough.

"You're joking," I say, because he has to be. He wouldn't go behind my back to get a job with the literal enemy.

"Felicity, I have to work. He got me a job. You can't be mad at me for taking it."

"Watch me," I say. "You know how I feel about him!"

"So that means I can't work at his mom's store?"

"That's exactly what it means! He'll get in your head, Roo. Infect you with all of his toxic masculinity."

"Yes, that's my greatest fear working at *Totes Adorbs*," he says, emphasizing the store name.

"He'll find a way," I insist. "He's the literal worst, Roo. How could you spend the entire summer with him?"

"First of all, you're the one who left me," he says.

I interrupt him. "For my mom's wedding; that doesn't count."

"Second," he continues, "it's. A. Job. Not all of us have family money we can fall back on."

I don't know why he's being this way. It's not like his family is struggling or anything. I mean, I know things are tighter with his sister in college now, but it can't be that much of a change. Can it?

"Are things okay at home?" I ask. "I can help if that's the—"

He groans. "No, I'm not asking for a handout. I want this job. I want to be able to pay for gas and help out with car payments. I'm just saying you don't get it because of the way your family is."

Well now I'm back to being angry. It's not my fault that my mom has done well. Between her early tech success and *Sleepy Dog*, I don't have to worry about money. And I'm grateful for that, don't get me wrong. I just don't like that he's trying to use it as an excuse now, like I need to be guilty about this thing that is entirely outside my control.

"Get a different job then," I say.

"Deal with it."

"I will not deal with it! You are actively betraying me right now."

"Felicity," he says my name like I'm a small child who's broken a well-established rule. "Seriously, what's your problem with him? When has he ever done anything wrong? Was it when he dared to help me get a summer job? Or was it that time he offered to drive you home?"

"He pushed me during tag," I point out triumphantly.

"If your most recent example is from kindergarten, I'm going to need you to do some reevaluating."

Roo doesn't understand. I worked so hard for the Social Friends Committee, staying late and helping make sure every project was finished, volunteering for all of the events, and then Brody just slid his way into the leadership position. He didn't get the title because he was qualified for it. How could he? He's always too busy joking around and making excuses for why he can't be at all our events. Meanwhile, I show up and take things seriously, and that still isn't enough. I can't compete.

There's this other part of me that's worried about the two of them spending time together, this nagging thought at the back of my mind: *What if Roo likes Brody more than me too?* Because that's what happened with the election. More people liked Brody, and I was left behind.

I don't need to have an explanation for Roo. Best friends are supposed to have each other's backs, no matter what.

"If you care about me, you'll quit this job," I say.

"That's ridiculous. I care about you, and I'm going to keep working. End of discussion." He sighs. "Are we still on for our *Murder She Solved* debrief next week?"

I want to say no, that he's lost all friendship benefits. Instead I nod. "We never miss a finale," I say. "Plus, I'll need to gloat when it turns out the vice principal did it."

"The school stuff is a misdirection; I'm telling you, it's the family." I can see Roo adjust on the screen, rolling his shoulders like he's trying to get rid of some tension. Which, I guess, he is. "Okay, talk later. Love you."

"Likely story," I grumble. "Love you too."

I don't realize that I didn't bring up my internship until he hangs up.

THIRTY-SEVEN DAYS UNTIL THE WEDDING

Mom's chamomile tea can't even fix my mood.

I cradle the cup with one hand, holding the refrigerator door open with the other like breakfast might jump out, fully cooked. Mom offered to "make" me cereal, but I'm not in the mood for her greatest culinary offering. Plus, I don't want to add any potential distractions while we discuss wedding dresses.

"What? Are you going to walk down the aisle naked?" I ask.

"I could pull it off," she says.

I take out the cream cheese and grab the frozen bagels from the freezer. "You're going to have to get something off the rack no matter what now. I don't even know if you can get a fitting. The more time we waste, the worse it's going to get."

I pop the bagel into the microwave.

"Lissy, chill," she says. "We'll figure something out."

I'll figure something out, more like. The microwave beeps, so I take the bagel out and cut it in half before putting it into the toaster oven.

"What if we look at some dresses together? I did a little research last night, and there's a place in Boston that has a pretty comprehensive website. We can narrow it down, maybe find something you'd want to try on," I offer.

"I'll have my people call your people," she jokes. She takes her already empty cereal bowl to the sink and rinses it out before putting it into the dishwasher. At least I don't have to clean up after her.

I pull out my phone and check out the website again. The mobile version isn't the most functional; it was a lot better when I looked on my laptop last night. I search through some of their dresses, trying to decide which ones I'll show her later.

"What are your feelings on ivory?" I ask.

"I don't condone harming animals," she says without missing a beat.

I groan. "The color, Mom."

"Feels very off-white to me," she says. She walks over and kisses the top of my head. "You've got a one-track mind, child of mine." Then she turns and looks at the toaster oven. "Also, your bagel's burning."

Great. Guess we'll start over with that one.

I toss the smelly burnt bagel into the trash and grab another one from the freezer. "You should be proud that I'm focused. It's a good trait."

"You have enough good traits," she says. "Live a little; take on some bad ones."

"That's not very motherly," I point out.

"Who says I always need to sound motherly?" she asks.

"My birth certificate."

"Now, if that started talking, I'd be concerned." She sits down at the kitchen table to finish her coffee.

I focus on making the bagel this time, so as to avoid further gross burning fumes. I watch it in the toaster and take it out once it shows the first sign of getting a little brown on the top.

I join her at the table with my non-burnt breakfast.

"I have an idea," I say.

"Sounds concerning; stop having those."

I ignore her. "I've figured out how to reach you with this wedding stuff."

She takes a sip of her coffee. "Yeah?"

"We're going to vision this," I say. "Close your eyes."

She actually listens. "How is this going to help?" she asks once her eyes are shut.

"The power of mindfulness is going to unlock your true desires," I explain.

"Oh, of course," she says in a mocking tone.

"Picture your wedding day," I say, channeling the smooth voice of the lady on this meditation app Bonnie recommended to me (that I sometimes remember to use). "Visualize everything around you. Imagine walking down the aisle and seeing Eric at the end. Are you doing it?"

She nods.

"Now focus on the details. Take a moment to look at your surroundings. What do you see? Feel? Smell?"

"That's easy, the burning bagel stench hasn't faded," she says.

"Not funny," I say. I slip back into my meditation voice. "All right, live in this moment. Look down at your vision self. What are you wearing?"

"Clothes," she answers. "I guess I won't go naked after all."

I mean, it's a start. "Do you see anything else?" I ask calmly. "Engage your senses. Really imagine all of the aspects, the sights, the sounds."

"I hear something," she says.

"Yeah?" I ask.

"The *Star Wars* theme," she answers.

"You can't walk down the aisle to the *Star Wars* theme," I say.

"What? It would be kind of epic."

"Mom, focus," I say, trying to salvage this experience.

She takes a deep breath in through her nose and lets out a little "om" noise like this is some yoga meditation.

"Mom," I scold.

She opens her eyes. "You know, there is one thing I see. Actually, caught me off guard a little."

"Yeah?" I ask.

"A chuppah," she says. "I guess it's one of those things I always pictured growing up. Getting married under a chuppah, breaking the glass at the end. The right amount of tradition."

My mom wants some tradition at her wedding? Bubbe will be thrilled. "We can have a chuppah," I say.

She smiles. "I'd like that." She takes another sip of her coffee. "Now let's cool it on the vision stuff; I'm not even really awake yet."

After breakfast, I start the process of getting ready for the day. I straighten my hair and put on a minimal layer of basic makeup, but I can't pick out what kind of eye shadow to add or lip color to go for if I don't know what I'm wearing. I grab a dress and even get as far as trying it on, but it's too . . . blah. All of my clothes are blah, probably because my best friend betrayed me by taking a job with the enemy.

I'm staring at three different potential outfits, all lying neatly on my bed, when my phone rings.

"My perfect girl," Bubbe says as a greeting.

"Hey, Bubbe."

"How are you, mamale sheli? I feel like we hardly talk anymore. What? Do you not love me?"

Jewish Guilt coming into the conversation in under a minute. That was fast.

"Hate is a strong word but . . ." I trail off. "I'm fine. Busy with all the wedding stuff," I add in my normal tone.

I tell her about everything I've gotten ready so far and run through some ideas I have for both the ceremony and reception.

"And the rabbi?" she asks.

Erm. I haven't gotten as far as thinking about the officiant, but knowing Mom and Eric, it's not going to be a Rabbi. "Undecided," I say. Mom did just say she wants a chuppah, so this doesn't feel like a complete lie. She *might* want one.

"Well, bubbeleh, you better get on it. You're already so far behind."

I take a quick breath. I *am* so far behind. I shouldn't have agreed to do this over the summer; weddings take more time than that. I got too caught up in the idea of coming here, having the apple orchard venue, seeing Nancy.

I'm so stuck in my head I almost miss that Bubbe is talking again.

"And Zayde and I will be walking her down the aisle," she adds, a statement, not a question.

"Of course."

"Oh, before I forget, I talked to Deborah at temple. You'll love her, I just know it. She told me there's an application for the internship, but not to worry, it's more of a formality. It's in my email somewhere. I'll send it over."

I wonder what the application is going to say. When is it due? When was Bubbe at temple last? Has she had this for a while? Did she forget to send it to me?

I end up asking, "Is the application long?"

"It's nothing," Bubbe says. "What school do you go to, GPA, why do you want to work here sort of thing. Really, the wedding will be a lot more important. What does a sheet of paper really tell anyone compared to the real thing?"

I guess she's right.

Bubbe doesn't wait for my response. "Everything sounds so beautiful already, nothing to worry about. Just keep me in the loop, please, dear," she continues. "You know, I always thought I'd be the one putting this together for your mother. I thought a lot of things about her life."

I think about that life Bubbe must have dreamt of: the stable and lucrative career in tech Mom gave up, the marriage before babies, all at the right time and the right age.

Sometimes I wonder if Mom ever wanted those things too.

Bubbe pauses before adding, "I know you'll make sure things are done right."

"Yeah, Bubbe," I say. I'm not sure if I'm agreeing to keeping her updated or to the fact that I can do things the right way. Maybe both.

Bubbe and I talk for a little longer. She tells me all about this dinner party she went to the other night and then absolutely has to run off or she'll miss an exercise class. She became so active after her heart surgery that I think she's healthier at sixty-eight than I'll ever be.

I put down my phone. I love talking to Bubbe, but it can be a lot. Especially with all the wedding stuff. She sets the bar so high and just assumes I'm going to meet it.

I *will*. I mean, that's why I'm working so hard on this. I'll throw the best freaking wedding out there *and* secure the fall internship.

There's just something about the way she says it all that makes me uneasy. Maybe it's the pressure. It feels like I have to do everything right or I've failed her.

I don't want to fail again.

<hr>

"What exactly is a rock quarry?" I ask Nancy from the passenger seat in her car. "It sounds dangerous."

"It isn't!" she swears. "I've been swimming there since I was little. It'll be fun."

I tug at the strap on my bikini top, which is poking out from beneath my cover-up. I'm wearing a retro-style, gingham swimsuit with high-waisted bottoms, which looks absolutely adorable but isn't the most comfortable for a car ride. "How many people have died there? Is it haunted? You legally have to tell me if it's haunted."

"The water is so deep that I've never even touched the bottom, and there are always tons of people there," she says.

I make a little humming sound, so as to properly convey my doubt before looking out the window. I keep getting shocked by how green it is in Vermont. Back home, the patches of trees are so broken up by houses that they're relegated to the background. Here, they're front and center, the stars of the show.

I try to appreciate being surrounded by so much nature. We're on a highway, but even that looks so different from anything I'm used to. Looming mountains out in the background, the occasional appearance of a ski lift that is currently not in use. I can't help but compare it to Massachusetts.

The problem with these comparisons is that now I'm thinking about home, which naturally leads me to worry about how I won't have a best friend when I go back.

It was one fight, I tell myself. Barely a fight. I just found out that Roo's spending the summer with my least favorite person. If anything, I should feel better. Once they spend time together, Roo will see how good he has it with me. No one else could possibly know him as well as I do. Who else would spend hours exchanging *Murder She Solved* theories or going down a reality show spiral? And what about shopping? There's no way that Brody is a good fashion consultant; I've seen how he dresses.

Nancy breaks the silence. "Penny for your thoughts?"

"Mine cost more than that," I say, still looking out the car window. I sigh. "There's the slightest chance I overreacted to something Roo said."

"About applying to the internship?" she asks.

"I didn't even get the chance to tell him," I say. "He decided to drop the news that he's working with Brody Wells over the summer."

"A betrayal!" Nancy gasps, voice dramatic like she's an actress in a classic whodunit film.

"Exactly!" I pause, trying to figure out how to say the next part. "I told him to find another job, and I think maybe that was the wrong move."

She doesn't speak right away, which probably means it was a terrible decision and now she's sided with Roo. At this rate, she might even unfriend me and track down Brody Wells as a replacement. "It's not the choice I would have made," she finally says.

"I don't know; isn't it easy to find a summer job? Aren't there a bunch of them? Like he could go be a camp counselor or work at an ice cream shop."

"Fe, it's not easy when the summer's already started," she points out.

I groan. "Fine. But Brody Wells? Why couldn't Roo work with literally anyone else?"

Nancy's still looking at the road, but I can see from her face that she's thinking. "Are we sure this wasn't just a way to put off having a conversation you were worried about?"

"Who are you? Bonnie?" Nancy knows all about Bonnie; she's just never channeled my therapist quite like that before.

"That means I'm right, doesn't it?"

I frown. "No," I say stubbornly. "We have a scheduled talk for the *Murder She Solved* finale. I'm definitely going to tell him then."

I will, it's not even that big of a deal. There's just a part of me that's still convinced he'll be weird about it. I imagine the possible reactions: he'll tell me not to apply, try to talk me out of it, immediately reach out to my mom. Or he won't even care, which somehow feels worse. There's also the chance that we don't even get to it because he's still angry about the job stuff and has decided to end our friendship and ghost me.

Nancy interrupts my spiral. "I don't know how you two listen to scary stuff like that. I feel like true crime always makes me think everyone is out to kill me."

"I mean, same, but it's still fascinating. Keeps you safe, if you really think about it. You're more aware of the danger. Like this one time, I knew a person who tried to murder me at a rock quarry."

She rolls her eyes. "I swear, you're going to like it there. You'll see."

The rock quarry turns out to be an absolutely massive stone formation with what looks like an artificial lake right in the middle. Nancy is right; there are a bunch of people already hanging out: laying on beach towels and sitting in foldout chairs and swimming in the water. There are at least three different families and a group of people who look about our age.

We walk around the edge of the water to get to the section where everyone else has set up their stuff. The path is overgrown with tall grass and weeds, leading right up to the stone. We have to do some minimal climbing from there before we can lay out our towels. I feel like I just went on one of those hikes Eric keeps talking about. I lose my footing not once, but twice and have to use Nancy's back to maintain balance.

We stop at the first section before the rock juts up, leading to a second outlook. I glance up just in time to see a kid, probably in the middle school age-range, jump off the cliff.

I watch as the kid falls right into the water, creating a huge splash. Their head pops out and they laugh, waving to their friends to join them.

"See, I told you it isn't dangerous," Nancy says.

I shake my head. "That poor child almost died."

Nancy gives me a look like I'm being dramatic. "How exactly is that what you saw?"

I point up to the cliff. "Do you see how high up that is? Look at all those rocks. You took me to a death trap."

"You don't have to jump from there," she says.

My eyes go wide. "But I still have to jump?"

"You could walk back around by the car and climb in. There's a ladder." She points to a spot almost directly across from us.

"So my options are to backtrack or jump in?" I ask.

"I mean, you could also chicken out and sit here alone while I swim," she offers.

"Nancy! Peer pressure is not a joke!"

"Fe, it's safe," she says. "I'll go first."

She slips off her shirt and shorts and leaves them in a pile by her towel. Her swimsuit is one of those one-pieces that looks like she stole it from her school's swim team. She glances over at me, like she's making sure I'm watching, and then dives in.

The water is too dark to see through. When she finally resurfaces, it's in a totally different area, like she swam underwater for a while before she deemed it time to get some air. "Told you," she calls to me.

She swims back over.

"You just survived getting in there. For all I know, there's some sort of monster lurking in the water."

Nancy gasps and pretends she's being pulled away by my suggested water monster, splashing like she's trying to resist. Then she stills. "I'm fine. It's just a tiny jump; you've got this. Wait." She looks serious. "You do know how to swim, right?"

"Oy, that's not the point," I say. "And, yes, thanks for just thinking of that."

"You're welcome."

I walk over to the edge of our shorter stone outlook. It's not even a pretty view, since the impressive stuff, the large rocks and the thickly settled trees, are behind me. From this spot, I can see a small green field and the parking lot. I look down, and there's nothing but murky water and an expectant Nancy.

"Fine, but I'll be a mean ghost," I warn.

I take off my simple white cover-up and fold it, then put it directly on top of my towel so it won't get dirty. I walk back to the edge.

I think the rocks grew; I'm definitely higher up than I was a second ago. Why am I so worried? It's not like I'm standing on the cliff, and, even if I was, kids are fully jumping off it. This is so much smaller, so much easier. Except the rocks are a little slippery, so I'll probably slip and crack open my head and suffer irreversible brain damage. Or I'll try to jump and instead go sliding in and land with a painful belly flop. Or I won't jump far enough out and end up slamming against the rocks and breaking every bone in my body.

I'm not sure how long I'm standing there, catastrophizing. I take a deep breath. It's okay to turn back. I don't have to do this just because Nancy brought me here. She even said I could sit up on these rocks while she swam. I am fully capable of making up my own mind.

So, I jump.

It happens so fast that I barely register what my body is doing. One second I'm panicking by the edge, and then I'm free-falling.

The moment I hit the water, my body feels very angry. It is absolutely freezing. Why didn't Nancy warn me about this? I'm shaking, and I'm not sure if it's from the adrenaline or the cold.

I swim up to the surface.

"Fun, right?" Nancy asks.

The thing is, it was fun. Maybe it's because I wasn't sure if I was actually going to get up the guts to jump, or maybe it was the way the air rushed past me in that split second before I hit the shocking cold or the relief of having done something scary and survived. I start to laugh. "Maybe," I say.

"Maybe works for me," she says. Her eyes light up. "Want to jump in again?"

"You're pushing your luck, Lim," I warn.

My body is already starting to feel numb. I paddle through the water, then try some different strokes, swimming on my back, then slipping under the surface. Now that the shock has worn off, the water feels good, cool in a refreshing-break-from-the-heat kind of way. It's actually calming, swimming and peacefully floating around the quarry.

For all the fuss, I'm happy I jumped.

THIRTY-SIX DAYS UNTIL THE WEDDING

Nancy gives me a confused look when I meet her outside the main house the next day.

"I thought I told you to dress comfortably? Clothes you can move in," she says. She pulls out her phone and checks. "Right here." She waves the screen at me.

I run a hand along my dress. It's made of a stretchy, breathable fabric that falls just above my knees. "I can move just fine in this, thank you very much."

"Not with what I have planned," she mutters. "I think I have stuff you can borrow in my bag," she adds, a little louder. She walks over to her car and grabs a gym bag out of the trunk. "Come on, we're walking."

I squint at her. "What exactly is our One Fun Thing today?"

"You'll see," she says. There's a mischievous look on her face.

We start to head through the orchard.

It keeps surprising me, how beautiful everything is here. I'm not usually a nature person. Maybe that's not right; I don't hate the outdoors or anything. I just find the idea of nature hikes cruel and unusual. But at Belmont Orchards, everything is so green; it's overwhelming in the best way. You look out and it's like we're in the middle of nowhere. Mother Nature is in control here.

Nancy stops walking.

I look at our new surroundings. "I'm sorry, do you have a soccer field in the middle of the orchard?" I ask.

"We have a field with an old goal my parents bought me for my birthday a few years ago," Nancy clarifies. She drops the gym bag on the ground.

"Where's the scoreboard? Where do your fans sit?" I look around, like I might find stadium seating. "Nancy, did you forget about your fans?"

She rolls her eyes. "We have them sit in the dirt here. Proves their loyalty." She unzips the bag and pulls out a pair of sweatpants. Then she looks back at me.

I wonder if she's judging if I can fit in her clothes. I tug at my dress, my whole body tensing.

Except it turns out I'm wrong, because what she says instead is, "You can't run in sandals, Fe."

"Hey!" I start. "This would've been a lot easier if you just told me what we were doing for fun today."

She sighs. "I'll wear the cleats, here." She kicks off her sneakers.

I pull the sweatpants on under my dress. They're tight around my thighs, and the shoes are about a size too big. I look silly with my mismatched outfit, but at least I can move around better. Not perfect, but manageable.

"All right, coach," I say. "What's on the agenda?"

She looks up at the sky, like she really has to think about it. "Quick warm-up, then a little one-on-one game," she finally says. "No score keeping, all good times."

"Counter offer, we kick the ball back and forth a few times and then lie out in the sun."

She shakes her head. "Who's the coach here?"

Well, if Nancy wants to see me make a fool of myself, I guess that's what she's going to get. I'm not sure I'd classify this as either "self-care" or "fun," but to each their own.

Nancy has us warm up with some stretches, then what she calls an "easy run," aka three sprints across the field. We take turns as the goalie, which she claims she isn't even very good at. I know I'm not supposed to keep track of goals for this exercise, but I can't help it. Final score: Nancy, seven—me, zilch.

By the time she decides we should take a break, I'm a sweaty mess.

"Wasn't that fun?" she asks, sitting down beside where I've essentially crashed on the grass.

I'm not sure whether it's better to laugh or cry to properly convey my feelings.

Nancy doesn't wait for a response. "Oh, come on. It's fun!"

"I'm glad you like soccer; let's never do that again," I finally manage.

"Exercise is a great way to de-stress and get your mind off things in general," she points out. "Therefore, this was a perfect idea for our self-care portion of the day."

"Shouldn't you think of this as work?" I ask. "You're on your school's soccer team; this should be the thing you need to de-stress from."

There's a look on Nancy's face, like she's considering this. "Yeah, I guess it used to be that way," she says softly. She isn't looking at me. I'm not even sure if she's looking at anything specific. I wonder if that's the expression I make when I'm stuck in my head.

"I didn't think I'd ever get to play again," she finally says.

"With your knee?" I ask.

She nods. I think she might say something else, but she keeps looking off at the field.

I want to say something. Should I apologize? Or is that silly? It's not like it's my fault she got injured. I guess part of what's making me so uneasy is Nancy's whole demeanor: she's usually joking around, easygoing. It's strange to see her so serious.

Eventually, she breaks the silence.

"I don't know," she adds. "After that, I guess I was so relieved to be back on the field. But it wasn't the same." She turns her gaze to me. "I was good," she says. "Really good, before everything happened. Like *definite scholarship* good. And then"—she snaps her fingers—"it was all gone.

"Maybe I could try harder to get back to where I was, I don't know." She pauses. "Right now, I kind of like just playing to play. Is that weird?"

I shake my head.

"Yeah, it's a little weird," she continues. "I feel like most people are supposed to feel all this pressure around sports."

"I mean, if you're me and you're bad at them, sure," I say.

"You weren't awful," she says, which feels like a big lie.

I sigh. "I was."

She considers this. "Maybe we'll find you another sport?"

"Well, I *am* on my school's golf team," I say.

She laughs.

"Hey, that wasn't a joke! *I am*. I needed a sport for my college applications!"

"And you chose golf?" she asks. "I can't believe this hasn't come up before. I'm sorry, I can't picture it."

I sit up a little straighter. "That's because you're not picturing low commitment, no tryouts, and a participation requirement of three tournaments a season."

"There it is," she says. Then she adds, "Maybe mini golf then?"

"I can get behind mini golf," I answer.

We sit there for a while longer, looking up at the sky.

I can't imagine going through something like that, being the best and then having it ripped away. All of my stress over the Social Friends Committee and Brody Wells taking my position feels so small in comparison.

I haven't had to reimagine what my whole life will look like. I mean, I even have a better opportunity in front of me now, with this whole internship thing.

I need to be more grateful about all that and stop turning it into a pile of stress.

I need to be more like Nancy.

THIRTY-FIVE DAYS UNTIL THE WEDDING

"What's on the agenda tonight?" Mom asks. "Family movie night?"

She's been trying to make a family movie night happen for the last few days.

For the first time, I don't have any excuses. I've already finished my wedding agenda today (a light load of vendor emails and some time on Pinterest). My plan for the night was to go on a YouTube spiral until I don't remember what video I started off on. "I can move some stuff around," I say.

"I finally get time with my daughter!" Mom says. "You've been so busy with Nancy, I thought you forgot about me."

My dramatic attitude is an inherited trait.

"You've been busy writing," I point out. "But, yes, I'll watch if you agree to do something for me first," I add.

"Hm, not sure that's how movie nights work, child of mine. What are you thinking?" she asks.

"You need to pick an officiant," I say. "I refuse to face the wrath of Bubbe; she wants a rabbi."

"Of course she does," Mom says. "Don't worry, I've gotten good at disappointing her. I can take it."

"You sure?" I ask. "This is a big task. It's one of those super important things you need to actually get married."

"I think I'm capable of handling a single thing for my own wedding," she says. "But thank you for the concern. Have I earned the movie night yet?"

I shrug. "I'll pass official judgment once your task is complete, but I guess I can preemptively reward you with my time."

"I raised such a little weirdo," she says lovingly, ruffling my hair like I'm a toddler. "I'll go get Eric so we can watch."

Eric ends up picking the movie, an overly cliché rom-com I've already seen. Not that that's a bad thing. I think those sorts of movies are meant to be rewatched, a formula so perfected that you can enjoy them even if you know what's going to happen because, let's be honest, you knew what was going to happen the first time too.

Girl meets boy. There are some cute and quirky hijinks. They like each other, but oh, no, there are obstacles! Those obstacles can't stand in the way of true love. Big declaration of said love, probably in a crowded place like a restaurant or at a news conference or an airport. They ride off into the sunset and live happily ever after.

The plot is comfortable in its predictability.

I think about Mom. A movie of her and Eric's love story wouldn't even make any sense. She already had a middle schooler and showed up to get her second tattoo. He was the one doing said tattooing. They started dating. There was no drama or quirky hijinks or airport love confession. They just slipped into a routine, like they jumped into the post-credit lives of the rom-com characters, which are too boring to garner any screen time.

I'm not going to be like that, I think.

I want the big romance; I want the cinematic feelings.

Except I might not ever get them.

I shouldn't think like that. There are plenty of people who are on the asexual spectrum who fall in love and get married and have all of those meant-for-movie moments. The problem is, there's always this underlying layer of fear when I think about potential relationships, this voice that tells me no one will want to be with someone like me.

Sometimes, I think I should just pretend to be normal. Like when Anesha Patel had a sleepover for her thirteenth birthday and we all went around and talked about crushes and kissing, I talked too. It was easier to blend in and say what I knew people wanted to hear.

Could I keep that up forever? Just learn the script and follow the formula and live happily ever after?

I try to imagine it. Find someone, flirt, act totally normal about intimacy. Yet the thought of even doing something tame like holding hands without a level of emotional connection to a hypothetical future significant other makes me cringe. If I'm to trust basically all of media right now, people do intimacy before feelings. Could I fake it? Should I?

I don't know if I could keep that up, all the pretending. Especially when it comes to a future partner.

I want someone who accepts me for who I am. I hope that person exists.

"Want to watch another one?" Eric asks.

"Sure, but I get to pick," I say.

Eric nods like this is a fair deal.

I choose a murder mystery. No time to queer panic when you're trying to solve a fictional criminal case.

THIRTY-FOUR DAYS UNTIL THE WEDDING

"You don't have to dye your hair red if you choose a mermaid gown," I say, already annoyed.

"I think I could pull it off though." Mom tugs at her hair for emphasis. The purple has faded, so I wouldn't be surprised if she changed it for the wedding. Granted, I was hoping for something like a simple brown, not Little Mermaid Red.

This is our FOURTH time looking at wedding dresses online, and I still don't have a good idea of what she wants. It's been a steady stream of "this one's too frilly" and "that's too tight" and "what, do you want me to look like a cake topper?" No. I would like you to look like a bride, thanks. At this point, I'd be fine if she walked down the aisle in a white garment bag.

If it had some delicate lace and an A-line silhouette.

"Or this," I say, showing her the next dress: a trumpet gown with a dropped waist.

"Pass," she says. "The shape is . . . just no."

The next one is a ball gown with beads, and the one after is a boho-style dress that looks like you could buy it at Target in their summer sundress section—way too casual, so I skip past it.

"I liked that one," Mom says.

I groan. She's so stubborn; she knows exactly what she's doing. "There has to be a dress—a real wedding dress—that you can wear. You can't be this picky."

"All those other dresses are so formal," she complains.

"How strange. It's almost like they're meant for *weddings*." It's bickering like this that ended our last three attempts at finding a dress, so I should be careful.

"What about that one?" she says to the next option.

"You can't—oh, that's not terrible."

We're looking at an A-line dress with loose lace sleeves that fall a couple of inches above the elbows. The front and back of the dress are both V-neck cuts, with the back dipping low and ending in a line of pearl buttons. It's formal wear meets boho chic with its flowing silhouette and lace and muted champagne color.

"Did we just find my dress? When am I allowed to say yes? Where are the cameras?" she asks.

"Cool it, you still need to try it on," I warn. Then I smile. "But, yeah, I think you just found your dress. I'll make an appointment."

"You're the best, child of mine," she says.

Agreeing on a dress feels *big*. Finding Mom's wedding dress is one of my most important to-dos still on my list. This is what's going to be in every picture, what's going to define not only her look for the day but the aesthetic of the whole wedding too. Getting this taken care of feels like confirmation that the entire event will be a success.

After a good deal of pleading and explaining our desperate situation and tight deadline, I'm able to book an appointment. Thank goodness the dress is off the rack because the only appointment available is exactly eleven days before the wedding. You're supposed to order your dress, what? A year in advance? Eleven days beforehand sounds like we're mocking the bridal dress industry.

I set an event reminder on my mom's phone and write the appointment down in my wedding notebook, so it's official.

Find a dress? Check.

I'm almost too good at this.

I'm still riding the wedding gown high when Nancy texts to ask if she can come over. We don't have any solid plans today, but I assumed we'd hang out at some point.

I start talking before she's even through the door. "Huge news," I say. "The biggest, most important news you might ever hear."

"World peace?" she asks. "Or wedding dress?"

"We found a dress," I confirm. "It's *so* pretty. I mean, I'd never wear it—it's a little too boho for me—but it's *so* my mom."

"Picture?" Nancy asks.

I get my laptop from the kitchen island and bring it over to the couch, then sit down next to her. The picture is still up on my screen.

"Oh, the lace is beautiful," she says, pointing to the loose sleeves on the gown. "And the color, very your mom."

"I can just see her wearing it, you know? Like if I think of the day, she's in this. It just makes sense."

Nancy nods, like she completely understands what I'm saying. "Is she going to try it on?"

"Appointment booked and everything," I say. Then I gasp, "You should come with us!" I don't know why I didn't think of that sooner. "It's just in Boston, not far at all. We can make a day of it!"

"You sure?" she asks. "I don't want to encroach on a special mother-daughter day."

I laugh. "You've done more for this wedding than she has. We probably owe you a dress."

She shakes her head a little in that *you're too much* kind of way.

I can't help but smile. We have the dress, I've booked the vendors, and we even have a bunch of the decorations. I feel like I've been thinking of this in the abstract, like there was too much to organize for it to feel real yet. I have details now. I can picture my mom in her dress, standing at the top of the hill that overlooks the orchard with the lights dotted along the nearby trees. She looks so happy in this hypothetical.

It's all coming together.

———

That night, Roo and I have our scheduled *Murder She Solved* debrief, meaning I need to work up the guts to tell him about this internship. I technically could have texted him beforehand, but in my defense, I was angry and also busy.

We agreed that we'd listen at the same time, then video chat. I call as soon as the credits start.

"The salutatorian," I say as soon as his face pops up on the screen. "That one came out of nowhere. Though I think I should get points for guessing the killer was school related."

"I'm doing fine, thanks for asking," he says.

Since when have we exchanged pleasantries? We're well past that point in our friendship.

"Roo!" I say, trying to get us back on track. "Big finale reveal, focus!"

He can't still be mad about how I reacted with his whole job thing, right? What? He's just going to drop the news that he's working with my known enemy and not expect a reaction?

Fine, there's a slight chance I blew things out of proportion, but Roo should understand. It's how we always talk to each other.

"I just can't believe it all came down to the yearbook. Though why'd we need that whole thing with his cousin? Just to get another episode out of the mystery?"

Roo seems so distracted. He's never like this when it comes to *Murder She Solved*. I mean, he isn't even looking at the screen.

I wave at the camera. "Roo, hello. Everything okay?" I ask.

He turns his gaze to me. "Yeah, sorry, I actually didn't finish the episode."

I put my hand over my mouth and gasp. "I ruined the season for you! I'm so sorry!" I pause. "We did agree to watch it tonight, right?"

"Something came up," he says. He doesn't offer any further explanation.

"We can reschedule. I mean, I know I gave you major spoilers, but it really does all come together in such a perfect way; you'll still love it. And then we can—"

He cuts me off. "Nah, I'm not really in the mood for podcasts."

Why is he being so strange? He's the one who got me into *Murder She Solved* in the first place.

He has to be angry at me for telling him to quit his summer job; it's the only explanation. My mind goes on: he's decided that he actually likes Brody more than me, they're best friends now, this is really a goodbye call because he's chosen sides and never wants to speak to me again.

Maybe I should apologize. Maybe I should say more mean things about Brody Wells. At this point, it's a toss-up.

I decide instead of doing one hard thing, I'll do another. "I have some news. Sort of," I start. "My grandma knows someone at this event planning company in Boston, and she's inviting her to the wedding. She thinks she can get me an internship."

"Cool," he says flatly. "If it works out."

Maybe I'm still frustrated from earlier, but I think his tone is sort of . . . bored. Or maybe annoyed.

Bonnie often tells me to be curious how other people are feeling, instead of jumping to assumptions. So, I will admit, I might be reading into things.

"I mean, I know it isn't a guarantee," I continue. "But this could be a big deal. So much bigger than anything at school. But now I feel like I have to pull off the most impressive wedding with, like, no planning time. I mean, my prospective boss, whose career is literally planning events, is going to be there."

"Sounds stressful," he says. I still can't read the tone of his voice. Is he worried? Does he think I can't handle it?

"Not really," I say quickly, just in case he's concerned to the point of telling my mom. "Plus, Nancy's helping me."

"Right," he says.

I'm so confused by his whole demeanor. He's usually more, I don't know, comfortable. It's normally so easy with us.

Maybe he's thinking about last winter. Maybe he heard everything I'm saying and he jumped to the wrong conclusions. I keep thinking about what my mom said to Eric before we left. This wedding is just another stressor I can't handle.

Of course he's worried.

"Is this a bad idea?" I ask him. "Weddings are already so much work. I could tell Bubbe to, I don't know, uninvite her. Call off the whole plan. Should I?"

"I can't figure that out for you," he says. This time there's definitely an edge to his voice, like he's exasperated with me.

"I'm not asking you to," I say.

"Aren't you?" He sits up on his bed, so I can see his black headboard now. Then he does the unforgivable: he mutes his microphone.

What am I going to hear that he wouldn't want me to know about?

He turns the microphone back on. "I have to go. Amira wants to watch a movie. Before I forget, I wanted to know if I could have a plus-one for the wedding. Since you're in the early stages and all."

I'm not exactly in the early stages, since everything about this is basically a scramble, but it won't be a problem if Amira comes to the wedding. I've missed her since she left for college last year; she was basically like my big sister when we were little. "Won't be a problem," I say.

"Cool."

Then he hangs up.

HANGS UP.

What is with him? He's being so . . . un-Roo-like. He was supposed to celebrate and tell me I can handle everything before we caught up and probably spend the whole night talking. But no, he hung up. We had longer conversations when he was visiting his family in Pakistan while babysitting his very needy younger cousins.

My problems are so much more important than some random movie.

THIRTY-THREE DAYS UNTIL THE WEDDING

I'm in Aunt Gwendoline's attic the first time I see Swift Wind.

Or, at least, I think it's Swiftie when I spot a blur of dark brown fur. "Either there are rats here, in which case we need to get out STAT, or Swiftie just ran by," I say.

"Definitely rats," Nancy jokes. "Tons of them. Snakes and cockroaches too." She bends down near an old, ornate cabinet. "Swiftie," she calls. She puts her hand out in front of her.

A tiny cat face pokes out from underneath the cabinet and rubs up against her hand.

"You have a cat," I say. "A real cat."

"You knew I had a cat." She scratches behind Swiftie's ear.

"Could've been an imaginary one. There wasn't proof before."

Swift Wind is tiny, the size of a kitten, even though I know he's already a few years old. His yellow-green eyes are so large that they make him look like he stepped out of a cartoon. He could easily trick someone into thinking he's a kid's stuffed animal dragon.

"He's a little skittish," Nancy warns. "Put your hand out."

I do as told, bending down closer to the cabinet.

Swiftie stays near Nancy, but his eyes turn to me, like he's evaluating whether or not I'm safe or interesting enough to walk over to. I stay still as he deliberates. Finally, he walks very slowly up to my hand and sniffs.

"I passed the test," I say. As if to confirm, Swiftie nuzzles my outstretched hand.

"Many don't," Nancy tells me.

Not that it lasts long. When I try to pet him, he darts away, back underneath the cabinet. It's a start; I'll win him over eventually.

Nancy and I didn't come upstairs for Swift Wind though. We're on a mission. An armchair mission.

I got the idea from a reality show. We were watching this one about weddings at Disney, and one of the couples had mismatched antique armchairs for their English garden Epcot ceremony. It was absolutely adorable, which is what I told Nancy.

"We can probably find enough here to do that," Nancy said. "Aunt Gwendoline has a whole bunch of stuff in storage and around the house that could work."

She was right. We found five armchairs just on our way *up* to the attic.

Nancy moves from her crouched pose by the ornate cabinet. "Ready to look?"

I nod.

The attic is massive, stretching the full length of the house. It's also packed. There's enough furniture in here to decorate two more homes and an apartment if we wanted to do so. I see some bed frames, dismantled and leaning against the side wall, dressers, bookcases, tables, both of the side and coffee variety, a couple of couches, and, yes, armchairs. There are some that are a little too modern, but I don't even think we'll even need them.

"Did we walk through some strange portal? Am I about to find every sock I've ever lost?" I ask.

Nancy nods, keeping her face serious. "Yes, we keep the lost socks in the back."

I love that Nancy always plays along with my bits.

"Some of this mess is because Aunt Gwendoline likes *collecting*, as she calls it," Nancy explains. "But it's also my parents' fault. They redid a lot of the house and got new furniture, but my dad never knows when they'll need something for one of their projects. I don't think anyone I'm related to can part with anything ever, *just in case*. Some raided yard sale trips, a few estate sales. Which all leads us to this." She waves a hand at the warehouse-like scene in front of us.

"Okay, I hear you, but"—I point across the room—"explain that."

She turns to look at the gigantic hot-pink Godzilla across the room.

"That's clearly a yard statue."

I can't help but snort. "For a future renovation project?" I ask. "What client asks for something like that? *Oh, hello, design team, heads-up, my aesthetic can best be summed up as flashy movie monsters; do with that what you will.*" I put on an exaggerated voice that was supposed to sound like a British accent but missed the mark. There goes my potential acting career.

"Oh, no, that one's all Aunt Gwendoline," Nancy says.

"Obviously," I supply.

155

With that, we get to work.

"You're sure they won't mind if we use these?" I ask, pulling a tufted, rolled-arm upholstered chair into our designated collection area. "I rented chairs for the reception. I could try to get more for the ceremony."

"I'm positive it's fine," Nancy says. "Better we use these than just leave them all up here collecting dust," she adds, shoving a love seat that looks like it came out of the drawing room from a period piece. "Would this work? Or is it too big?"

"Oh, it definitely works. Less to find this way. Plus, it fits the whole mismatched vintage style."

It's not easy getting to everything. I wouldn't say that the attic is a mess; there's an order to the chaos of the collection. It's just that some of that order is in the way of what I want.

"Hey, could you help me with this one?" I ask. There's a wingback with circular armrests that's stuck behind a square mahogany coffee table and bordered by a long cherry bookcase with doors along the bottom. On the other side there's a precariously balanced set of cardboard boxes.

Nancy walks over and examines the situation. "I think you have to climb on the coffee table," she says.

I don't like the idea of stepping on this very old-looking table, but here we are.

I put one foot on the surface to test it. The wood seems sturdy enough, fingers crossed, so I take the other step up. With light movements, I walk to the other side, closer to the chair. It's tight, but I think I can get it.

I take hold of the chair and try to lift it up, which is admittedly a bit awkward from my spot on the table. The boxes wobble a bit, so I stop and readjust, pushing the chair closer to the side with the bookcase. It works. I hold it up and walk it back across the table. Nancy helps me lower the armchair down and step off the wooden surface.

"A success!" I practically cheer.

I guess it's inevitable. When things feel this good, something has to come crashing down.

We hear the sound of the fall first, followed by the scream, so piercing I can practically feel it. At first, I think it's my fault, that maybe I knocked down those boxes after all. Except Nancy and I are fine and the boxes are in place. If neither of us screamed, it means someone else is in trouble.

"What happened?" I ask.

Nancy is already on her way out of the room. "Aunt Gwendoline!" she yells.

There's no response.

We run out of the attic and down the stairs. Nancy opens her great-aunt's bedroom door, but she isn't there. "Aunt Gwendoline!" Her voice is more desperate now.

Nancy bolts for the stairs to get to the first floor. I follow closely behind. We turn the corner. Nancy's already on the first step when I see Aunt Gwendoline, collapsed at the bottom.

No. My mind runs through a series of worst-case scenarios. She had a heart attack or a stroke. She fell and hit her head so hard she's in a coma. She died, and we're looking at a dead body.

"Aunt Gwendoline!" Nancy screams.

She whimpers from her spot curled on the floor. That has to

mean she's conscious; at least I think it does. If she's conscious, that rules out the worst possibilities.

Not all of them, but the worst ones.

"It's all right," I say. "It's all right, we can handle this. It's all going to be all right."

Except I have no clue. I've never been more terrified.

AN HOUR AFTER THE FALL

We've been sitting in the hospital waiting room for the last forty-five minutes. There was the whole process of getting Aunt Gwendoline checked in and trying to get in touch with my mom and Eric, who were both not answering their phones, and talking to the nurse practitioner who told us they were going to take Aunt Gwendoline into the back. It felt like time wasn't real, somehow too slow and too fast. Maybe that's just the way it is in waiting rooms, a weird liminal space.

I take Nancy's hand. "You okay?"

She gives me a little, unconvincing nod.

"You don't have to be, you know?"

This time her head bobbles, a nonanswer at best.

"I just don't know how she fell," Nancy finally says. "That's never happened before."

"She might've lost her balance," I say. "One time I tripped *up* the stairs."

"Hm, that sounds like a you problem." She offers me a weak smile. She doesn't let go of my hand.

There's a TV high up on the wall inexplicably playing a Hallmark holiday movie. It must be one of those celebrate-during-the-summer marathons, which I feel like they do just because they have so many Christmas movies. I can't tell what's going on in the plot, other than the fact that there's a lot of fake snow and not a lot of realistic winter wear. No one looks film attractive in a practical puffy coat.

A few other people are in the waiting room with us. There's a guy behind the check-in desk and a mother sitting with her young son. The toddler has commandeered her phone and is listening to what I think is a kid's cartoon, but it must be something new. I don't recognize the overly dramatized, high-pitched voices.

I wonder what these people must think of us, two teenage girls sitting on vinyl-covered chairs side by side, holding hands. Do they think we're dating? Do they think I'm just offering a friend support during a stressful time? Does it even matter?

There are other questions filling my mind too. What am I supposed to do right now? What does Nancy need? I don't like silence; I should fill it. Will that help her? Does she need silence right now? Or a distraction?

Probably a distraction.

Which is why I say the worst thing I could possibly come up with. "I haven't been to a hospital since last winter."

WHY? Why did my brain think that was the right thing to say right now? Does it run purely on association? We are in a hospital equals I was in the hospital, so let's share that story with Nancy!

Guess it's time to internally scream forever.

It's not that Nancy doesn't know I ended up in the hospital over the winter. When something dramatic like that happens, you're basically contractually obligated to tell your friends. I might have just . . . altered the story a bit.

"Oh, yeah, when you hit your head, right?"

Fine, I might have altered the story a lot.

"Yeah, my head," I say, except I obviously can't leave it at that. "Actually, I sort of worked myself too hard during midterms. There might have been some over exhaustion paired with what the doctor deemed 'an alarming amount of caffeine.' Which led to me fainting and hitting my head."

She doesn't respond, so I continue, "I think the worst part was that it wasn't even anything dramatic. I wasn't on drugs or doing anything illegal. All of the things that led to me going to the ER, well, I had done them before."

This is inappropriate, I think. We should be, I don't know, talking about Aunt Gwendoline. This isn't my time; I'm a bad person for even bringing this up.

"I'm sorry," I say. "I don't know why I said anything."

Nancy shakes her head. "No, I get it. It's just . . ." She pauses. "Why didn't you tell me all of that when it happened?"

I shrug. "I guess I was sort of embarrassed. I didn't tell anyone outside my family, I mean, except Roo. Who does that to themselves?"

She should be judging me harshly right now. She should be angry at me for not knowing my limits and doing something so ridiculous.

Except when I look at her, I don't see anger or judgment. Admittedly, she does look a little confused.

"Wait, coffee sent you to the hospital?" she asks.

"I might have had a higher than recommended number of Four Hour Energy Boost drinks," I admit.

I think she might make fun of me for that part. Maybe I should joke about it and call myself a frat bro wannabe. Maybe I should curl up into myself until I disappear forever.

I should have known better. Just because I could buy them, didn't mean it was safe. I feel like I'm some ridiculous plot twist on a teen show that's gone on too long. I can practically hear an imaginary showrunner pitch, "What if the overachiever almost gave herself a heart attack? Trust me, it'll be ratings gold!"

I can't look at Nancy right now. I was supposed to be helping her. Now I just feel small and ridiculous.

"Hey," she says, "thanks. For sharing that with me."

I nod. My head feels heavy.

I'm not sure why I said any of that. I guess it's all the worry, since we still don't know what's going on with Aunt Gwendoline. Maybe it's because this is the first time that I've been to the hospital since everything happened.

I take a breath. "She really will be okay."

Nancy nods.

"All right, um," I try again. "Let's talk about something else. Best episode of *She-Ra*?" I ask.

"Rude question, but also it's a tie between the princess prom and the D&D episode."

"That feels like 'Save the Cat' erasure," I say.

I try a few more things to fill the time. After a heated *She-Ra* debate, we talk about some books and video games. Nancy's more into video games than I am; I never got past the kiddie-learning kinds, so she tells me about some of the ones that she thinks I would either love, because of the storytelling, or hate, because they're too complicated.

Nothing we do feels logically connected. I think it's often that way when you're trying to fill time.

Eventually my mom shows up. "Lissy baby, Nancy, have you heard anything yet?" she asks.

"They're doing some tests," I say.

Doing some tests. I wonder what that actually means. Probably blood work or some kind of scan, but I picture Aunt Gwendoline sitting down to finish a timed essay and write short answer responses.

"She hurt her arm, maybe her head too, but we don't really know much else," Nancy adds. "They're trying to rule everything out."

"Did you get in touch with your parents?" Mom asks.

Nancy nods. "Called them on the way over. They're in the car, but it's a long drive."

There's this relief to Mom being here. She doesn't even do much other than sit and wait with us, but it feels good to have an actual adult around. It's good to have someone to defer to.

Deferring to *my* mom . . . desperate times and all that.

I'm not sure how long it is until the doctor comes over; it feels like years have passed.

"Gwendoline Lim's family?" she asks.

Nancy gets up.

"Your aunt's fine. She fell on the stairs; apparently a heel on her shoe broke. Told me all about it, *in detail*. Quite the personality," the doctor says lightly. "She has a mild concussion, and she fractured one of the bones in her left arm, but we've ruled out everything else. We'd like to keep her a little longer to observe, but she should be good to go home in a couple of hours." The doctor puts down her chart. "She's okay," she adds, voice comforting, "you can go see her."

I get up, standing next to Nancy. "She's okay," I repeat.

Nancy hugs me. "Yeah, yeah, she is."

She's not crying, but her eyes look a little glossy. "Let's go see her."

Aunt Gwendoline isn't just okay; she's downright lively. When we walk into her room, we find her sitting up in her hospital bed, animatedly telling a story to one of her nurses.

". . . so I say, 'Not in this robe,' and I make him wait while I change before—oh, girls, you're here!"

Nancy goes over and carefully hugs her aunt, avoiding the arm placed in a standard blue sling with a crisp white strap.

"I'm fine. Playfully dazed and confined to this fashion faux pas, but otherwise unharmed." She adjusts the strap on her sling. "You know it's a broken humerus . . . how funny."

"She's made that joke three times already," the nurse says, like he's in on the whole thing.

"Humorous," Nancy supplies. "Glad you didn't knock that personality out."

Aunt Gwendoline smirks.

This too is a relief, though my brain is having a little trouble registering it all. I blame the liminal space.

We wait with Aunt Gwendoline until she's allowed to leave the hospital. Mom talks to the doctors and handles the forms. There's a whole stack of paper about caring for someone with a concussion and what Aunt Gwendoline should do if she's in pain and which specialist she should see about her fractured humerus.

"I'm going to go with them," I say to Mom as we're leaving. "You okay to drive back alone?"

She pulls me into a one-armed hug, the stack of documents in her other hand. "I can manage," she says. Then she adds, "You did the right thing today, child of mine."

I didn't really do anything though; it's not like I'm one of the doctors or nurses. Still, I say, "Thanks," before following Nancy to her car.

I take the back seat so Aunt Gwendoline can sit in front with Nancy.

That's usually my spot. I picture us driving to the rock quarry or the bookstore, the sun shining brightly through the slightly dirty window, hot against my right shoulder and arm. Can you get a sunburn in a car? I feel like the answer is yes, but I'm not sure.

Not that it's a problem now. We were in the hospital so long that it's already dark. It must be cloudy, I think, as Nancy starts the car. I can't see any stars.

When we get back, we help Aunt Gwendoline get settled in her room. According to the doctor, it's okay to let her sleep, even though I thought you had to keep people with a concussion awake. Maybe that's just for really severe cases.

The last thing she says before going to sleep is, "Utterly knackered." She turns out her bedside lamp with her uninjured arm before we're out of the room.

Nancy and I walk downstairs, stopping near the front door.

"Hey," Nancy says. "Thanks for staying with me."

"I don't have to leave now; I can stay longer," I offer.

"It's okay," she says. "My parents will be here soon. You can meet them tomorrow."

"All right."

We stand there by the door for a moment, silent. Should I stay? Does she need me? Is it better for us to get some rest? It's been such a long day.

I settle on giving her a hug.

She nestles her head against my shoulder. "Thanks," she repeats softly.

"Anything. Anything for you," I whisper back.

We stay like that, holding each other by the door, until her parents arrive.

THIRTY-TWO DAYS UNTIL THE WEDDING

Nancy: Lunch with my parents? We're making homemade bibim-bap, you'll love it.

I don't want to encroach on Nancy's time with her mom and dad, since they've been gone for most of the summer.

I guess I sort of met them last night, but I don't think that counts. We basically said hello and good night in the same breath; that's hardly enough time to make an impression.

I send her a quick text back.

Felicity: yes and yum

I wonder what I'm supposed to wear.

All of my dresses are pretty meet-your-friend's-parents friendly. I tame my messy hair so it falls straight and try on a couple of different outfits before settling on a navy sundress with a stripe of beige along the hem. It looks like the sort of thing I might put on to go yachting. A boat-ready dress has to be parent appropriate.

I find Eric sitting on the couch upstairs. He's reading a book, but I can't tell what kind from the way he's holding it.

"I'm heading over to have lunch with Nancy," I tell him.

"And her parents," Eric adds.

"Yes, and her parents," I confirm.

Eric puts his book down on the coffee table. "They'll love you. You're very lovable."

"You're obligated to say that," I point out.

"No," Eric corrects, "I'm happy to say it. Your mom, she's obligated. That's the bonus of marrying into the family: I get to make choices. I could go all evil stepmother on you."

"Evil stepmother? Something you want to tell me, Flores?" I tease.

"Psh, it's a trope. You know what I mean." He picks his book back up. "Have fun, Lissy. Don't stress it."

Saying "don't stress" to a person whose baseline is anxiety is never helpful. He probably just jinxed the whole meal. They're basically required to hate me now.

I walk over to the main house, worried about this lunch. I should turn around; I don't have to do this. Nancy probably wants her space anyway, and they should just be together now after everything that happened yesterday. This is a bad idea; we don't need to do this now.

I knock on the door.

"Felicity!" Nancy's mom says as she opens the door, so loud that it seems like she's announcing my arrival to all of Vermont. "Get over here." She pulls me into a hug.

So far, no hate. I'll take it as a good sign.

Nancy and her dad are finishing cooking in the kitchen. "Hey, Fe," Nancy says. "Egg or just veggies?" she asks.

"Oh, however you usually make it is fine," I say.

"Egg then," she tells her dad.

She walks over to me and gives me a quick hug.

"How's Aunt Gwendoline?" I ask.

"She can't even get dressed by herself, but she told me she's hosting a bridge tournament tomorrow. I just . . ." Nancy trails off. "She seems fine. She's out to lunch with a friend right now, refused to reschedule. Said it's rude to break plans."

"I'm barely home and she's already sick of me," Nancy's dad jokes.

The two of them finish cooking as Nancy's mom and I set the table. It all feels strangely normal, like we've had lunch together a million times before. I guess I didn't have to worry; Eric was right.

It's a comfortable lunch. I've never had bibimbap before, which I immediately clock as a poor choice made by past Felicity. It's delicious, packed with flavor from the fresh veggies and the strong sauce that is nothing like anything I've had before: spicy and salty and sweet all at the same time.

I'm mesmerized by the way Nancy is with her parents. They seem so happy, the perfect family coming together to help one of their own in need. Not that Aunt Gwendoline would look at herself as someone in need, of course. They're the kind of family I always wanted when I was little. Two parents who look and act like real adults. Both of them have to step away to take phone calls, but they're super apologetic about the whole thing. "Awful timing," Nancy's mom says. "So many moving parts. Though I have to say, it *is* good to be home."

It feels like I'm getting a glimpse into Nancy's normal life. This is her home, her standard, something that's always been a guarantee. I bet she's never had to fight her school secretary because her mom wouldn't wake up or scrubbed hair dye out of her parents' shower because no one else would be bothered to do it.

Nancy is so lucky.

———

Nancy's parents are staying for two days. I try to keep busy so she has some alone time with them. It's weird how quickly I got used to spending all of my time with Nancy, especially after our year physically apart. What am I supposed to do without her showing up and telling me I'm ruining my summer if I don't eat a maple creemee?

I check my email. There's a new message from Bubbe.

Dear Felicity,

Here's the application, darling!

All the kisses and hugs,
Your Bubbe

I open the attachment right away. I can't believe I forgot about the application. I scan the document quickly. Bubbe was right; there isn't a lot on there. Name, address, school, GPA—a bunch of easy fill in the blanks. I'm not worried until I see the question.

Why do you want to work for Hartman and Company?

I sit there at the desk in my summer bedroom, looking at my screen. Why do I want to work for them? Okay, this is easy, I can write an answer. I want to work for them because . . . my grandma told me it would look good. Nope, can't write that. I want to work for them because Brody Wells stole my leadership position at school, so now my resume looks terrible and I'll never get into a good college. Another poor attempt. I try again. I want to work there because Bubbe has a connection and—all right, made it worse.

I watch the cursor blink on the screen.

Maybe I need to think bigger. Why did I want the Junior Committee President position on the Social Friends Committee? That one is easy. I mean, obviously part of it was that I wanted something to add to my résumé, but I could have joined a ton of other clubs. Hell, I could've gone for something on the golf team; I'm already *technically* a member. Queer Club doesn't have any officers, but I could have joined, I don't know, the yearbook or the school newspaper. Those would've looked good to colleges.

Except there was something so exciting about being in charge of those big high school moments, the dances and celebrations everyone will remember for the rest of their lives. I could help craft those. I could make memories.

I google Hartman and Co. again and flip through some of the pictures of their past events: holiday parties and fundraisers and, most importantly, weddings.

Am I doing enough for this wedding? This isn't just a means to an internship; this is also about my family. This is something we'll remember forever. Am I doing enough for Mom and Eric and even Bubbe?

I think about my mom, who has missed out on most of the adult landmarks she was supposed to hit. I think of Eric, dreaming about his perfect traditional wedding since he was a little boy. Bubbe, who only wants the best for our family.

They need this wedding to be perfect. *I* need to be perfect.

I turn off the computer. The application isn't even due until the week after the wedding. I'll finish it later.

ONE MONTH UNTIL THE WEDDING

I run through my to-do list. I need to finish the seating chart so I can start making the place cards. I need to find something to include that is either Red Sox or generic baseball related for Eric. I need to finish ordering decorations for the reception. *I need to, I need to, I need to*, the list goes on.

I should tell Nancy we have to cancel our One Fun Thing today. There aren't enough hours to get everything done as is.

A weird thing happens when I walk up to Nancy outside the main house: all of that worry fades away.

I blame the hot-pink Godzilla statue.

"Why?" I ask, eyeing the statue standing next to Nancy.

"Hear me out," she starts. "Mini golf." She says it dramatically, like this explains everything.

It decidedly does not.

"I'm hearing, I swear, but understanding . . . not so much," I say.

Nancy leans against the statue, like she's settling in for a long explanation. "I've given it some thought, and, what if, instead of our whole One Fun Thing activity, we do One Fun Project this week?"

I pause, like I'm giving this real consideration. Which is admittedly hard to do when I'm looking at a monstrous pink garden statue. "Aren't we already in the middle of a super-duper fun project?" I point out.

"But," Nancy counters, "and this is a very important 'but,' Godzilla deserves something epic. Like an entire homemade miniature golf course."

Can't argue with that logic.

I take a moment to really look at Nancy. She's wearing her brace, so it must be a bad knee day. Her long black hair is obscuring part of Godzilla's flashy face. She has her arms folded like she means business.

She's adorable, I think, then immediately panic. Is it okay to think of your friend as adorable? That's normal, right? Sure, I've never looked at Roo and thought wow he's cute, but that's different because of reasons I can't think of right now. Good reasons.

Bonnie would probably tell me I should focus on the present right now. I'm too in my head.

I look back at Nancy and the gaudy statue. "What exactly does that entail?"

Nancy smiles. "I'm glad you asked."

It turns out that Nancy has given this a lot more thought than she let on. She bends down and picks up a sketchbook by the statue's monster feet, then walks over to show me. There are pages and pages of designs.

"So, as you can see, I think if we use some old piping my mom has in her workshop and spring for some turf, maybe do some crafting, we could probably get a small course. Five holes, at least."

I look at her pictures. "How long have you been working on this?" I ask.

She bites her lip. "Don't make fun of me."

I hold up my right hand like I'm swearing an oath.

"That night that we went to the hospital, I couldn't sleep after you left. Somewhere in the stress"—she points back at Godzilla—"this happened."

She's stressed? I think back to that night we took Aunt Gwendoline to the ER. Should I have stayed with Nancy, even after her parents arrived? Should I have checked in more since? I thought giving them family time was the right move, but I have a whole set of miniature golf designs in front of me proving otherwise.

"Are you okay?" I ask.

She straightens her shoulders. "Yeah, I'm . . . yeah."

I wait for her to continue.

"I don't know," she admits. "Is that silly? She's fine, I should be fine."

I shake my head. "Not silly at all."

Nancy looks serious, like she's considering this or maybe just lost in her thoughts. When she finally speaks, she says, "I couldn't stop thinking about what would've happened if it was worse or if we weren't there. That it could happen again." She takes a breath. "I needed to focus on something else."

"Like designing a homemade miniature golf course," I say.

Nancy looks down at the design facing up on her sketchbook. "Apparently," she says.

I am in no way handy. I know my way around a DIY project, sure, but this feels bigger than designing centerpieces or decorating posters. If I were to pick a relaxing activity for my day, it wouldn't involve manual labor and construction.

I look from Nancy's design to her face. She needs this.

"I mean, mini golf *is* fun," I concede.

"Thank goodness you're on board; I already ordered a set of cheap clubs," she admits, her voice sounding lighter.

I laugh. "Guess we're really locked in then."

"Guess we are," Nancy confirms.

It takes us five days to finish the course. Five days of running to the home and gardening center and raiding the attic at the main house and rifling through the workshop. We end up with seven holes in a grassy opening between some of the apple trees and a wild-looking patch of blueberry bushes. It's not exactly professional, but Hot Pink Godzilla has a home.

"We did it," Nancy triumphantly announces. She has a streak of dirt across her forehead. I wonder if I have any dirt on me too.

"That we did," I say. "Should we . . . I don't know? Celebrate?" I ask. "Is there a maple treat you haven't told me about yet?"

Nancy ignores this. "A game?" she proposes. "I'll get Aunt Gwendoline, you get your parents?"

It's weird hearing "parents" as a plural and it not being a mistake. "Sounds like a plan," I say.

When I get back to the barn-cottage, I find Mom making tea in the kitchen.

"Hey, child of mine," Mom says, mid-squeezing honey into her mug. "Why do you have dirt on your arms?" She puts down the bear-shaped bottle.

Well, that answers my question about the dirt.

"Right, so, Nancy and I made a mini golf course, and we thought you guys could come test it out."

Mom's eyes light up. "That's what you two have been up to? I thought you were still running around looking for, I don't know, lace or china or something." She sounds too pleased by this revelation.

"Nope, it's been all mini golf," I say.

"You know," she starts, stirring her tea. Her voice sounds like she's about to tell me some fun new piece of trivia she read online. "You haven't asked me about the wedding in *days*."

I frown at her. "That can't be true."

She shrugs. "Pretty sure it is."

It's fine. I'll just focus on the wedding twice as hard for the rest of the week to make up for it.

I'm not about to leave Nancy waiting so I can argue about my apparent lack of productivity with Mom. "Are you coming?" I ask, tone bordering on snippy.

She takes a sip of her tea, totally unmoved. "I'll go grab Eric; give me a sec," she says calmly. "He's been painting outside. It's so adorable I might just marry him."

As we walk over to the course, I wonder if I should feel guilty. I could've spent more time working on wedding errands. I haven't even finished the Hartman and Co. application yet.

Except it's hard to stay worried when I see Nancy's excited face.

"If there's anything you think we should change, be honest," she tells the group. "This isn't final."

"Really, you should all think of yourselves as guinea pigs," I add.

"I was going to say lab rats," Nancy continues. "Talking ones, who give feedback."

She hands out the clubs from a brightly colored pack. They look remarkably like they could pass at a real miniature golf place. Or at least a cheap one, I note, looking at the quality of the plastic on my green club up close. It's already peeling around the edges.

The game is fun, if not a little cutthroat. Aunt Gwendoline insists she doesn't need any help, even with her arm in a sling. That is until hole three when Eric gets the ball in after two tries. Not that it makes much of a difference; Nancy is squarely in the lead.

"I won, right?" she asks at the seventh hole. "I definitely won."

"I thought this was just a test run," Aunt Gwendoline points out. "Rematch!"

Nancy ignores this. "I won," she sings. "I wonnnnn!" She starts to do a little dance that is so dorky it passes into adorable territory.

It's a perfect moment.

Most of the time, my mind is on the future. *This is what I need to do next, this is why it matters, this is how it'll shape my entire life.* Even if a task is small, it feels big and important. It's like there's this voice in my head saying I have to do everything right or I'll ruin all of my carefully laid plans. No perfect wedding, so no internship, so no college, so no job, so no future at all.

When I'm with Nancy, it's like that voice disappears.

TWENTY-ONE DAYS UNTIL THE WEDDING

Eric's sitting on the couch sketching when I walk upstairs. I'm supposed to meet Nancy at the main house for our latest One Fun Thing surprise, but I got ready a little too early. I have some time to kill.

"Whatcha up to?" I ask, sitting down on the armchair off to the side of the couch. My dress is new; I ordered it online, and it only arrived this morning. It's made of a pale blue fabric with a pattern of delicate daisies and a swing-style skirt. I smooth it out, trying to prevent wrinkles.

"Working," he says, his eyes focused on the paper in front of him.

"Excuse you," I say. "You're supposed to be on summer vacation."

"Could say the same thing to you, Lissy."

"I'm about to go out with Nancy for an entirely non-wedding-related activity," I point out.

"And before that?" he asks, putting his pencil down on the coffee table.

"Vendor emails," I admit. "You two are meeting with the photographer in a couple of days, by the way."

He places his sketchbook next to the pencil. "What if I have plans?"

"Do you?" I ask.

I guess I haven't really been paying attention to what Eric's been up to. He said he was going to focus on his art while we were away, but I haven't even seen any of his new pieces. For all I know, he's been doing nothing but binge-watching shows and baking empanadas.

"You're looking at the latest guest artist at Tattoo-Een," he says.

"Tatooine? Like from *Star Wars*?" I ask.

"It's a themed shop," he explains. "About an hour away. I booked a few appointments for next week. So no plans in a couple of days; you're lucky this time."

I guess I should have checked before committing Mom and Eric to anything. But Mom's writing time is super flexible. Even though she's back on deadline, she can pause her writing whenever she needs to, at least for something like a photographer meeting. As for Eric, well, I thought he was just working on creative projects.

"You make *Star Wars*–themed art?" I ask.

"I make what the clients want," he says before adding, "Or I try to. Want to see some of the designs?"

I nod. I get up and walk over to sit next to him.

He picks back up his sketchbook and flips through some pages. I notice that it's a lot nicer than the one Nancy has. There's something about the quality of the paper that looks more professional.

"I'm mostly working on spaceships and their placement among the stars and planets. This one has an asteroid field. There are a few more simple designs, just the ships, a couple of droids." He pauses at each piece. The lines are so delicate. Some are in black and white while others pop with color. They're beautiful, I realize.

It's not that I haven't seen Eric's work before. He has a couple of paintings up at home. These feel so different since they're designs for actual tattoos.

The only real tattoo of his that I've seen is the one Mom has. It's on her rib cage, so I haven't seen it much since she first got it. There was the one time we went to the pool with Bubbe, and Mom wore a bikini, but that barely counts since Bubbe made her cover up pretty quickly because she apparently looked "lewd" and the visible tattoos were "an embarrassment to our whole family." There were a couple of times when we were shopping and shared a dressing room; I guess I saw Eric's work then too. I remember thinking that the piece Eric designed for my mom looked impressive. I just didn't approve of her taking that art and scarring herself permanently with it.

In my mind, Eric's tattoos weren't real art. Tattoos have always been something I don't approve of. When I pictured them, I just thought of skulls and infinity symbols. Not that my mom's tattoos looked like that—she has a floral design on her arm, and the one Eric did is a landscape—but I had to disapprove of those on principle alone. The mere fact that she had any tattoos in the first place felt like further proof that she didn't know how to be a real mom. None of my friends' parents had tattoos; she shouldn't either.

Eric's designs catch me off guard. They're nothing like I'd

expect. Instead they're delicate and pretty. I can see why someone might want to walk around with his art on their body for the rest of their lives.

"They don't have anyone over there who specializes in fine line tattoos or watercolors, like I do," Eric continues. "I've done spaceships before and tattoos of stars and constellations, but I like that this is something new. Something specific. Not to mention the fact that your mom and I have that whole thing with *Star Wars*. You know, I hadn't seen any of the films before I started to date her? She sat me down and made me watch all of them in a weekend. In a weird order too." He has this small smile on his face, like he's stuck in the memory.

"You're good," I say. "I'm putting you on sign decoration duty."

"The truest stamp of approval," he says. "A part in a Felicity project."

I shrug. "I have a feeling you can handle the signature cocktail display. It's no fine line droid, but it'll have to do."

"Signature cocktails?" he asks.

"Appletinis and a specialty cider," I say. "Aunt Gwendoline took control of that one."

"What are you up to tonight?" he asks.

"I don't know," I say. "But I'll find out in"—I take my phone out of my pocket—"a few minutes, actually. Got to go."

I take one last look at the design on the page in front of me. Eric's sketchbook is open to a picture of the *Millennium Falcon* flying among the stars, made entirely out of intricate, thin lines and dots.

I head to the main house to meet Nancy. She was very specific on the timing tonight, which makes me even more curious about our One Fun Thing activity.

I find her standing by her car.

"So," I start. "Do I get the reveal yet?"

"Drum roll, please," she instructs.

I give her a look.

She holds up her hands. "Fine, no drum roll." Still, she pauses to prolong the suspense. "We're going to a movie in the park!" she finally says.

"Very summery," I note.

She nods, then opens her car door. "They're showing *Captain Marvel*, which, as we all know, is a sapphic movie."

I walk over to the passenger side. "I think the people at Marvel might disagree."

"Two women raising a child together," Nancy says. "Right. So straight."

We get into the car. "Gals bein' pals," I say as I buckle my seat belt.

Nancy laughs.

We talk the whole car trip. Nancy explains how each superhero is probably at least a little queer and then goes on to explain a fan fiction she read once that took place at the Avengers Compound, which essentially confirmed this theory. Then she moves on to tell me about past movies in the park she's been to, some with her family and some with friends, and how they've all been amazing, which naturally means we're going to have a great time. I love listening to her like this, so enthusiastic and silly and excited.

When we get to the park, Nancy takes out a large blanket and some snacks. She brought both popcorn and chocolate because she is a true hero. "No maple," she says. "I thought you might want a break."

The movie doesn't start until it's dark, and the sun is only just setting now. Nancy explains how this is the perfect time to arrive since you can get the best viewing spots. We lay out our blanket and watch the sky change colors, vibrant oranges and pinks framed by the surrounding trees.

Other moviegoers start to arrive. There are a few families spread out among the crowd and a couple of groups of friends, but other than that, it looks like there are mostly couples. I guess a movie night under the stars is a peak date-night activity.

If I were going to date someone, I think I'd want it to be like this. I'd want to be with someone like Nancy who makes me feel so safe, so comfortable. Who is silly and kind and adorable. Who comes up with plans like swimming in a rock quarry or designing a miniature golf course or watching an outdoor movie.

It's funny, because all these fun activities could sort of be dates, I realize as the movie starts. If our relationship was like that, of course. Except it can't be, I remind myself. I'm not the kind of person Nancy wants.

Because I know what she looks for in a romantic relationship. She wants passion and intimacy, things that I might not be able to give her.

I remember when she started dating her ex, Quin. Nancy told me everything, what it felt like the first time they kissed and what it was like to feel so attracted to another person that all you could think about was getting closer to them. I couldn't relate.

There are other things on top of being too ace, like the fact that my hair is too red and I'm too chubby and too tall. I recognize that some of those are just general insecurities, but some are very real. She met Quin through soccer, so Nancy has to like other athletic types. I am decidedly not athletic. I'm not her type.

Which is why even if these activities are fun, they could never be real dates. I could never be a real romantic prospect for Nancy. I know what she wants, and it's not me.

But maybe, just for tonight, it'll be okay to ignore all of that and pretend. I look over at Nancy, her eyes focused on the movie. I know she's seen it before, but she looks so excited, so wrapped up in the story, like at any moment it could change.

If this were a date, it would be a perfect one.

FIFTEEN DAYS UNTIL THE WEDDING

"Lissy, wanna help us up here?" my mom calls from the kitchen. "We're making falafel empanadas!"

While seeing Mom attempt to cook would be amusing, I have plans with Nancy. We're going shoe shopping so I can find something to match my new dress, and then we're going to hang out at the main house.

"Can't," I yell, walking up the stairs. I lower my voice once we're on the same floor. "Going to spend time with Nancy."

Mom leaves the kitchen area and heads over to where I'm standing by the stairs. "You're always spending time with Nancy. This is a family vacation too. We're not all that terrible to hang out with, you know."

I notice she has flour on her chin. How did she manage that? Poor Eric, it must be so much easier to cook when he doesn't have to keep an eye on her.

"You'll come to dinner," she adds, less a question than a statement. "It's Shabbat. You missed the last two."

I guess that's true. I haven't really thought about keeping up with traditions here. I blame it on being away. Days of the week don't count over summer.

"Can Nancy come too?" I ask.

"Only if she loves delicious home cooking!" Eric calls from behind the kitchen island.

"Awfully high on yourself, Flores," I shoot back. "You're lucky she does."

So, I guess we're going shoe shopping and then having Shabbat dinner with Mom and Eric. Love a last-minute change to my day.

⸺

Shoe shopping is a bust. There are a lot of Crocs and not a lot of fancy footwear. Nancy has fun suggesting all kinds of options we could both wear—tie-dye sandals and sneakers covered in tiny spikes and glitter rain boots. Needless to say, I don't buy anything.

"I've never been to Shabbat," Nancy says as we're driving back.

"Not sure this one counts. We do like zero of the actual requirements," I explain. "Though I think Eric went out and bought challah."

"See, I've never had challah," she says.

I let out an exaggerated breath. "Well, that's a crime."

We weren't out long, but dinner is already set up like we've created a delay. Eric's falafel empanadas are piled on a plate in the middle of the table with a bowl of cucumber and garlic tzatziki set next to it, for dipping and drizzling purposes. There's an Israeli salad too, cubed pieces of tomato and cucumber mixed with tiny chunks of red onion. Mom and Eric even put out plate settings and preemptively poured everyone water.

Maybe that should have made me suspicious.

"Nancy, did Lissy tell you about our Shabbat tradition? Positive talk only," Eric says.

"And you have to eat a lot of challah," Mom adds.

"I think that one is less of a rule and more of a natural occurrence," I explain.

Once we're all seated, I make sure Nancy gets the challah first. "Thoughts?" I ask.

"Oh, it's sweeter than I thought it would be!" She takes another bite. "So good."

"We've snagged another one!" Mom jokes. "In no time at all, you'll be obsessed with latkes and matzah ball soup too."

We settle into eating. Eric's food is, as always, delicious. There's the warm and earthy taste of the cumin in the falafel, which are still crunchy even though they've been packed in pockets of dough, then the crisp cubes of cucumber and tomato from the salad, paired with the creamy garlic sauce, which come together to add a cool, refreshing layer. I could eat the whole plate of these by myself.

I'm caught up in my food when Mom ruins everything.

"So, great news," she starts. "I have a team meeting coming up. Editor, agent, publicity, marketing team, the whole crew. Things are looking really good for this project." She pauses. "It's Tuesday at eleven."

Tuesday at eleven . . . the same time as our dress appointment in Boston.

"No," I say. Because she can't do this. I have to believe she wouldn't schedule a business meeting at the same time as her wedding dress appointment. There's no way she'd be this incompetent.

"Don't be mad," she says, which is a surefire way to make me cross the line into being fully livid. "I forgot, and I'm basically the least important person on this call. It can't be moved."

She forgot? FORGOT? We're driving to a completely different state; how could that slip her mind?

"It can't be moved, or you don't want to move it?" I ask, voice accusatory.

"That's not fair," she says. "This is my career."

"It's practically a hobby," I mutter under my breath. "It took us so long to find something. How can you ruin this?"

"You're being dramatic, Lissy. We'll just reschedule."

"When? For after the wedding? We have no time."

She shrugs. "Then you can go yourself."

"To try on *your* wedding dress?"

She's quiet for a moment. "Let's discuss this after dinner," she finally says.

I glare at her. "That would've been better timing in the first place."

I can't believe she chose dinner to break the news. She had to have known what she was doing. What did she think, I wouldn't argue with her because it's Shabbat? Has she not met me?

It's even worse because Nancy is here. I don't want her to know that my mom is like this, forgetful and irresponsible. I don't like being embarrassed.

Mom and I are silent for the rest of the meal. Nancy and Eric make some meaningless small talk, but I'm not really paying attention.

I take another bite of bread. Not even challah can save this Shabbat.

——

I offer to walk Nancy back to the main house, largely so I can avoid a further confrontation with my mom. It's not like Nancy doesn't know the way home.

"I'm sorry about that," I tell her once we're outside.

"You broke the positive talk rule," she points out.

"Technically, my mom started it," I defend myself. "But, yeah, guess we both have to go to Shabbat jail."

We walk for a few moments quietly. Dinner was early, so it isn't even dark out yet, which makes our trip a little easier. I'm not exactly in the mood to walk into a tree or trip over a fallen apple tonight.

"You okay?" she asks.

I groan. "Can I say no? Or does that make me too *dramatic*?" I'm still bitter about what Mom said. It's so invalidating, like my feelings can just be summed up as drama and dismissed.

Nancy gives my shoulder a little squeeze as a response.

Aunt Gwendoline is in the kitchen when we get inside, filling a teapot.

"Cuppa?" she asks, without turning away from the sink.

"A lifesaver," I say. "I could definitely use some of that good-good calming goodness."

"Oh dear," she says, intrigued. She walks over to the stove, holding the teapot on her uninjured side, and turns on the heat. "That sounds like a story."

"Felicity's mom backed out of going into Boston," Nancy explains as she sits down at the table.

I sit down beside her.

Aunt Gwendoline looks unphased. "So, go yourselves."

I let out a snort. "To try on her dress?"

Aunt Gwendoline is turned toward one of the kitchen cabinets, selecting mugs. She has to take them out one at a time because of her sling. "Nancy, you're about the same height as Hannah," she says, looking over her shoulder at her great niece. "A little more muscle, but we'll blame that on youth. You can be her model." Aunt Gwendoline says this so easily, like we should have thought of it in the first place.

"We can't just go alone," I point out. "It's not like we'd be visiting a neighboring town; we're talking about *Boston*."

"And?" Aunt Gwendoline asks. She's moved on to selecting tea.

"We're too young," I say. You aren't supposed to visit a city unsupervised when you're a teenager; it's basically against the law.

Aunt Gwendoline waves this off. "Nancy has a license. You both are responsible. I don't see why it would be a problem."

This time Nancy speaks. "What about you? I wasn't going to go now that . . ." She trails off.

"Because of this?" Aunt Gwendoline looks down at her sling. "I've managed with worse, darling. I've lived quite the life."

Nancy doesn't look convinced.

"I presume Hannah and Eric could assist, should things descend into chaos in your absence." Aunt Gwendoline lets out a sigh. "One fall and suddenly I'm in need of supervision."

"I don't know," I say.

"The secret to life, dear, is that no one knows," Aunt Gwendoline says. "We must make up our minds all the same. I encourage choosing the fun options."

We sit there for a moment before the teapot starts to hiss.

Nancy looks over at me. "Let's do it," she says. "I mean, it has to get done anyway. We can make sure the dress isn't horrible in person and then just find a tailor here so it will actually fit your mom."

"Are you sure? This is a big ask." It's not like I'm bugging her to drive us to the thrift store. We're talking about hours in the car. I barely like driving to the supermarket with my mom in the passenger seat; I definitely couldn't manage a trip like this if I was the one behind the wheel.

"Opens up a lot more activities for our One Fun Thing that day," she points out.

This wasn't the plan. Everything will end up being a complete disaster. It's too much to ask from Nancy, and it basically gives my mom permission to keep being irresponsible. I'm sixteen, and Nancy is seventeen, so if we go alone, then we're probably going to get kidnapped. I'm pretty sure kidnappers keep an eye out for unaccompanied minors. This is a bad idea; we shouldn't go.

"I guess we're going," I say.

Aunt Gwendoline smiles as she hands me my cup of tea. "I'm glad we got there."

So, I guess Nancy and I are going into Boston. Alone.

ELEVEN DAYS UNTIL THE WEDDING

Nancy and I arrive at L'Boutique Bridal with two minutes to spare. We should have been even earlier, but we had trouble finding a spot to park by Newbury Street.

This is one of my favorite places in the city—the street, not the bridal store. It's long, with alphabetically arranged cross streets—Arlington, Berkeley, Clarendon, all the way to Hereford before hitting Mass Ave. Bubbe likes to joke that the farther you go down Newbury, the worse it gets, since most of the really fancy stores are right there in the beginning and you find things like the comic book store near the end. L'Boutique Bridal is just past Clarendon.

We have to be buzzed into the building, which feels very official. Only serious customers through these doors.

"Becker, eleven o'clock appointment," I say through the little speaker box.

"Becker, Becker, let's see," I hear someone mutter. "Ah yes, right here."

The door unlocks with a *click!*

There isn't anything special when we first walk in; it just looks like a small residential lobby. There's a sign in gold with black lettering that lets us know that the boutique is on the second floor.

We take the elevator up. Stairs would have been manageable, but I didn't actually see any when we walked in. Don't all buildings have to have stairs? Fire safety and all that.

The elevator doors open, and we're still not at the boutique. There's another sign at the end of a short hall with the store's name engraved in a looping script.

I feel my heart start beating faster the closer we get. What is this even going to be like? I've never been around so many beautiful gowns. Will they kick us out once they realize we aren't with an adult? Will the dress be perfect? It better be.

Nancy opens the door.

I immediately feel like I'm underdressed, even though I purposefully wore my lucky green-and-white checkered dress for this. I should be wearing, I don't know . . . a ball gown?

There's something so formal about the white-and-gold decorations, consistent from the walls to the main desk, and the attendants' sophisticated all-black attire. The biggest thing, unsurprisingly, is the fact that we are surrounded by dresses. I underestimated how different it would feel to see them in person. They're too pretty, like they all deserve to be on a runway or carefully arranged in an exhibit instead of packed together on hangers.

"Ms. Becker, welcome," the attendant says. "The file says the appointment is for a . . . Hannah?" She looks between the two of us like she's trying to figure out which one of us might be the bride.

I guess I'll take this one. "This might be super unusual, but the bride isn't here. We're on a tight deadline, and something came up at work, so we're her stand-ins. I'm the daughter of the bride," I explain. "Sorry, this is so weird."

The attendant smirks. "I've had weirder appointments. One time the bride brought a medium to make sure her late parrot approved. This is practically boring in comparison." She claps her hands together, like now that we got that out of the way, we can get started in earnest. "Tell me about the big day."

I run through some quick details: the venue, the setting, and most importantly the date. "Yes, we know there's no time," I assure the saleswoman. "But we saw one of your off-the-rack options that we're hoping will work." I show her the picture.

She nods, like we've made a sage choice. "I'll bring it right out."

She leaves Nancy and me in our own dressing room, which is about the size of my bedroom back home.

"You excited?" Nancy asks, sitting down on the gray velvet loveseat in the corner of the room.

I don't answer right away. Am I excited? I was so stressed about getting to this point it barely feels real that we're about to see *the* dress.

I sit down next to her. "I think I'm mostly relieved."

"I get that," Nancy says.

It doesn't take long for the saleswoman to come back, holding the dress. "Beautiful, isn't it? What a lovely choice."

Seeing it in person is so different from the tiny picture online. The gown has a slight glint from the understated bead-work, and the lace seems more intricate along the sleeves. There's only one problem.

"Online it said it was a size ten," I say, because this dress is definitely not that. She must have brought out the wrong one.

"Yes, a wedding dress size ten. Can vary by designer, but this one is about"—she holds up the dress in front of her to examine it—"a street size four."

Mom's thinner than me, roughly a size eight or ten depending on the brand. I thought at worst we'd have to get the dress taken in a little, not that we'd need it to double in size.

What are we going to do?

I look over at Nancy, like maybe she'll have an answer. She gives her head a quick shake to indicate that she's also confused.

Let's try this again. "Does it come in a larger size? If not for sale immediately, we would be open to getting it rushed." *Rushed*, I repeat in my head. I highly doubt a wedding dress can be rushed in a week, even if we drop an absurd amount of money on it.

The saleswoman doesn't seem to realize the severity of the issue; she seems nonplussed. "Hm, not this one. It's discontinued, which is why we're selling the sample size. I can pull some other options," she offers.

So this is what it feels like at the start of an apocalypse movie.

I don't answer. How can I? This is a problem that can't be fixed.

"Sure, let's take a look," Nancy says after a beat. Then she adds just for me, "Maybe we'll find something better? We can send your mom some pictures."

I don't think there's a dress in this store that she hasn't already vetoed online. What difference would it make now?

"I guess," I say, because we booked this appointment. We came all this way. We have to see something, at least.

The saleswoman leads us out of the dressing room, into what looks like a hallway lined with gowns. "The ones on this rack are a street size ten," she says. "Not a lot, but there are some stunning options."

She pulls out a trumpet dress with a dropped waist. I can practically hear my mom complain that the shape is "blah." The next one is too frilly, and the one after has blue stitching along the skirt.

"Your mom might like that one," Nancy says to the blue-and-white gown.

She has to be joking; that's clearly not a real option. It's exactly the sort of thing my mom *would* defiantly suggest right before I pulled the veto card. Your *something blue* can't be a wedding dress. "We're looking for something a little more traditional," I say.

There are only two left on the rack. The first has long sleeves and silver detailing that makes it look too wintery, and the final one is a simple yet elegant halter that would highlight the tattoo on her arm too prominently.

Nothing works.

"Should I try any on?" Nancy asks. She looks over at the saleswoman. "I'm the sizing model," she explains.

"The halter really shines once it's on a body. Deceivingly simple on the rack," the saleswoman tells us.

I feel like I can't say no. We have to try on at least one or they'll send us to shopping jail, since it would be such an absurd waste of time. You can't book an appointment and then just leave. "Okay, that one," I say.

We head back into the dressing room. There's a little space off to the side curtained off where Nancy gets changed. When she steps out, the saleswoman clips the back of the gown with industrial-looking clamps. I wonder if she got them at a hardware store. It seems like such a disconnect from the rest of the store.

Nancy turns around. "Thoughts?" she asks.

There's a part of my brain that notices the particulars, like the fact that the dress does fit her pretty well, even though it would have to be taken in a little at the back and around the neck, and that it does look so much better on than it did hanging up. She looks like she stepped out of a classic movie.

The other, louder, part of my brain is freaking out. This is Nancy in a wedding gown. Naturally, that makes me think of her getting married. To me? My mind flashes to the conversation I had with Roo while we were on our wedding reality show spiral. If I'm the one she's marrying, does that mean I couldn't wear a gown? Or that we'd have to find matching gowns? Is that how it works?

It takes me a moment to realize what I just thought. I swear, this is Roo's fault.

Nancy and I are friends. Nothing more.

I have to pull myself together. This is no time for a breakdown. "You look stunning," I say. "This is Audrey Hepburn levels of classic. But . . ."

"Not right for your mom," she finishes.

I scrunch up my nose. "Not right for her."

We take some pictures, just to be sure, and send them to my mom. Not that she'll see them before we leave because of her meeting. Then Nancy goes back behind the curtain to change.

This is devastating, I think as I wait for her to finish. It might just be the biggest disaster to ever happen to any wedding in the history of the world. I don't see any feasible way that we'll find a replacement. We were already on such a tight deadline; we've run out of time.

Nancy walks out, back in her simple athletic shorts and cotton shirt.

"Thank you so much for helping us," I tell the saleswoman as we leave, voice apologetic.

We head out of the store, back to the elevator.

This is an unfixable problem, I conclude. I've failed at one of the most important tasks on my list. The wedding is officially doomed.

ELEVEN DAYS UNTIL THE WEDDING, CONTINUED

Despite my suggestion that we head back to Vermont and end this miserable trip, Nancy insists that we do our One Fun Thing. "You won't regret it," she swears, looking up the directions on her phone.

Nancy loves a surprise, so she refuses to say exactly where we're headed. I try to predict based on the driving route, but it's a bust. I never drive in the city, I barely drive with my permit in the first place, and I have a general inability to understand directions as a passenger.

She pulls into the parking lot for the Museum of Fine Arts.

"I *have* been here before," I tell her. I certainly hope she doesn't think this is something new; it's one of the main Boston museums. "You know I live a half hour away. My mom used to take me to art classes here once a week when I was little."

Nancy is focused on finding a spot, so she doesn't turn to look at me. "Art museums are amazing no matter how many times you go," she says like she's a teacher trying to convince an uninterested student.

"I don't know, art doesn't change," I say. "No point in going back."

She scoffs. "I'm pretending I didn't hear that."

"Maybe if there was some variability," I continue the bit. "Like, if while you were looking at a painting, it moved."

"La-la-la," she pretends to sing, as though that will block out what I'm saying.

"Or if they turned the museum into some sort of roller coaster that takes you past the art before spinning you upside down."

This time she doesn't fake sing, but that's mostly because she's concentrating on parking. As soon as she turns off the car, she looks straight at me. "Your little joke doesn't work because art *does* change. There are temporary exhibits and collections on loan and that sort of thing. But, more importantly, you change. When you visit an art museum, you bring with you all of your emotions and experiences. You're different each time, so the way you view and connect to the art changes."

"Hm." I pause like I'm thinking about what she just said. "A little too philosophical for me. Friendship over."

She rolls her eyes, then gives me a little smile. "You're insufferable," she says.

We walk around the side of the museum to get to the main entrance on Huntington. It looks like we're entering an ancient Greek temple that's been transported through time and placed in Boston.

After we deal with tickets, we decide to start on the second floor. I like doing that because the staircase is so grand I feel like I'm on the way to some fairy-tale ball. I wonder if they actually have events like that here . . . like a less famous Met Gala.

I bet Hartman and Co. would put something like that together.

"I'm walking in the general direction of the Impressionists. If there's something you want to see, speak now or forever look at Monet," I tell Nancy.

She makes this little *oh you* sort of face, like I've misunderstood the assignment. "It's not like we're going to see one exhibit and then bolt; we've got all the time in the world. My vote is we just wander and see what we see."

Usually, whenever I'm here with my mom, we follow a certain order. Finish one exhibit, move on to the next, say hello to our favorite paintings (or, in her case, the mummies, which I think she makes us go see because she knows I'm convinced there's a chance they'll come to life and murder us), visit the gift shop, and maybe grab a snack.

It turns out that visiting the museum with Nancy is completely different. There's no clear path to our route through the exhibits. We walk into Art of Asia before heading to the Impressionists, then stop to see Renaissance art, before walking back to finish our path through Impressionism. Contemporary blends in with ancient Greek works and portraits from Regency England. There's a lot of "oh, look over here's" and "I think we missed a room" and "let's turn around"; it's chaotic, but in a fun way.

Half the time, she isn't even looking at the art. "Have you ever noticed how the ceilings all look so different?" she asks, before making us turn around to see the decorative vaulting in a small room dedicated to the Renaissance, then heading to an exhibit that looks like a ballroom was transformed into a gallery. "The ceiling is so much higher in here," she points out. "And look how the light marble contrasts with the dark, decorative wooden design at the very top. It changes the entire feel of the room."

She notices things I've never paid attention to before. The changes in the styles of the display cases and the frames, the colors of the walls, the use of paint versus wallpaper, the light fixtures, the flooring. I've been here so many times before, but I've never noticed how the materials of the room change depending on the era or origin of the art.

I think part of what makes it so different is Nancy's unexpected enthusiasm. I had no idea anyone could get this excited by looking at the transition from the Art of Europe collection to the first room of Contemporary Art. She walks back and forth between the two, pointing out new details each time, like the textured wallpaper compared to the white-painted walls or the line where the wooden flooring changes. She bends down to examine it. "Is this a rug? The material seems almost like a plastic, except it's woven. Even that feels modern," she says.

I'd find it funny if she wasn't so genuine.

I'm not sure I've ever seen Nancy as in her element as she is now. Maybe when we played soccer? But even then she wasn't as excited as she is talking about the museum.

I wonder if I sound this way to her when I talk about mismatched china and centerpieces.

We decide to take a break and grab some tea in the café on the first floor. There are less fancy options, but I feel like this one is too iconic to pass up. We're in a huge room that looks like a high-end train terminal. There's an absolutely massive lime-green glass sculpture with giant spikes off to the side that Mom always pretends is about to fall so she can do a little bit about how it's going to crush us. I don't find it funny.

We're seated at a table for two along the edge of the café. The space is sectioned off but still in the open hall so we can see guests headed into galleries or walking over to the visitor center. I don't think I realized how long we've been here until I sat down. My legs feel like they're ready to take a nap.

"Want to share something?" Nancy asks. "We kind of skipped lunch."

We look over the menu and decide to share a flatbread. It's a little expensive here, but not terrible if we split the bill.

"Ugh, I just love it here," Nancy says.

"You do? I never would've guessed," I joke.

"Hey! It's beautiful. I mean, look." She points to the large glass windows across from us. "They managed to fit in an entire space of greenery between the galleries and this hall, essentially bringing the outside inside. Where else are you going to see something like that?"

I pause to think. "A greenhouse?"

This doesn't seem to stop her. "I can't get over the attention to detail. Everything is so specific to the exhibit, essentially making the building a part of the art. Plus, there's the fact that the museum itself encompasses so many designs. It's as though you're walking through entirely different spaces, even though you're in the same building."

"I never really thought of that before. I was just like, 'Oh, yes, this is the museum. Let's look at the paintings.'"

"That's the thing though," she continues. "You don't have to notice any of that for it to impact your experience. The fact that you didn't notice before really shows how seamless those details are when you look at the museum as a whole."

I smirk at her. "Weird thing to be so interested in, Lim," I say.

"I was raised by two people who design homes," she points out. "If I didn't notice these things, I'd be disowned."

"Oh, that can't be true," I say playfully. "Maybe grounded, at most."

She looks thoughtful at this. "I love my parents' work, don't get me wrong," she says. "I just feel like this is so much . . . bigger."

I think about making a joke about how it is, in fact, bigger than a standard-size house, but I don't want to ruin the moment.

We spend another couple of hours in the museum after we finish eating, this time exploring the first floor. I try to pay attention to all of the details, like I'm seeing things through Nancy's eyes.

It's kind of magical.

"Oh, you must love this," I say, when we get to a re-creation of an old American estate bedroom, since we can actually walk through it along a clearly marked path.

"Too obvious. I'm all about the ceilings," she jokes before heading to the next room.

I should probably be more tired than I am by the time we leave; we've been walking for so long. Except I don't want this to end.

How strange, I think. Even after the dress disaster, I'm still capable of having a good time.

"Ready to head back?" I ask.

She shrugs. "What's the rush?"

It's one of those moments where I feel like we really *are* on the same page. This trip doesn't have to end if neither of us wants it to.

So we walk around outside the museum. There are a bunch of signs for Northeastern, stylized *N*s hanging on banners on the lampposts and along buildings. We pass stores and restaurants; we cross streets. It's strange walking around Boston without a clear destination in mind.

"Want to check it out?" Nancy asks, nodding to a path with a bunch of school buildings. We've turned around, back near the museum.

"Wouldn't that be trespassing?" I ask.

"Definitely not," Nancy assures me. "For all they know, we're prospective students."

Mom and I are planning to go on an extended school tour next year, so I guess I'm almost a prospective student. I might go to Northeastern, who knows?

I don't have a dream school yet. When I get to the right campus, I'll feel it, like a gut instinct telling me I found the right place. You can't know for sure if you've never been to the actual school, right? I'll figure it out when we go on that tour.

Not that it will matter if I don't get the fall internship and therefore have a lackluster résumé, I remind myself.

The first thing that really surprises me is that it's a legitimate campus. As we keep walking, it's like we've left the city entirely, as though we've walked through a portal and landed in some small collegiate town. I thought the drawback of going to a school that's actually in Boston was that you miss this, the secluded bubble of a university.

"Did you know that Northeastern has a five-year program?" Nancy asks. "It's longer than most schools because you do something called a co-op, where you get real-world experience in your field. I think it's kind of like an internship, but it's actually a part of the curriculum."

"I didn't know I was with a tour guide," I tease.

"Hardly," she says.

"An expert on museum design and schools. I feel like I should take you somewhere else to test your knowledge. Fancy going to the aquarium?"

"I *did* watch a documentary on seals last week, but it's probably closed by now," she says.

Is it? How long have we been walking around?

The sky isn't dark yet, but the colors above us are shifting, muted now, like a prelude to the official sunset.

"I super wasn't paying attention to the time," I say. "We have such a long drive."

"It won't be that bad," she says.

I've seen Nancy drive at night before. I know she knows how to do it, even if I personally get scared by how bright headlights are once it gets dark. Except now I wonder if she's even allowed to drive at night. Legally, I mean. I have no clue what the rules are in Vermont for junior drivers.

There's this fear too. We can't drive at night; it's too late. What if she gets tired? I can't help her, I only have my permit. What if a tire pops? Maybe we shouldn't have come here in the first place because now we're going to get stranded on the highway or on a mountain road in the middle of the night.

"We could just go to my house," I offer. "We're not too far out of the city."

"I haven't been to your house before," Nancy says.

"No apple trees," I warn. "So, it's terribly boring."

"I have trouble believing anything your mom's involved in is boring," Nancy says.

She's got me on that one.

When we get back to the museum parking lot, we make some phone calls. Mom promises to check in on Aunt Gwendoline, and Aunt Gwendoline tells us to stop worrying, she'll be fine for the night, she's lived alone before, and she can do it again.

I plug in the directions to my house. I guess the trip really isn't going to end yet.

TEN DAYS AND ONE NIGHT
UNTIL THE WEDDING

Seeing a three-dimensional Nancy walk into my home is like watching a glitch actively occurring in the system. Error, does not compute, please refresh.

"Why's there a framed picture of *Sleepy Dog* on the wall?" Nancy asks.

I look at the art print hanging in our entryway, a special piece my mom had commissioned after the movie deal. "You know *Sleepy Dog*?"

"Um, who doesn't? It's basically Diya's favorite game," Nancy says. "What? Is your mom the game's number one fan?"

"Something like that," I say. "She's the creator."

Nancy gasps. "Shut up! How did I not know this?"

I shrug. "I don't tend to walk around saying, 'Hi, you know that old phone game with the dog? My mom made that.'"

"You should," Nancy says. "I think that makes her a celebrity. Should I ask for her autograph?"

I roll my eyes. "Please don't."

Luckily, Nancy moves on. Unfortunately that's because of the Halloween wall. "Stop it, are those all you?" she asks, spotting the shrine to Halloweens past, aka pictures of me in all of my old costumes through the years, set in kitschy-themed frames and lining the wall up to the second floor. Lovely, guess it's time for some embarrassment.

"Roo's in a few." I point out some of our more imaginative costumes like the year we went as Marvel characters halfway through their superhero transformations and the time we left the house and were seen in public as "haunted flowers."

"Did you go as a different Disney Princess five years in a row?" Nancy asks.

"I can only partly be blamed. Mom wanted to get to them all, and, I mean, come on, who didn't want to be a princess when they were little?"

"I don't know, I was more into the animals and monsters and aliens. Like I was convinced that I could *be* a lion when I grew up," Nancy explains.

"Chaos from the start," I say with a sigh.

I give Nancy a quick tour as we make our way to the kitchen. Living room there, bedrooms upstairs, here are the bathrooms. I'm conscious of the fact that the entire place is significantly less impressive than anything on the orchard, especially the fancy barn-cottage.

I wouldn't even say that there's a particular style to our home. Mom's wall décor ranges from travel postcards to my childhood artwork to the Halloween timeline. She has all of her book covers framed in the living room, but they don't have her name on them, so it looks like she's just really appreciative of movie novelizations. The furniture is comfortable, but nondescript. The kitchen has a vague rainbow theme, including Pride hand towels and oven mitts. It all feels too eclectic compared to what Nancy's used to.

"Are you hungry?" I ask. "I cleared out the fridge before we left, but I think there's some pasta and maybe sauce in the cupboard. Maybe a granola bar?"

Nancy's eyes brighten. "Oh, I love this. It's like one of those cooking show challenges. You have one hour to make dinner using only the ingredients left in a house where the occupants have gone away for the summer. Your time starts now," she says in a fake game show host voice.

"We don't have to compete, do we? Because I would very much lose," I say.

She considers this. "It's a team challenge," she decides.

After assessing our supplies, Nancy decides to combine dollar ramen noodles with some of the frozen vegetables that live in the freezer. After I boil the noodles, she fries them in a pan along with the veggies. She adds teriyaki and a little sesame seed oil, before tackling the spices—garlic powder and cayenne and even a pinch of truffle salt. She finishes it off with a garnish of cashews that come in little snack-size packs.

"Ta-da," she says, stepping back from her creation.

I grab bowls and forks. "That smells so good," I say. "I'd eat that even if we weren't suffering from a case of limited ingredients."

"That means I won the challenge. It'll give me an advantage in the next round."

She's so ridiculous.

We sit down to eat in the living room so I can turn something on for us to watch. "A movie?" I ask. "Or should I look for your pretend cooking show?"

We end up watching *Night at the Museum*, which seems fitting.

At least when the mummy comes to life in this one, he doesn't try to murder everyone.

Once the movie's over, we head upstairs to get ready for bed. We're not tired yet, but pajamas are always the comfiest option.

"So, this is your room," Nancy says. "It's exactly what I thought it would be like."

I'm not sure what she means by that. She could be talking about the pressed pastel pink-and-blue bedding or the framed set of geometric pattern prints I found from an artist on Etsy that hang on the wall. Mom is big on letting me decorate my own space, so this is definitely my favorite room in the house. It's organized and simple, just the way I like it.

"I feel like that's an insult," I say.

"No," she swears. "It's just so . . . perfect. And clean. I don't think my room has ever been this tidy."

She hasn't even seen my closet or dresser yet. I started arranging my clothes by color last year, warm to cool tones, and even Roo thinks it's a step too far.

It's strange because I feel like Nancy has been here before. I've spent so many nights lying in bed and talking to her about my day.

I look for a pair of pajamas for Nancy. Most of my nice summery stuff is in Vermont, but there are some T-shirt and lounge pants combos that could work. They'll be big on her, but I guess that's better than the other way around.

I hand her a pair of pants and an oversize shirt from an old school fundraiser. At least the pants have ties, and an oversize shirt is supposed to look big on everyone.

We both go through our nighttime routines. Makeup off, teeth brushed. She's a nighttime shower-er, so I show her how to turn on the annoyingly complicated faucet in my bathroom. It's easy, like we've gotten ready for bed together a million times before.

"You tired?" she asks once we're all done getting ready.

"Not yet," I say, even though I am starting to feel a little sleepy.

"Sequel?"

I nod.

I have a TV in my room, which I got for Hanukkah a few years ago. I don't actually use it that often because it's normally just easier to pull out my laptop . . . which I don't have because it's currently in Vermont.

We find the movie and turn it on.

Nancy sits back against my headboard, so I join her.

We start chatting mid-movie. She tells me about this trip she took to DC, and then we're on to superheroes and what kind of superpowers we would want, and it goes from there. We talk in that seamless way that I think only exists during a sleepover. We turn the TV off and then the lights and still keep going.

It feels so natural. Until suddenly it doesn't.

"Hey," she starts, "is it okay if I say something that's been on my mind? You don't have to respond or anything; I just feel like I can't not say it."

Well, that can't be good, I think. What sort of thing would she need to ask permission to say?

"Yeah, of course," I tell her.

She doesn't continue right away. I think I can hear my heart beating, the anticipation is too much.

"Okay, I'm just going to say it," Nancy finally manages. "I like you. More-than-a-friend like you. And I really don't want to make things weird because our friendship comes first, obviously." She takes a breath. "You don't have to say anything now. Or ever. Or you can—*sorry*, I'm really bad at this. I just wanted you to know that I have these romantic feelings. There's no pressure at all; I just thought it was important to let you know."

Then she stops talking. Or I've gone into shock. Maybe both.

The problem is, I have no clue what to say. This is Nancy. *My Nancy.* Of course I love her, but do I *like* her? Like that?

This is what you wanted, I think. *Of course you like her. Say that you like her.*

My mind wanders back to all of those conversations Nancy and I had when she was dating Quin. Sure, Nancy knows that I'm on the ace-spectrum, but I don't think she realizes what that means.

She wants intimacy; she wants passion. I can't be the one to give those things to her.

There's this sinking feeling in my chest. If I were ever going to be in a relationship, I'd want to be with someone like Nancy. I could have that, if I were different.

My mind races. Maybe I should pretend to be normal. I wouldn't mind trying things like kissing or cuddling with Nancy. But if my hypotheticals only extend to objectively tame things like that, we'd never work out. She'd expect more, and I might not like it, and then our friendship would be ruined.

I have to say something. I am obligated in this moment to open my mouth and produce sounds that are recognizable as human speech. Even if my brain looks like %@&*!~?^+.

"Thanks," I say. "For letting me know."

If anyone is ever curious why I ended up in the Bad Place, it's because of that ridiculous nonresponse.

"Sorry, really tired," I add. "Sleep?"

I can see her nod in the dark. "Yeah. 'Night, Fe."

"Good night," I say back. I turn on my side, facing away from her.

Why? Am? I? Like? This?

TEN DAYS UNTIL THE WEDDING

I slip out of the room before Nancy wakes up. I put on some makeup my mom left in her bathroom and change into a wrap dress that is technically also hers, but it's one of her old summer ones and she didn't even pack it for Vermont, so I doubt she'd mind.

I go downstairs to the kitchen. Am I supposed to cook something for Nancy? I don't think there's anything I could put together with the limited supply right now. Maybe dry cereal that's likely already gone stale?

Nancy comes down, still in pajamas.

"There you are," she says. Her voice sounds sleepy, like she still hasn't properly woken up. "Sleep well?" she asks.

No, I couldn't stop thinking about what you said, I think. Except I can't say that out loud.

I shrug instead. "I'm sorry, I think there are zero suitable breakfast options," I tell her.

"We'll just pick something up on the road," she says. "We can head out soon."

I still feel tense as we get ready to go back to Vermont. Last night felt so much more seamless; I don't even know what the difference is now.

Other than the fact that Nancy apparently has romantic feelings for me and I'm the literal worst for not being able to respond.

"It was so nice to see your home. I'm happy we ended up on this detour," she says as we walk out to her car.

I wish I could say the same thing.

I force myself to smile instead.

―――――――

I text Roo once I'm back in Vermont and safely in my summer bedroom.

Felicity: SOS

something happened

i need you to tell me i'm being ridiculous, because i'm like 98% sure i am

. . . or not? the world might never know

i should make matzo toffee

update: there's no matzo at the store? apparently they only keep it in stock for passover, like total monsters

ROO

This isn't working; this is too big to wait for a response. It's not like I need to tiptoe around him and wait for a text back. I'll just call. If he answers, he's free.

He picks up after a couple of rings.

"Are you okay?" he asks, voice appropriately concerned.

Good, he still cares. He was probably just thinking of a response when I got impatient and called.

"I don't know," I admit. "I'm not even sure if I need to address it. Or how I feel about her confession."

"What are you talking about?" Roo asks.

I sigh. Jumped into the middle of the problem with that one, huh?

"So," I start again, "Mom bailed on our trip to Boston to try on what was supposed to be her wedding dress, huge disaster there, but that's another story, and Nancy came with me, and we hung out in the city, but it got late, so we decided to crash at home. Except then Nancy confessed she has feelings for me. Of the romantic variety. Which has led to this particular bout of panic."

"You came home?" Roo asks.

That seems like the smallest part of this story, but okay.

"Barely," I say. "Just in time for dinner, and then we watched some stuff before *she confessed she has feelings for me.*"

"Why didn't you tell me you were coming home?"

What is going on with him? It's like he isn't even listening to me.

"I didn't know we were going to actually be back. This was just supposed to be a wedding dress trip, but, as mentioned, huge disaster there. I doubt my mom will even have a dress at this point."

He doesn't let it go. "You could've told me. You decide to go away for the entire summer, but you can't even manage to tell me the one night you're nearby."

"Because I didn't know I would be," I say defensively. "It's not like anything changed when I left. Phones exist, Roo."

"You know that's not the same thing," he says.

"It could be," I say. "Except you actually have to respond when someone reaches out."

I know I shouldn't have said that the moment the words leave my mouth.

"I didn't text you back right away, big deal. Sometimes I'm just not in the mood to put up with the Felicity Show."

Whoa, what does that mean?

He keeps going before I can say anything. "Did you stop and think that maybe I have stuff going on in my life too? I'm not just here to be your sounding board or offer emotional support. That's not how friendship works."

"That's not fair," I say. "I come to you with my problems, and you come to me with yours. It works both ways. What am I supposed to do, read your mind? How the hell am I supposed to know how you feel if you don't tell me?"

"Yeah, well, a lot of the time it feels like I can't say anything to you. You're always in the middle of some crisis."

I want to hang up on him. "That's not true," I say. "It's just how we talk, both of us. I am always here for you. Always."

"Yeah, except for when you come home and don't even tell me."

It feels like he just slapped me across the face. "Cool, Roo. Point made. I'm a terrible friend. Glad we sorted that out."

"That's not even what I said." I can hear the annoyance in his voice. "I have to go."

"Don't you always," I say.

He hangs up.

My vision feels blurry. I'm not sure when I started crying,

probably around the time he called me the Felicity Show, essentially saying he hates me.

Has he always felt this way? Has our entire friendship been a lie? Am I just being dramatic again, like I apparently always am? Because that's what I am, *dramatic*. My feelings are too much; I'm a burden to the people who care about me.

My best friend hates me. I'm too much.

I can't do anything right.

———

Nancy asks if I want to come over to hang out, but I tell her I'm too busy.

Nancy: Want any help?

I don't text back right away. Normally I'd say, "Yes, come help; let's redo the seating chart together." Except what do I say after that? "Oh, yeah, I'm redoing seating arrangements because Roo probably won't be coming now that we got in a huge fight after I called him panicking over the fact you confessed you have feelings for me, so, to sum it up, I ruin things and you probably should end our friendship right now?"

None of that works as a text.

It's fine, I just told her I'm busy. I'll respond as soon as I know what to say.

"Hey, child of mine," Mom says, walking into the living room. "Want to come with me to the thrift store?"

Being out of the house seems like a legitimate response. "Sure," I say. I turn toward her; she has this excited expression on her face, like she's up to something. "Wait, why?"

"I thought maybe we could look for . . . drum roll, please . . . a wedding dress!"

"At a thrift store?" I ask.

"I'm putting it out into the universe," she says. "I have a good feeling about this."

"A misguided feeling," I say. Still, I get up and head to the car with her.

We're already on our way to the store when she asks, "Is everything okay?"

I shrug. "Totally normal."

She frowns, but her eyes stay on the road. "I don't know, you've seemed a little off since you got back."

"I'm not," I say.

"A mother always knows."

Her voice sounds so smug.

I don't say anything at first. What does she think she knows? She can't read my mind, the same way I can't read Roo's. She has no idea what's going on with me, not with Roo or Nancy. I should just let it go.

I don't let it go.

"I can't believe you let me go into the city alone. You're not supposed to do that," I say.

She raises an eyebrow. "Am I getting yelled at because I trust you?" she asks.

"I'm not yelling," I point out.

"Geesh, what's gotten into you, Lissy?"

"I just don't think it was responsible," I say. "Moms aren't supposed to let that happen."

"Noted. Get back to me when you're a mom."

She changes the station on the radio. "Oh, I love this song," she says.

That's it, argument over, we've moved on. It's always like that with Mom.

Sometimes that's a good thing, like we've said everything that we needed to say so it's safe to leave whatever was bothering us behind. But right now I kind of want to argue. I want to blame her for my anxiety over what happened with Nancy. I want it to be her fault.

I wonder what Bonnie would say about all of that.

Neither of us says anything else for a few minutes, the sound of the radio filling in our silence. Mom talks first.

"This is nice," she says, even though we're just in the car and I basically called her a bad mom roughly a song ago. "We should do more of this."

"Drive around?" I ask.

"Sure, why not? We can drive around, see what else Vermont has to offer. You could practice your driving. Eric really wants to go see something called a fire tower; maybe we could all go together."

I'm about to say that I'm busy, but that isn't true. I mean, what else would I do? Talk to Nancy? No thanks.

"That sounds nice," I say.

Mom grins. "Great, I'll tell Eric when we get back."

We pull in front of the store and park.

I know this isn't going to work as soon as we walk in. This is not the kind of place that sells wedding dresses. While the bridal boutique was all elegance with its neat displays and white-and-gold color palette, this place looks like a leaky rainbow held a dance party with a disco ball and some glitter. It's pure chaos. The lights are fluorescent, and there's a sticker-based pricing system; we're not going to find anything fancy in here.

"See, they have a formal section," Mom says like this proves some point, walking over to a row near the back of the store. The dresses are arranged by size and tightly packed together, so you can barely tell anything about the actual designs from the rack.

She immediately starts pulling out dresses. "Maybe this, hm, that could work, oh, I'd love to see that on," she mutters as she looks through the selection. "All right," she says once she has an armful of dresses. "It's got to be one of these."

Why is she like this? She's only picked one that could even pass as a wedding dress, a white summer maxi with small floral details around the hem. Nothing else will work; there's no champagne or ivory in the bunch. At this point I'd even accept something in a soft blush.

"Maybe that one," I say, touching the cap sleeve of the white maxi dress.

She doesn't respond. Instead, she heads to the other side of the store so she can try everything on.

The dressing rooms are unreasonably small, so I wait outside. I don't want to feel any anticipation or excitement because this is obviously not where she's going to find her wedding dress.

The problem is that she's taking too long.

"Mom, you have to actually show me," I whine.

"The last one was too small; it would've caused a scandal if I walked out in it," she says through the door.

"When have you cared about scandals?"

"Call me old-fashioned, but I draw the line at showing my underwear."

I can hear the shuffle of dresses and the sound of a hanger moving from one spot to another. Then Mom mutters, "Oh, wow."

I hate to admit it, but I'm excited . . . even if we *are* in a thrift store.

I try to adjust my vision of the big day. Mom walks down the aisle in the white summer dress with tiny, colorful flowers along the hem. It's casual, but we'll make it work by getting her hair and makeup professionally done, perhaps a sleek low bun with the veil pinned underneath and some dramatic eye shadow.

There's a creak as she opens the door.

"This is it," she says, twirling so the skirt fans out around her.

She's wearing a baby blue, vintage-style swing dress with off-the-shoulder sleeves that cross around the low neckline like a faux wrap. It's tea length and satin. In any other circumstance, I'd find it lovely.

"That's a great cocktail dress," I manage. "Maybe you could wear it to a party?"

"Lissy," Mom says, voice playfully scolding. "Imagine it with a petticoat underneath," she adds, back to her normal tone. She fluffs up the skirt for emphasis.

I squint at her. Is this some elaborate joke? She can't wear a short blue dress to her wedding.

Except there's this look on her face, a mixture of joy and determination. I know that look. She's already made up her mind.

"What if we keep looking? I'll even go to another thrift store," I try.

Mom ignores this and walks back into the dressing room, leaving the door open this time. She checks out the dress in the mirror, swinging the skirt and moving her shoulders so she can see the back. "This is it. This is *definitely* it."

She walks back out. "I know, it isn't traditional. But when have I ever been traditional?" She pauses. "What do you *really* think?"

I think wearing that would be a huge mistake. I think none of the pictures will make any sense since she looks more like a wedding guest than the bride. I think everything is wrong with it, from the color to the length.

I *know* that nothing I say will change her mind.

I have to make the most of it. This, at least, is a script I know how to follow.

"You look beautiful," I say. Because she does; she's stunning in that dress. The look isn't complete—she'll need the petticoat and a nice pair of shoes, maybe a statement necklace too—but that doesn't take away from how good she looks, even if she is standing under fluorescent lights in a thrift store.

The dress looks amazing . . . It's just not a wedding dress.

She smiles at me. "Yeah?" she asks, turning back to the mirror. "It just feels so right."

"Yeah," I say.

I might not know how to function as a friend, but at least I know how to be a good daughter.

NINE DAYS AND ONE NIGHT
UNTIL THE WEDDING

I throw myself into work mode once we get back. At least if Nancy asks what I'm doing now, it won't be a lie to say that I'm busy. I follow up with the vendors. Photographer, DJ, hair stylist/makeup artist, caterers, all set. There's a delay from the tent folks where they seem to forget that I ordered chairs and tables from them for the reception, but even that gets sorted out. I go as far as figuring out a baseball surprise for Eric, which doesn't take nearly as much time as I think it's going to.

There are other things that I need to do, like writing out the place cards (which I ordered online and still haven't arrived) and finishing the wedding favors. Then there's all of the decorating and coordinating I'll need to do in the few days leading up to the wedding, but for once I've finished my to-do list early.

I could get started on one of my other projects, like finalizing the seating chart (which I keep tampering with) or assembling the centerpieces.

Instead, my gaze falls to my phone. I open Instagram and, because I objectively make poor life choices, search through Nancy's old photos. I find the one I'm looking for. It's a group shot, which is why it lasted the post-breakup purge. There's Nancy, standing off to one side with some of her friends from the soccer team. Quin is right in the middle of the group.

She's stunning. Her dark hair falls in perfect waves past her shoulders, and her makeup looks flawless in a way I feel like I'd need hours to achieve. It's simple and understated, but I can tell she has some on from the highlight set against her olive skin and the clearly defined eyelashes. Her outfit is sporty yet stylish, nothing at all like my go-to vintage dresses. I might not feel attraction myself, but I can certainly understand Quin's aesthetic appeal. I remember how she looked from the other pictures too, the ones Nancy deleted after they ended things. She always seemed so cool and at ease in a way I could never achieve.

I keep the comparison going. She's shorter than me, more athletic, more confident. I start to think of the conversations Nancy and I had back when they were dating. "Quin can do such amazing things with her mouth, Fe. I swear, it turns my whole body to mush. And the way she looks at me, I'm talking pure desire. It's so hot."

This is what Nancy actually likes, I think. She wants someone to look at her with passion. She likes girls who are athletic and cool and easygoing.

I think about all the times we've spent together over the summer. If that was the extent of what a romantic relationship with Nancy would look like, I wouldn't be afraid. But I know too much. I know that I won't be able to give her all those other parts of a relationship. Maybe I'd feel comfortable with things like kissing, but I don't feel attraction in the same way she does. I will never look at her the way Quin did.

That makes it all worse. It's like I'm so close to having the perfect romance, the relationship I've always dreamed of. Nancy said she likes me. She said it.

Except there's no way she realizes what a relationship with me would actually look like.

If we try dating, she'll want more than I may ever be able to give her. She'll have expectations, and I'll break them. Then I'll just be another person she deletes off her Instagram page and out of her life.

I need to do something bigger to distract myself. I take out my computer. I still have my email open to the confirmation for the chairs and tables. Then I notice the minimized document at the bottom of the computer screen: the application I've been putting off.

I click on the icon so the document fills the screen. I'm still not sure exactly what I want to say, but I have time to figure it out.

———

I can't figure it out.

I try different approaches to answer why I want to work at Hartman and Co. I write about the experience of being point person for the Arbor Day Dance, and it sounds so small, so boring. Then I write about being a part of the Social Friends Committee in general, but that only boils down to a list of my club responsibilities. I even attempt to write about what it's like planning my mom's wedding. That feels like it should be a unique angle, but the words all come out wrong.

I add Bubbe to the document around 2:00 a.m. with a quick

email asking for some input. She'll know the best way to approach something like this. I try to go to sleep after, but my mind is buzzing with so many fears, worries about Nancy and Roo and even the wedding get jumbled together in my sleepy mind. So I open the computer again. It's much better to distract myself with the application.

I don't fall asleep until after 4:00 a.m.

NINE DAYS UNTIL THE WEDDING

I know something is wrong as soon as I walk upstairs. My mom is cleaning. That's never a good sign, especially this early in the morning.

"What did you do with my real mom?" I ask. "Were you brainwashed by aliens?"

She stops sweeping and turns to look at me. From her expression I can tell that it's even worse than an alien brainwashing. "My mother is going to be here. In an hour," she says.

"Bubbe's visiting? Why didn't you tell me she was coming?"

She shakes her head. "Nope, not my fault. She texted me at six a.m. to say she was on her way. Who even wakes up that early?"

"Bubbe, apparently," I supply.

"No time to be smart," she scolds. "Go wipe the counters."

"Good morning to you too," I mumble. I don't know why I'm the one in trouble here; I always keep up with my chores.

I help Mom finish her speed clean and do a rushed version of my morning routine so I can look marginally presentable. Bubbe isn't the kind of person you can greet in pajamas. Then I walk over to the main house since she'll have to park in their driveway.

I make it just in time to watch her car pull in.

"Oh, there's my perfect granddaughter!" she calls before she's even closed her car door.

"Hi, Bubbe," I say.

"What, do I not get a hug? Get over here." She holds out her arms.

Hugging Bubbe is like trying to cuddle with a rock. I know she goes to the gym a lot, a lifestyle change she made after her heart surgery, but I still don't understand how she's *this* muscular. I guess I didn't get those particular genes.

Bubbe takes a bag out of the trunk of her car. She's an efficient packer so I can't tell if she's planning on staying a night or the week.

"I'll take that for you," I say.

She smiles and hands it to me without a word.

We walk to the fancy barn-cottage, which gets the right kind of reaction from Bubbe. She can appreciate good interior design.

"Oh, you have to give me their number," she says.

"Sure, yeah, it's just Nancy's parents," I tell her.

"Right, Nancy," she says. "It's so nice that you have a little friend with you this summer. You're always hanging around that boy; you need some more female influences in your life."

There are many things wrong with what she just said, ranging from the fact that she definitely knows Roo's name to the whole female influences thing. I don't push it; it's never worth it to correct Bubbe.

"Hey, Mom."

"Hannah," Bubbe says. "What, did you just wake up? Please tell me you don't go out like that; I raised you better than that."

I knew it was a good call to get dressed before she arrived.

Mom is still in her pajamas, long flannel pants and a tank top that shows off her arm tattoo.

"Haven't gotten ready yet," Mom says.

"This late in the day," Bubbe says. "You were always like that growing up. I thought if you could sleep all day, you just might."

Mom ignores this. "So, Mom, what spurred the surprise visit?"

"I need an excuse to see my daughter? Before her wedding at that?"

"Not what I meant," I hear Mom mutter.

"Well," Bubbe continues, "I just thought you two might need some help. The mother of the bride is supposed to help, you know."

Mom has a fake smile on her face. "Great," she says.

"Felicity, what are we up to today?" Bubbe asks.

I actually do have something scheduled. "Cake tasting," I say. "I booked the bakery in advance, but since we're on such a tight deadline, we haven't actually picked the flavor yet."

"See, it's perfect. I can come along and help you decide," Bubbe says.

"Perfect," Mom repeats, voice higher than normal.

She's always so weird around Bubbe.

Mom leaves to get dressed, so I keep Bubbe company. I tell her about all of the wedding stuff I've gotten ready since we last spoke, and she tells me about her summer, what's going on at temple and her gym, and some long story about one of her friends losing her car in the mall parking lot.

By the time we're ready to leave for the tasting, I feel like I just sat through one of our Sunday brunches.

Mom says she'll drive, so I get in the back seat of her car. Grandmothers automatically get the passenger seat.

Once I'm buckled in, I check my phone. I have a new text from Nancy.

Nancy: Free today? I have an idea for a new fun thing

I think about the picture of Quin. I know what Nancy wants, and I know that her idea of a romantic relationship is entirely different from what I can give her.

I don't know anything at all.

What we really need to do is talk. I have to tell her how I feel and why I've been freaking out. Except I still haven't figured out what exactly I want to communicate.

Should I explain to her what it would really look like to date someone like me? Would it be easier to just tell her we should stay friends? Or should I tell her I want this too, give it a shot, and then inevitably lose this friendship that means so much to me?

I need to plan out the best way to approach this. I need to figure out what to say, what I'm willing to risk.

Not that I have to rush this. Bubbe is here; I have a built-in family-based excuse.

Felicity: my grandma showed up last minute, it's a whole thing, might be busy for a few days with family and wedding stuff

I hit Send.

Her response is quick.

Nancy: Have fun with your grandma!

I feel awful; I should have definitely invited her. When her parents were here, she invited me to have lunch. I'm supposed to do the same.

Maybe in a few days.

I'm aware that I'm avoiding Nancy; I know that I shouldn't be doing that. Except . . . Bubbe *is* here. One could argue that I'm just being a good granddaughter.

When we get to the bakery, I walk up to the counter to tell them we're here for a tasting.

"Yep, Becker party, got you right here," the guy working behind the counter says. "Take a seat, I'll bring out the samples."

The samples turn out to be five different slices of cake. I wonder if I can work wedding cake tastings into my daily schedule.

"What do you think of the lavender one?" I ask.

"It tastes like soap," Mom says.

Bubbe purses her lips. "You would say that." She takes a bite of the lemon raspberry slice. "Oh, this is delicious. Bright, summer flavors."

I reach over and try it. She's right, it's good.

"No," Bubbe says, trying another slice. "This one is definitely it. Champagne and strawberries. Perfect for a wedding."

Mom frowns. "I don't know, the chocolate cake tastes better."

"For a summer wedding?" Bubbe practically laughs. "Definitely not."

Mom groans. "What does it matter? Cake is cake."

"This is the most important cake of your entire life. Of course it matters." Bubbe looks over at me. "At least you understand."

I do; I've been thinking about the wedding cake since Mom got engaged. "I was actually thinking we might go for a mixed berry filling so they can decorate the side with fruit. It looks really beautiful," I say.

I reach for my phone in my purse so I can show Bubbe what I was thinking.

Bubbe takes a bite of the mixed berry and vanilla slice before I can even find an example picture. "No, it's got to be the champagne and strawberry one. And they're going to decorate with flowers, not fruit. It's better to choose the classic option. Trends pass."

It's not what I wanted, but Bubbe is probably right. It's better to go classic.

"I'd rather get an ice cream cake," Mom says flatly.

"She's kidding," I tell Bubbe.

"Am I?" Mom says.

Bubbe ignores this. "I'll tell them what we want," Bubbe says. "And I'll pay for it, no protesting. I'm the mother of the bride. You have to let me do something."

She gets up and walks toward the bakery counter.

"I'm going to murder her," Mom says quietly.

"No, you're not," I say.

"I'm going to drown her in champagne and choke her with strawberries."

"Be nice," I warn. "You wouldn't make it in jail."

"You don't know my life," she grumbles. She's always so childish around Bubbe.

After Bubbe finishes putting in our final order, she walks back to the table. "What's next?" she asks.

"I was hoping to go to this craft store, but it's kinda far," I say. Now that I know how skilled Eric is with his art, I have a few more ideas for signs I want him to make.

"What's a long trip with family? I'll drive," she says. "Hannah, you always go too fast. It's like you don't care about your daughter's safety."

"I've been trying to get rid of her. I think they make them sturdier these days," Mom says.

"I would never make jokes at your expense," Bubbe tells me. "Let's get you to that craft store."

I should've come up with something else. Being trapped in the car with the two of them could end in disaster.

At least I can take care of some errands.

I should go to bed early. I barely slept last night; I need to rest. It's the healthy thing to do, and I know how to make choices that are right for my body.

Instead, I'm sitting in the living room, working on the centerpieces.

I can hear Bubbe walk up the stairs before I see her. She's already dressed for bed, hair set in rollers and a satin robe tied around her matching pajama set. I've only seen her like this a couple of times before when I stayed over at her house. It feels special to see her like that, as though she trusts me enough to let me see her no matter how she looks.

"Want any help?" she asks, sitting down next to me.

"I can't tell if I want them all to look the same or if there should be slight differences, to differentiate the tables," I explain. "It'll be more work, but I think there's a way to make them look purposeful and unique, yet still cohesive."

"Why not try it out? We have all night," she says. "I'll put on a pot of coffee, and we can get to work." She leans over and kisses the top of my head. "My perfect bubbeleh, such a hard worker." She gets up and heads to the kitchen.

It's small moments like this that make me love my grandma even more. She knows exactly what I need. Mom would probably complain or tell me that it doesn't matter how her centerpieces look. Bubbe doesn't just support me; she pushes me to be my best too.

We work on the centerpieces all night.

EIGHT DAYS UNTIL THE WEDDING

"Are you okay?" Mom asks the next morning when I walk into the kitchen. "You look like you're coming down with something."

"Thanks," I say, annoyed. "You always know what to say to make me feel beautiful."

She puts her hand on my forehead. "No fever."

I swat her away. "I don't have makeup on yet, are you happy?"

She squints at me. "That's not it," she says. "You're definitely coming down with something. Take a nap today."

"I'm not five," I remind her.

"You'll always be five to me." She coos like she actually thinks I'm an infant.

I walk past her to get to the fridge. Maybe I should take a nap. Bubbe and I stayed up working on those centerpieces so late that the sun was starting to rise when I finally made it to bed. It's just one night though; it'll be fine.

Except that's not right. I stayed up the night before too.

I decide I'll just take it easy today. But Bubbe wants to run to the grocery store and then take a tour of the reception space and walk through the orchard, all before driving to a shoe store she found online that's an hour away because I mentioned in passing that I still hadn't figured out footwear.

We're so busy, there's no time for a break.

My head starts to hurt around noon. I'm sure it's just the car ride because sometimes I get a little nauseous on long drives, especially if I'm looking at a screen. I put my phone in my purse and look out the window, but it doesn't help.

It's all in my eyes. The pressure starts to build as we drive, getting even worse when we're back at the cottage. I imagine poking a little hole right between my eyebrows and just releasing all the pain in a poof of air, like some cartoon character. Is that a real thing doctors do? Should I look into that?

"Do you have any ibuprofen?" I ask my mom instead.

She's standing in the kitchen, holding a spoonful of Nutella. She must be deep in her revision now if she's eating right out of the jar. "What's wrong? Do you have a cold? Is it the flu?" she asks. "I told you that you weren't looking well."

If I was feeling especially mean, I'd tell her that she sounds like Bubbe right now.

"It's just my head," I say.

"You don't get headaches," Mom says.

"Sure, I do," I say. I'm not lying. I've gotten headaches before, from long car rides and staring at my computer too long.

"Not lately," she points out. She walks over to the cabinets, takes out a glass, and heads to the sink. "Drink some water," she says, already filling the cup.

"I don't need that," I say. "I can take something; it'll be fine."

"What about soup? Eric started the empanadas already, but I can ask him to make soup too. You should go to bed."

"Mom," I groan. "Drop it. You know what, I'm actually feeling fine."

240

She gives me this look like she doesn't believe a thing I've said and might attempt to swaddle me to sleep, just to be safe.

"Drink the water," she says as she leaves the room.

It's so condescending. I'm not allowed to have something as small as a headache without her freaking out. She doesn't trust me, doesn't think I know how to take care of myself. I do; I've shown her over and over again.

I take the glass of water and pour it down the sink.

I'll push through this, I decide. I can head to my room after Shabbat and sleep it off.

By the time dinner rolls around, my vision is starting to spot.

It'll be fine. How long can dinner take anyway? I think as I pull out my chair. People eat fast. I'm almost through the worst of it.

I haven't had Shabbat dinner with Bubbe in years. The last time was at her house. She does it all, the prayers and the traditions that we usually skip over. We basically just have a weekly family dinner. She does the real thing.

"Where are the candles?" Bubbe asks as she sits down at the table. "And the kiddush cup? Do you even have any wine?"

"Yes, wine. I could use some wine," Mom mutters, walking toward the kitchen.

"We don't usually do that," I explain to Bubbe. "We always have challah," I add, like this might help.

"You're raising my granddaughter without any faith? It's like you don't even care about our culture."

Eric steps in. "We're so happy you're here, Judy. Can I get you something to drink?"

Mom puts a bottle of wine on the table. "I've got it covered," she says.

Bubbe insists on blessing the challah and the wine. I feel like I've failed as a Jewish person since I don't know the words by heart.

We start eating, slipping into the kind of silence that usually comes as a side with a delicious meal.

I take a bite of my mashed potato, pea, and onion empanada. The flavors feel comforting. I'd enjoy them a lot more if my head didn't feel like it was going to burst.

I close my eyes. The worst is almost over. We'll finish eating, and I'll go to my room and turn out the lights. I can put on my pajamas and lie down. Maybe I'll put on a podcast; I've been meaning to go through the latest season of *Murder She Solved* one more time to listen for any clues I missed the first time around.

I run through all of this in my head. Maybe I'll just keep my eyes closed now and the pressure will get smaller and smaller until it's gone. I'm sure no one will notice; they're so focused on their food.

But then Bubbe speaks.

"I should meet the rabbi."

I open my eyes and look over at Mom across the table. This one's all on her.

Bubbe continues, "You're getting married and I don't even know the rabbi. We should go to the temple, at least."

"Actually," Mom starts. "We decided to go in a different direction."

"A different direction," Bubbe repeats. "Are you telling me my only child isn't going to have a rabbi at her wedding?"

I knew this was going to be a fight, but I had hoped to be very much not in the room when it happened.

"Well, I like Eric's family better, so we're going with a priest," Mom says. "Joking, sorry," she adds quickly.

She should know better than to try to break the tension with something like that.

Bubbe is still focused on the rabbi reveal. "I can't believe you'd do this to me. Did you tell your father? Oh, he's not going to like this one bit."

"Why would Dad care? He probably won't even show up."

I know Zayde works a lot, but there's no way he'd miss Mom's wedding. That's just not something parents do.

Bubbe's mouth drops open. "Of course he will," she says curtly.

"It's not like he did for anything else," Mom says.

"That's not true. You can't be angry at your father for being a proper provider."

"That's a fun way of saying workaholic," Mom shoots back.

I glance over at Eric. Poor thing, I wonder if he's regretting attaching himself to all of this. I notice that he has his hand on my mom's knee. She puts her own hand on top of his.

"I don't need to sit here and listen to you talk about our family like this," Bubbe says. "You're always so disrespectful. No rabbi, raising Felicity without any tradition. I've failed as a mother."

"Thanks, Mom. Glad to hear it. Why'd you even come here? Just to berate me?"

"No," Bubbe says stiffly. "I came because I got Felicity's email and I missed my girls."

Mom looks over at me. "What email?"

No, this can't be happening. I turn to Bubbe like maybe I can telepathically will her to stay quiet. It doesn't work.

"About the internship," Bubbe says. "She asked for my help with the application, and I just thought that she could use even more help. The wedding is so close, and I know how you are. Always irresponsible. If you couldn't even read over her application, well, what does that say about everything else?"

Mom ignores the gibe. "What internship?" she asks, her gaze still on me.

Bubbe answers. "The fall internship at Hartman and Company. Remember, I added Deborah Segal to my list so she could see Felicity's work and I could introduce them properly at the wedding. Hannah, we talked about this ages ago."

"No, we didn't," Mom says. "Because if I knew anything about an internship, I sure as hell would've had a conversation with my daughter about whether or not she was up to it."

"Up to it," Bubbe repeats. "What does that even mean? Kids have to have full schedules. It's like you don't even want her to succeed in life."

"I want her to not wind up in the hospital again!" Mom yells.

I hate this. I hate everything about this. They're acting like I'm not even here, like I'm something breakable that needs to be controlled. Like I don't know my own limits.

My mind flashes to the hospital. It feels like I'm there again, hearing the doctor say on a loop that I was at risk for a heart attack. Because I don't know my limits, I can't be trusted, I shouldn't be in control.

And here I am, overworking myself again.

I know exactly why I didn't tell Mom about any of this. Because I thought she would stop me. Because I thought that this might be a bad idea. Because I wanted it all so badly that I didn't think I could take it if she told me no.

The pressure behind my eyes feels even worse. The lights are too bright, and my thoughts are too loud. I'm a risk to my own health, I'm in so much pain, I feel sick, I feel—

Which is exactly when I throw up.

Bubbe lets out a little scream and jumps up from the table. At the same time, Mom yells, "Lissy!" and rushes toward me. Eric immediately goes into cleanup mode, disappearing to the kitchen and returning with a roll of paper towels and disinfectant.

"I need to lie down," Bubbe announces. She folds her napkin and puts it carefully on the table, then pushes her chair in before walking away.

Which leaves me sitting with Mom and Eric.

I attempt a joke to lighten the mood. "Would you believe it if I said I was pregnant?"

Mom ignores this. "Go to your room and lie down," she commands. "I can't deal with you right now."

Right, because I'm something she has to deal with.

I get up and head to my room. With that, I've officially ruined dinner.

———

I'm about to turn off my lights when Mom knocks on my door. She doesn't wait for a response before opening.

"Can we talk?" she asks. Her voice sounds a lot calmer than it did over dinner.

I nod.

She walks in and sits at the edge of my bed. Before saying anything, she hands me a bottle of Advil and a glass of water.

"I emailed Bonnie," she starts.

Great, I'm such a mess she needs to consult with my therapist before talking to me.

She continues, "I don't like that you kept this from me. I think you've been pushing yourself too hard again, but that's on me. I should have been paying more attention. Which is why I also emailed my editor and told her that I need an extension."

"Mom," I start to protest. Because that feels too big. My choices shouldn't affect her like that.

She puts up a hand to stop me. "I already did it. I should've done it sooner; I just thought I could manage it all. Some example I am, huh?" She pauses before adding, "If this internship is something you want, I support you."

I can't believe she's being so calm about all of this.

"But," she continues, "you still kept secrets. Which is not okay in this household. And you pushed yourself way too hard today. If I tell you to drink some water or take a nap, I'm going to need you to listen."

I nod, then prepare myself for punishment time. I wonder what we're talking here . . . no phone? No TV?

"No wedding planning," Mom says. "For five days. If there's anything pressing, I'll do it. You can forward me any vendor emails, but that's it."

"Mom, that hardly sounds like—" I start.

"Nope," she cuts me off. "My rules. You have some workless days ahead of you, child of mine. Rest, go spend time with Nancy. Play mini golf, go swimming in a lake, or watch a movie. Just have fun, enjoy the summer."

She squeezes my arm and leaves the room.

Enjoy the summer? Like that's possible now.

ONE WEEK UNTIL THE WEDDING

I wake up to a knock on my door. I sit up groggily in bed. What time is it? My alarm hasn't even gone off.

Bubbe opens the door before I respond. "My perfect girl, I hope I didn't wake you."

She did, which is probably very obvious from the fact that I'm still under the covers. "It's not a problem," I say, propping myself up against the headboard.

"Are you feeling better?" she asks.

I nod. It turns out I really did just need a night of rest. The Advil didn't hurt either.

Bubbe sits down at the edge of my bed. "I just wanted to say goodbye before I head out," she says.

"You're leaving already?" I ask.

"I know when I'm not wanted," she says. "I'll come back in time for the rehearsal dinner. I booked a nice bed-and-breakfast last night," she adds. "Hopefully that will give your mother some time to calm down."

"Yeah," I say.

"You know," she starts, "I'm not as bad as she makes me sound."

"I don't think—"

Bubbe puts up her hand to stop me. "No, I know exactly what your mother thinks. It's not the truth, Felicity. Is it a crime to want what's best for your daughter?"

I'm not sure how I'm supposed to respond to that. Of course it isn't. I've always known Bubbe wants the best. Isn't that what I'm trying to give her?

She continues, "I had a lot to live up to with my ema. Your great-grandmother, she only ever wanted me to have a good life. A safe life. It was so different with her. There were a lot of secrets, a lot of things she didn't feel like she could tell me. She escaped Poland during the war, you know. I don't know a lot of the details. She wanted to protect me from them. I guess I wanted to protect you girls too. Nothing is a guarantee; we need to work to be successful. If I was hard on you, if I pushed you in the right direction, I knew you'd have good lives. Safe lives."

I sit with that for a moment. I don't know a lot about Bubbe's family; I never got to meet them. Mom tells stories sometimes but said stories are never very . . . warm. Was that because they were trying to protect her from the truth of what they had gone through? Is that why they always come across as distant in Mom's stories? What *had* they gone through? I can't even begin to imagine what it would be like to flee a country, especially during the Holocaust.

Bubbe straightens. She reaches out and smooths some of my hair, messy from sleep, then pats my cheek. "I just want you to have a good life. Understand?"

I nod.

"Good, motek." She looks away. I wonder what exactly she's looking at.

"Now, you can always call," she continues. "I know your mother isn't helping with any of the preparation. If you need me to buy anything, let me know."

Sure, only problem is I've been banned from all that. Which is something I definitely can't tell Bubbe.

She'll be angry at my mom, and she'll feel like I failed her. It's easier to stay silent.

"I know you'll be fine," she adds. "I just feel terrible that it's falling on you. Not that it will be a problem. My bubbeleh, so talented."

I'm not sure how I'm supposed to respond. "Thanks," I say.

She kisses my cheek.

"Love you, Felicity," she says. "You have a good head on those shoulders. I trust you."

I'm not sure if that's necessarily the right call, but I don't protest.

"Love you, Bubbe," I say. "Do you want me to take out your bag?"

"See," she says, "just proving my point. I can do it by myself; don't get up." She gives me one last kiss before she walks to the door.

"You always know what to do, my perfect girl," she says as her goodbye.

I wish that were true; it would make my life a lot easier.

With my no-work punishment in place, I have nothing to do, at all, but stress about Nancy's confession.

I mean, yes, technically, I also have Netflix, but how many times can you watch *The Legend of Korra* before it gets out of hand?

The biggest problem is I can't figure out how I feel now that I know Nancy likes me. Here are the facts: I love spending time with her, she makes me feel happy, and I'd like to keep feeling happy and spending time with her.

What's the difference between a friendship and a romantic relationship, for someone like me? A lot of what Nancy and I have been doing could seem date-like. Would the difference be physical? If we started dating, would she expect more from me? Would she want to cuddle or hold hands or kiss or even more? Is that something I want too?

Theoretically, I'm fine with those things. I've never daydreamed about making out with a future partner, but I don't hate the idea of doing that with someone like Nancy, who I'm comfortable with. Except maybe that's all she'll ever want to do, and then we'd never have time to just hang out or decide spur of the moment to design a miniature golf course. I know she cares about the physical parts of a relationship. My mind flashes back to our conversations about her ex. I lived through all of that, and I have the facts to back up my fears.

Except the more I think about it, the more I realize that Nancy has her facts as well. I might have heard how she talks about attraction and relationships, but she's heard me talk too. I think back to that night at the retreat when we went up to the roof. I shared so much with her, things I haven't even talked about with Roo. Nancy is so thoughtful and kind; there's no way she hasn't thought about the proverbial ace elephant in the room.

I'm just convinced she doesn't fully understand what it would mean in practice.

Is it kinder to turn her down immediately? I know the kind of relationship she expects. If I don't know whether I can ever give that to her, I shouldn't lead her on.

I could be wrong; she might have changed her mind about liking the physical stuff. Or she might say that she changed her mind and be lying and eventually resent me for being the way I am. It's entirely unclear.

If I say we should date, that puts our whole friendship in jeopardy. I can't lose her.

Except I'm basically putting our friendship in jeopardy by isolating like this.

I should probably talk to her, even if I don't know what to say just yet. She told me there wasn't any pressure on answering; she wouldn't lie about that. I need to stop being ridiculous.

I make it all the way to the main house before I chicken out.

"Felicity darling, can I help you?"

I jump. I had no idea Aunt Gwendoline was out here.

"Oh, I'm fine, I'm . . . getting some fresh air," I manage.

She's crouched down in her garden. She still has the sling, now paired with what I think must be a cocktail dress.

She must notice what caught my eye, because she says, "You know, this was stuck in the back of my closet." She smooths the skirt with her free hand. "I never seem to get reasons to wear this sort of thing anymore. The day we met, I pulled out that gown as a little joke; I knew how Nancy would take it. But I always felt so glamorous in clothes like this. I hope you can indulge an old woman with a mere moment of fancy."

"You *do* look fabulous," I say. "I admire that," I add. "The fact that you don't care about what you're supposed to wear or when you're supposed to wear it."

She looks at me, up and down like she needs to take in my outfit and maybe my entire being. I suddenly feel like my vintage-inspired sundress is completely inadequate.

"The thing about appearances," she finally says, "is that you can't stop other people from making assumptions. From judging and having opinions. How boring would it be, if we all looked the same or thought the same?

"You admire me; someone else says I'm too quirky or strange. It's always going to be something.

"I was a Korean girl growing up in a small English town. My father moved us all for a job opportunity when I was three years old. I stood out; my family stood out. And then I fell in love . . . more than once. What a scandal." She stands up. I notice some dirt along the side of her dress.

"You know, this orchard originally belonged to my third husband. Richard, the love of my life. He was on vacation when we met, backpacking through the English countryside. We got married before the week was up. When you know, it can be that simple," she says with a smile. "We had twenty-two perfect years together. When he died, I couldn't bring myself to leave this place. It was our home. I can still feel him here, his presence.

"It might have been easier to move somewhere less . . . homogenous. Or even to blend in, make myself smaller so other people would feel more comfortable. But I realized something. People would stare anyway, so why not give them a show? Why not have fun doing it? And I have a lot of fun." She winks at that.

"A big personality, dear, is not a sign of weakness," she adds. "There will always be people ready to shame you for having opinions, likes and dislikes . . . for having a voice. I'd love to say screw the haters, but it's so hard to see that at your age. Sometimes it's hard to see that at my age too. Remember to be your beautifully flawed self and know that others will be flawed too."

She takes my hand and gives it a squeeze. "Would you like me to tell Nancy you're out here?"

I shake my head.

Aunt Gwendoline lets out a little sigh. "Neither of you wants to talk, it seems."

What does that mean? What's going on with Nancy? Did I make her so entirely miserable that it's obvious to her great-aunt and probably random passersby?

I should go inside and talk to her. I should fix this.

Except I have no idea what the solution looks like.

"I, um . . . I should head back," I say.

She gives me that look again, like she can read my entire being. Without another word, she picks up her gardening tools and heads inside.

SIX DAYS UNTIL THE WEDDING

I'm sitting in the living room, in the middle of season two of *The Legend of Korra*, when Eric walks over.

"Want to go grocery shopping?" he asks.

"I don't know, I'm only allowed to do fun things," I say, voice flat. "Probably not allowed."

"Get dressed, kid," Eric says. "We're going grocery shopping."

I mean, I'd rather stay on this couch in my pajamas all day, but Eric is clearly not going to let that happen. I shouldn't be surprised. We're well past due for one of his classic heart-to-hearts.

He doesn't pester me until we're in the store. "So," he starts, pushing the cart. "How are you doing?"

Not great, Eric, thanks for noticing, I think. "Fine," I say out loud.

"Your mom, she means well. Your grandma too. I know it's never fun to see the people you love fighting, but—"

"Eric, really. I'm fine."

This doesn't seem to stop him. "Spending time with your grandma is always hard for your mom. Your bubbe is really tough on her. I'm not sure there's a choice they've ever agreed on."

Like my general existence, I think.

"Like when your mom decided to freelance so she could spend more time with you," Eric says.

I turn my head to face him, confused. "She did that because she wanted to," I say. I look back to where I'm walking. I don't want to barrel into a display of cereal.

Eric shakes his head. "Not entirely," he says. "I mean, your mom, she's been so successful, you know. Right out of college making all that money, and then she had this big job lined up. Long hours, serious corporate life ahead of her. It was everything your grandma wanted her to do, but she turned it down. Got in a huge fight with your bubbe about it."

I knew she had other options after she left school, but the way she's always told me the story was that she sold that software she made and decided she wanted to have me and that was it.

Eric keeps going. "Your grandma has never approved of writing, especially the kind your mom does. Even the *Sleepy Dog* stuff wasn't the right kind of success. She was supposed to be a doctor or a lawyer or some kind of CEO. But she chose her own path. Kind of a rock star, if you ask me."

"Are you just saying all this so I'll stop being angry at her for this whole 'go enjoy summer' punishment?" I ask.

He shrugs. "Is it working?"

I don't respond.

"She means well, is all," Eric adds. "Her relationship with you, that's the most important thing in her life. Just thought you might need a reminder."

I sigh. He has to say all that; it's like a soon-to-be-husband requirement.

Eric takes my silence as an excuse to change the topic. "So what *are* you up to this week? Anything exciting?"

No, I can't do anything fun because Nancy told me she has feelings for me and I'm a monster who doesn't know how to process that, and now I can't even distract myself by planning your perfect wedding, I think.

I shrug, which feels like a better response.

"Your mom says you'll go hiking with us," Eric continues. "That'll be fun."

"Super," I say, with as little emotion in my voice as possible.

He turns the cart down the next aisle. "I'm here if you need to talk," he finishes.

I sigh. He's trying so hard right now, I know he is, but I'm not about to dump all of my Nancy feelings on my soon-to-be step-father. "Thanks," I say, voice a little kinder. "Noted."

He smiles, like maybe his talk made a huge difference. "All right, Lissy. What should we cook tonight?"

I'm happy he's moved on. "Something sweet and objectively bad for us," I say.

"I think we can manage that."

We end up with the ingredients to make my favorite sweet empanadas, condensed milk and cream cheese and strawberries, so the grocery trip isn't a total failure.

FIVE DAYS UNTIL THE WEDDING

It turns out that it's hard to avoid a friend when you're staying in her guesthouse for the summer.

"Lissy, Nancy's here," Mom calls from upstairs.

I don't move from my spot at the desk. If I stay here, it might look like I'm working, even though I'm just watching YouTube, which apparently counts as mandatory fun.

I pause the video.

"Hey," Nancy says, walking into the room. "Sorry to just drop by; I feel like I haven't seen you in ages."

"I've just been right here," I say. "Nothing to report."

"Is your grandma still here?" she asks. "I didn't see her car earlier."

Right, I told Nancy I was busy with Bubbe.

"She left," I say, deliberately not specifying the when of it all. "She'll be back for the rehearsal dinner."

Nancy nods. She sits down at the edge of my bed. "Whatcha working on?" she asks.

"Oh, nothing really," I say. I don't add the fact that I'm currently mid-punishment for keeping the whole internship thing a secret, so I really am working on nothing. "We're actually about to go on a hike," I say.

"Wow, Eric finally roped you into it, huh?"

I nod. "Hard work and persistence pays off."

She pauses, like she's thinking about her next words. "Can we do a dinner sometime this week? Just the two of us. Hang out . . . *talk*."

My throat feels tight. She wants to have a dinner with just the two of us so we can talk? What does that mean?

This should be a good thing, communication and all. I shouldn't assume what Nancy wants.

I just can't get over how loaded the word "talk" feels.

"Yeah, sure," I say.

"We can work it around your schedule," she promises. "Let me know, okay?"

"Uh-huh," I manage.

She smiles, but it looks fake. I can tell from her eyes.

"All right. Text me tonight to let me know when you're free."

"Yep."

She gets up and walks over. What does she want, a hug?

I don't have to worry. All she does is give my shoulder a light squeeze. "Have fun on the family adventure."

"Thanks," I say.

It's not that I lied or anything. Eric really is taking us to see this fire tower thing, which he swears will be "so much fun" because we'll get to see "basically all of Vermont" from the top.

I don't think that's technically possible, but he seems so excited. I'll let him have that joy; at least someone in this house should be happy.

I close my computer. I should change for the hike. I've heard it's best not to go in pajamas.

Mom and Eric look especially dorky when I get upstairs. They must have coordinated, from their matching blue baseball caps and army-green shirts all the way down to their navy bike shorts and too-white sneakers.

"Is there a dress code for this outing?" I ask.

Mom laughs. "Total mistake, but kinda cute, right?"

"I was going to say creepy."

Eric does that thing where he looks right at Mom as though, by doing so, I can no longer hear. "She finds us adorable," he tells her.

"She's just embarrassed to admit it," Mom agrees.

This better calm down once they're officially married; I can't live in a house filled with this much sickly sweet nonsense.

We head to the car. Mom asks me if I want to drive, which is a solid no. I'm not even sure if I can drive in a different state with only my permit. I haven't looked it up.

"You've got to practice," she warns, but then drops it. She gets in the driver's seat.

The car ride is the right amount of long for my mind to wander. Nancy asked to do this dinner and sounded so nice when she said we could work it around my schedule, but I don't like the fact that she made me commit to when I'd tell her. Telling me to text her tonight felt like a command. Like I was in trouble because I've been avoiding her.

I should be in trouble; it's my fault. I *have* been avoiding her. Except maybe that's not it. I've needed some space to work out my thoughts, to figure out why I reacted the way I did. Is that so terrible?

I don't know.

It would be different if she knew what this was all about. I picture telling her over dinner, running through various possible reactions. *Hi, Nancy. I don't know how I feel, and I'm worried you won't be okay with that.* She's angry, she's accepting, she's . . . Nancy. She's my Nancy. I don't have to be afraid about this.

Mom stops in a small parking lot in front of the trail.

We get out of the car and start walking along a wide, dirt-lined path. It narrows, curving around a lake and twisting into the woods. The farther we go, the more convinced I am that we're going to get lost. It feels like we're leaving our normal world behind. I bet there isn't any cell service out here.

Mom and Eric are both talking as they go. They ask me a few questions, boring stuff like what's been my favorite thing so far this summer and whether I know my class schedule yet for next year. It's rude to try to uphold a conversation when the path gets steep. I can't talk and breathe under these conditions.

Their chatter gets so out of hand, I actually have to say, "Guys, chill. These aren't talking conditions."

"Lissy, this isn't a race," Mom says. "You can slow down and have a conversation."

I thought the whole point of this was to see all of Vermont, not have a flimsy discussion about whether or not I got into Civilizations of the Ancient World for my junior history requirement.

"What about your club?" Mom asks. "Are you excited for the . . . what is it? Halloween Haunted House?"

Is this really the time to bring up the Social Friends Committee? Why doesn't she just invite Brody Wells, Junior Committee

President position stealer slash arch nemesis, to come join us to really amp up my misery?

"Hallway," I correct. "It's a haunted hallway."

"Yeah, that," Mom says.

"I don't even know if I'm going to participate next year," I say dismissively.

Neither Mom nor Eric say anything to that, though they both have concerned looks on their faces.

I'm saved by the fire tower. From the conversation, that is. From a hiking perspective, things get a lot worse.

The fire tower turns out to be an old metal structure so tall it peeks out above the massive surrounding pines. There's a lookout at the top that's partially rusted. It's got to be too old to be safe.

"You expect me to climb that?" I ask.

"Come on, it'll be fun," Mom says.

Has Eric brainwashed her? She's never been that enthusiastic about exercise. I can feel my legs preemptively ache just by looking at all those stairs.

"Nope." I fold my arms, which means business. I am not going to die in the middle of the woods in Vermont.

"Lissy, if you back out, you'll miss the view," Mom says.

"Shucks," I say. "Try to have fun without me."

"She'll change her mind when she sees us up there," Eric says. "You'll see."

They start climbing.

I don't like that they're being peer pressure-y about this. I'm the smart one here. I don't care how awesome the view is; that doesn't look safe. They'll see when it falls apart.

"Oh, wow," Mom calls out once she reaches the top. "Lissy, you can't miss this."

"I'm good," I yell back.

"It's breathtaking," Eric adds.

"Yes, in that it could take your breath away forever," I mutter to myself. For them, I give a thumbs-up. I wonder if they can even see that clearly.

I can't decide whether I'm being stubborn or smart. They've been up there for a while, and nothing has happened. If I don't try things that seem a little scary, I'll always miss out.

I'm always going to miss out because I'm too scared and too dramatic, because I take normal things and turn them into catastrophes. This little thing shouldn't be a problem, yet I've turned it into one. I'm always going to be the Felicity Show, just like Roo said.

This is ridiculous. I've jumped into a rock quarry; I've made it through my mom finding out about the internship. I can climb this fire tower if I want to. I can talk to Nancy and tell her everything that's been going on in my head. I can be brave. I *am* brave.

I walk all the way up to the stairs but stop. The steps look too rickety. This is bad, this is dangerous; if I do this, the whole structure will collapse. My vision isn't that clear, and my heart is racing. *I can't do this, I can't do this, I can't do anything right.*

I stay at the bottom.

THREE DAYS UNTIL THE WEDDING

I wonder if there's a dress code for destroying a friendship . . .

It would be easier if I could talk to Roo about this. He'd have something logical to say, like "calm down" or "it's just dinner" or "you're overthinking things." I haven't heard from him once since our fight, not even something harmless like a baby animal GIF text. For all I know, we'll only ever see each other passing in the hall at school from now on. Maybe he'll move to avoid the Felicity Show altogether. I wouldn't be surprised.

I decide on my lucky dress. I'll need all the luck I can get tonight.

Nancy's waiting for me at the main house. "Hey," she says, opening the door. "Hope you're hungry; I went a little overboard."

I follow her into the house.

"Just us tonight. Aunt Gwendoline is at a charity bingo event. I asked her what charity, and she didn't even know, which I thought was kinda silly. But, yeah, um, just us. I splurged and got Chinese takeout. You came over just in time; it's fresh. I was all about the timing tonight."

I can tell she's nervous from the way she's talking. It's all ramble. Does it make this any easier now that I know she's nervous too?

We sit down at the table in the kitchen.

I wonder how this is going to work. Should I preemptively tell her everything? Should I apologize for being distant and explain why I'm freaking out? Will she understand? Or should I wait for her to talk first . . . let her say whatever she's going to say and then react from there? Maybe it's smarter to eat, especially if the food is fresh, before we have this talk.

The takeout is still in containers, but Nancy already put plates and silverware and chopsticks out for us. We serve ourselves, spring rolls and lo mein and fried rice and scallion pancakes and cubes of tofu tossed with steamed vegetables.

I take a bite of my spring roll. I'll let her go first. I have no idea what she wants to talk about, and I need to stop jumping to assumptions. Plus, it would be rude to let the food get cold.

There's a moment where we're both quietly eating before Nancy speaks. "I want to talk to you about something," she starts. "Since we went to Boston, I feel like I can't pretend it isn't what I want anymore."

I hate that I was right. I don't like that I could tell she was disappointed that I haven't properly responded to her confession; I don't like that I let her down in the first place.

"I know," I say. "But I just don't know what to say."

She gives me a quizzical look.

"You deserve a response, a real one," I continue. "But the more I think about it, the less I know how to respond."

"Oh, Fe, that's not what this—"

But I don't let her finish. "I just need time to figure it out. You're so important to me; I can't ruin our friendship. I just need time, okay? I need time."

She nods. There's this sad look in her eyes. I can tell she's disappointed in me.

My chest feels very tight. I'm crying now, and I don't really know why I'm crying. It's probably all the disappointment.

"Fe," Nancy says, her voice pleading, like she's trying to understand me.

How can she understand me if I don't understand myself?

What would Bonnie say to do? She'd tell me to communicate, but I don't know how to do that. I don't know how I feel. Because the more I think about it, I do want a romantic relationship with Nancy. I want to spend all of my time with her and listen to her excitedly talk about the design elements involved in making a museum. I wish that all of our One Fun Thing activities really were dates.

Everything I want feels so close.

Everything I want feels impossible.

I hear Nancy's voice run through my head as she talks about her past relationship, her old crushes. I see all the ways I could disappoint her. I think about what it would be like to turn her down. I imagine us dating and breaking up and that breakup ruining our entire friendship. I picture Nancy deleting me out of her life the same way she did to Quin.

Every single option I have feels like a risk I'm not ready to take.

What else would Bonnie say? She'd tell me I could ask for space so I could figure out my feelings.

"I can't do this right now," I say, getting up from my chair. "I'm sorry, I can't. I need space."

I need to be safe, I need to get out, I need to be alone. I don't even want to be with myself right now.

"I can give you space," Nancy says softly, staying seated. Her voice sounds so hurt. I did that, I caused that pain, I hurt her. It's all my fault.

So I leave.

THE DAY BEFORE THE WEDDING

Now that I'm allowed to focus on wedding stuff again, I try to keep busy. What else am I supposed to do? Hang out with my friends? I've ruined every meaningful relationship in my life, so that option is out.

My phone buzzes on the desk, and for a moment I hope that it's Nancy. It's not, just Bubbe telling me she's almost here. I don't know why I'm disappointed; I'm the one who asked for space. I should be happy that Nancy's respecting that.

I grab my phone and put it into my back pocket. I don't even know what I want.

I walk upstairs. "Bubbe's almost here," I yell to Mom. "She's stopping by on her way to her bed-and-breakfast." I thought Mom was in the kitchen, but I don't see her.

"Eric's family's already at their Airbnb," she calls back from downstairs. Oy, I must've walked right past her.

Mom stomps up the stairs, stopping at the top step. "Are you wearing jeans?"

"No, my legs turned blue," I say, deadpan. "I asked the florist to deliver the chuppah early so I can make some last-minute tweaks, and I'm okay getting these dirty."

She looks me up and down. "You're dressed like me," she says in the same tone she might use announcing that aliens had landed on the roof.

I *am* wearing one of her shirts, so the observation's not wrong.

We don't have time to discuss outfits. "Now that you're here," I say, as though her appearance isn't a direct result of me yelling from the living room. "Would you mind going to wait for Bubbe outside the main house?"

"Don't think she'll be any nicer if I get to her first," she warns, as though this was something I was worried about. It's not like I'm the one who dyed her hair navy blue last night . . . like that's going to go over well with Bubbe.

Mom kisses the top of my head. "I'll go get her."

I run through a list of everything I have to do. The chuppah is going to take the longest out of my tasks for today, because I decided I want to string lights along the wooden beams in the front and along the top. The tables and chairs for the reception are getting delivered around four, so I'll need to make sure they go to the right place. There's some more decorating to finish too. Then I'll have to shower and change for the rehearsal dinner, which I arranged at the fancy Italian place a town over.

I need to get to sleep early, since I have even more to do tomorrow. There's setting up the tables and arranging the mismatched armchairs and getting everything I don't finish today into place and making sure things are okay with the DJ and caterer and photographer, not to mention all the time it's going to take for hair and makeup.

At least I prepared for all of this.

I can see Bubbe and Mom walking over from out the window, so I head outside to meet them.

"My perfect girl!" Bubbe calls, walking over with her arms already open for a hug. "What are you wearing?" she quickly follows up.

I give her a big hug. "Stuff I can get dirty," I reply. "Don't worry, I have a nice dress for tonight."

She nods her approval and takes a step back.

"I don't know why you wear your hair back like that; it looks so much nicer down." She taps the neat bun that's resting at the back of my neck. "Such pretty hair," she continues. "You know, you get that color from me. I wasn't always gray. Thank goodness for your hair; can you imagine if you got it from the other side? You'd never know. Lucky girl with our lucky family hair." She glances over at Mom's newly navy locks and gives her a look that's so disapproving it should be censored.

"Now," she continues, "show me everything."

I take her downstairs so I can show off all of my work. "The string lanterns and lights are going up this afternoon, then there are lanterns to line the aisle, here's a sample place setting, the favors are over there, here are the centerpieces." I point out each thing around the room.

"You've outdone yourself," she says.

"Yeah?"

"Oh, definitely." She pauses, bending down to look at the *Mr. and Mrs.* sign I asked Eric to paint for the sweetheart table. "Not that I'm surprised. I told you, I knew this would all work out with you in charge."

I'm nowhere near done with my work; there's still so much to do before the ceremony tomorrow, but Bubbe's approval feels big, like this whole summer has been worth it.

"All right, I don't want to take up your time, my little wedding planner." She kisses the top of my head, the same spot Mom did before. "I have to go check in. I'll see you tonight."

"Love you," I say.

"And I love you more."

I look over all of my completed projects, spread out around my summer bedroom. I *have* outdone myself. I've worked hard and it's paid off.

I can do some things right after all.

———————

I'm in the old orchard store turned workshop, standing on a ladder and stringing fairy lights between flowers on the chuppah when I hear a knock on the door.

For a second, I picture Nancy. She walks in and I apologize and we hug. I can see it so clearly, it almost feels real.

It's probably just Mom. The tables and chairs for the reception arrived early and took much longer than they should have, so this chuppah decorating is cutting into my prep time. I should've headed back to get ready for the rehearsal dinner already.

"Come in," I call, eyes still trained on the lights. Is this too much? The beams are already covered in flowers; it's not like they need the lights too. I don't want the chuppah to look too busy.

"Are you wearing jeans?"

I stop what I'm doing. I didn't think I'd hear that voice today.

"Roo?" I turn around. There he is, leaning against the door-frame, looking so put together he easily could have headed to the workshop from a runway show. "You came," I say, surprised.

"I couldn't miss your mom's wedding," he says. "She told me you were out here."

I climb down the ladder and run over and give him a hug. There's so much I want to say, so much I should say. I want to apologize for making him feel like he couldn't talk to me and then ask him what's going on. I want to tell him everything about what happened with Nancy. I want to just stand here and hug my best friend until it's time to leave for dinner.

He speaks first. "Hey, there's something I should've told you earlier."

I pull away. This is it; I can prove to him that I'm able to lis-ten, that I'm here for him just like he's there for me. "Yes?"

He turns his head and looks out the door. "This is my plus-one," he says.

At first I think he's being ridiculous; I already know his sister. Amira's the one who taught me how to give myself a perfect at-home manicure. How could I forget such an icon? Except the person who walks over is decidedly not Amira. He's a *he*, for starters. His skin is a few shades darker than hers too, and, from the looks of his nails, I doubt he knows the benefits of a good base coat.

My brain must have stopped functioning, or I accidentally ingested a strong hallucinogenic, because I *have* to be seeing things. There's no way that the boy walking over to Roo is really here. I squint at him, like maybe that will make sense of things, studying his tight cornrows and too-small-for-his-muscles school athletic department T-shirt. He's holding two garment bags in one hand and has a duffel bag draped around his opposite shoulder that has tiny lacrosse sticks stitched on the front.

"Brody Wells?" I say out loud.

"Hey, Felicity, so chill that you invited me," he says. He leans over and kisses Roo on the cheek. "Babe, we've got to hang these. Don't want them all wrinkled tomorrow."

Kissing? Babe???

"Can you drop them off in the room? I'll be right there," Roo says. His voice sounds different, too sweet. I haven't heard his voice sound like that before.

"I got ya," Brody says. He gives Roo another quick kiss and leaves the workshop.

WHAT THE HELL IS HAPPENING?!!!!!!!

"So," Roo says, filling the silence. "Surprise?"

I have no clue what he thinks that's going to accomplish. How the hell did he keep this from me? BRODY WELLS? My mortal enemy? How could Roo do this?

I have so many questions running through my head. How did this start? Why didn't Roo tell me earlier? I told him everything that was going on with Nancy. How dare he? Is there a jail for former best friends?

I don't even get the chance to ask him anything because my phone starts ringing. I hold up a finger in that *give me a moment, I'm not done with you* sort of way, and take my phone out of my back pocket.

"Hello?" I start.

"Hi, is this Ms. Becker?" a voice asks.

"Yep," I say.

"Hi, Ms. Becker, I'm Maya calling from Villa Osteria. Unfortunately, our hot water heater broke earlier this evening. As per Vermont health code, we are unable to open without a working hot water tank, which is for the health and safety of our guests. This means that we will be unable to accommodate your party this evening. We will of course return your deposit in full. I'm so sorry. Please let us know if we can help you find a replacement venue; I know this is all so unexpected."

Unexpected. She's got that right.

"Thank you so much for letting me know," I say. "Is it all right if I call back about helping us find a new place? I have to talk to the bride." Saying "bride" sounds much more official than saying I need to consult my mom.

"Of course," Maya from Villa Osteria says.

I hang up.

Well then. Brody Wells is here, *and* we don't have a venue for the rehearsal dinner. What else can go wrong?

SEVEN HOURS BEFORE
THE WEDDING DAY

Mom doesn't understand the urgency of this no-restaurant dilemma. She's carefully putting on eyeliner like I didn't just tell her that her rehearsal dinner is ruined. If it was me, there's no way my hand would be that steady.

"What are we going to do?" I ask. I can hear the stress in my own voice. "Should I call the restaurant back? They said they can help us with another reservation, but it's so last minute. Where would we even go?"

"Lissy, it's fine." She moves on to her other eye. "We can just go to that burger place down the road."

That burger place is a stand with picnic tables outside. We are not going to trade an upscale Italian restaurant for a place without chairs.

I snort. "Yeah, no."

"Why not?" She puts down her eyeliner and examines her work in the mirror. The wings must be uneven because she picks it up again.

"Mom, this isn't funny. We're talking about your rehearsal dinner."

"Yes, *my* rehearsal dinner," she says. "I've been craving a good milkshake; it's sort of perfect." She steps away from the mirror and turns to me. "Did I fix it?"

Her eyes are perfect; her plan is not. "We can't have your rehearsal dinner at a burger joint."

"I think we can," she says like she's made a valid point. "There's something for everyone—salads, milkshakes, fries. Eric and I tried their portobello burger; it's so good. Plus, there are what? Fifteen of us tonight? It's just family. We'll definitely be able to grab enough tables for it to work. Problem solved."

I groan. "You don't get it. That's not how weddings work. We're supposed to go to a restaurant, a *real* restaurant."

She shrugs. "Agree to disagree." She walks over to her bedside table and picks up her phone. Is she texting in the middle of our conversation?

I can't believe she's being like this. I worked so hard to organize everything for her, and she's being dismissive? No, that's not acceptable.

"You can't just come in and change the plans last minute like that," I say. "I've worked so hard to make sure all of this is perfect; we're not going to ruin it over milkshakes. We'll find a suitable place for tonight."

Mom looks up from her phone. "Don't worry, I already texted the group the new location. Nothing to stress about."

Oh, so now I'm unnecessarily stressing? It's like she can't even hear me when I talk. "You made it worse," I point out. "Never mind, I'll take care of this. As always."

I storm out of the room.

I can fix this, I think. *I have to, no matter what Mom says.* There has to be another option, some place in rural Vermont that can handle a rehearsal dinner with zero notice.

I call Villa Osteria back, but the line is busy. It doesn't even ring; it goes right to this infuriating *beep, beep, beep.*

This is fine. I'll just start getting ready and call them back. This is going to be fine; I can fix this.

As soon as I get in the shower, my mind starts to wander. I think about the clock ticking and running out of time, of failing everyone. Of working so hard only to have said work destroyed by a flipping hot water tank. I should have had a backup planned. Why didn't I think of that?

I keep getting ready for a rehearsal dinner that probably won't happen. I blow-dry my hair and change into my dress, a navy fit and flare that falls just past my knees. My simple heels are lined up by the door. I put on a full face of makeup, more than normal, and add a bold red lip color, like that might help.

I pick up my phone to try to call the restaurant again. This time, it goes right to voice mail.

This isn't the end of the world; I can still fix this. There's still a chance. I open my laptop and look up restaurants near me. We're getting catering from the French place tomorrow, so we can't have that two days in a row. There's a highly rated place near the book-store . . . that just serves breakfast; never mind. How far is too far? Is it okay if we drive an hour and a half for this?

"Lissy, we're headed out! You ready?" Mom yells.

No, no, this isn't happening. I open the bedroom door.

"I haven't found us a new place yet," I say.

She's standing by the door to her room, right down the hall, wearing jeans and a *Star Wars* T-shirt. She's got to be kidding me with this.

"Matty's already grabbing seats at the burger place; what are you talking about? We discussed this already."

"I vetoed that idea."

"Lissy, that's not how this works. It's *my* wedding."

Oh, now she's going to act like she cares.

"Your wedding? You barely seem to care. Where were you when the seating chart had to be made or the wedding favors organized, huh?"

"I never asked you to do that. You know I didn't."

"You didn't have to," I say. "It had to get done. I would've been doing it anyway."

She sighs. "All of this, it's just not me. It's not either of us. Eric thought getting away would be good for you, but honestly, I would've been happy going to the courthouse to sign papers and be done with it. Don't get me wrong, I'm glad that we get to share this special moment with our family, but we never needed the fancy party."

Fancy party? I can't believe she's saying this now. It feels like she lied to me, like she betrayed me. "So this was just a ruse to get me away."

"Lissy, it's not like that."

"Really, because you basically just said it is."

She folds her arms. "Yeah, and all of this doesn't have anything to do with that secret internship you're trying to get," she says. "I didn't want this to become another stressful thing; I told Eric that. This vacation was supposed to be bonding time for all of us. But

I'm pretty sure I'd remember asking for, what? Mismatched china and assigned seating? Blah."

Did she just say "blah" to my vintage chic plate settings and seating chart? It feels like she slammed a door on my head.

"Eric wants a traditional wedding," I say, like this will make a difference. "He told me."

"No, he doesn't, Lissy. He just wants what's best for our family. Neither of us need anything flashy, you know that."

It's her nonchalance that pushes me over the edge. Her ridiculous outfit, her calm tone. It feels intentional. She's trying to mess with me, trying to make me angry, trying to invalidate everything I worked on this summer.

Fine, I can be nonchalant too. "Go without me," I say. "I can't deal with you right now." I'm too furious. I want to punch something, like a pillow or the wall. I want to run outside and scream as loud as I can. I want to rewind time and send a hot water tank repair person to Villa Osteria so none of this is even a problem.

"Felicity," she says my name sharply.

"What? It's not like you even want me there. It's not like you care."

"That's not true," she says.

I feel this tension, like we're building up to something. We should scream at each other, throw things, cause a scene so huge that Aunt Gwendoline comes over to make sure we're okay. I want everything to explode.

Which is why it's so much worse when Mom says, "You know what, fine. I'm leaving." She turns her back on me and walks up the stairs.

I don't move. I hear her say something to Eric upstairs. There are too many voices; maybe Roo's up there with them. They're all using hushed tones. They must be talking about me. *Jerks*.

Then the door opens and closes and there's the muffled sound of the car pulling away.

I'm alone. This is exactly what I wanted.

This is the worst thing that could possibly happen.

I have to get out; I need fresh air.

I'm not sure how I end up in the middle of the orchard, but it feels fitting to aimlessly walk along the tree-lined paths.

They left me. I told them to go ahead without me, and they did. I'm missing my mom's rehearsal dinner. I'm a failure as a wedding planner and a daughter.

I run through a list in my head of everything I've destroyed. There's my friendship with Nancy, good job there. Everything with Roo is probably my fault as well; I wasn't exactly welcoming with the whole "hi, here's my boyfriend" thing, though I'm not sure I can be blamed when said boyfriend is my mortal enemy. Now, to really top it off, I've destroyed my relationship with my mom and Eric forever by skipping out on their milkshake-filled rehearsal dinner.

I wish I could make matzo toffee right now.

I think about that "blah." Mom's lying. She's just saying that because she's nervous; it's the day before her wedding. Brides are supposed to be nervous. She doesn't mean it.

Of course she means it; I've gone overboard. This is the Felicity Show all over again. I took over and didn't think about what she actually wanted. I only cared about making it look good so I could get the internship at Hartman and Co. I'm a selfish monster who just ruined one of the most important days of my mom's life.

I ruin everything. I always ruin everything.

The thing is, deep down, I thought she cared. I thought she was incapable of putting any of this together herself, but that, in the end, she'd be so grateful to have the whole experience. I was giving her something everyone wants.

Everyone except my mom, apparently.

Should I have seen it sooner? She was so disinterested in the wedding tasks, but I thought that was just Mom being Mom. She's always like that when she's on deadline. Of course she'd rather have a family movie night than talk about her reception; it's who she is. And Eric seemed supportive of my ideas, but Eric is always supportive.

I go through all these small moments in my head, like when she backed out of the Boston trip only to find a blue cocktail dress at a thrift store. I should've known then that I was making a mess of things. I mean, mismatched china for the two of them? It seems ridiculous now.

I want to be furious. She should have told me all of this before we got here; she should have been up front about what she expected. Except the thing is, I'm not even angry; I'm just tired.

Maybe it's more than that. I feel *defeated*.

I keep walking, not really intending to go anywhere. My arguments with Nancy, Roo, and Mom run through my head. *All your fault*, I tell myself.

I end up in front of the workshop again. I never finished decorating the chuppah. This, at least, is something I know my mom wants. Maybe if I make it perfect, I can fix something between us. A sign that I really do listen, a sign that I care.

I open the door and walk in.

The chuppah looks too big for the cluttered space. I haven't moved the armchairs yet, so they're stacked up by the side wall, next to a display of tools. I wonder what Nancy's mom would think if she saw her workshop now.

I was trying to intertwine the lights and the flowers along the front three beams when Roo showed up. I've already finished one of the supporting sides, so this won't be too hard.

The ladder is right where I left it. I climb on and search for the end of the strand, safely tucked in along the flowers. The wiring is green; I bought that kind so it would blend in with the floral arrangement once I'm finished, except now it's making it hard to find. I push aside one of the flowers, and it falls to the floor. *Oof.*

I step off the ladder to retrieve the fallen flower, bending down to look for it. It's a white peony, so it shouldn't be too hard to find against the dark wooden flooring.

I spot the small white petals directly underneath the ladder. I reach over and pick it up.

"There we go," I mutter to myself, like I've accomplished something very important with my flower retrieval. Then I straighten my back and, in the process, knock over the ladder.

The ladder goes crashing into the chuppah with a loud clatter, and everything topples down.

I jump back, even though it fell away from me. *Oh, no.*

The sight in front of me looks like a tornado came through the converted store. Two of the beams broke off the chuppah, and the majority of the flowers are now crushed underneath the weight of the wood and the ladder.

No, no, no.

Something inside me snaps. I sink to the floor, my fingers reaching out to touch one of the smushed peonies. I start to sob, the kind of cries that rattle my body. I'm shaking. This is unfixable, and I'm shaking and my makeup is probably ruined.

I destroyed the one thing my mom asked for. There is no fixing this one.

THE NIGHT BEFORE THE WEDDING

I'm not sure how long I'm there on the floor, absolutely bawling, before someone comes running in.

"Is everything okay?" Brody asks in a rush. "I heard this loud sound and—oh, that's not good."

I'm too worn out to even care that it's freaking Brody Wells here. "No, it's not," I say.

"Was that the wedding arch?"

I stand up, brushing the dust off my knees. There's no way I look presentable; my face has to be splotchy red. I wipe under my eyes like that'll help.

"Chuppah," I correct.

Brody nods. I wonder if he knows the difference.

He walks over and examines the wreckage.

"Why are you here?" I ask. I'm not even sure what I mean. Why is he here right now, when everyone else is leisurely enjoying milkshakes? Why did he show up to the wedding in the first place?

He answers the former. "I told Roo to go ahead with your mom. I was taking too long getting ready."

I notice that he's wearing a button-down shirt. I've never seen him in anything so formal.

"I heard the crash and got worried," he adds. "Are you okay?"

I nod. "Physically, sure."

"Yeah, this is a mess, huh?" He picks up one of the broken beams. "Fixable, though."

I laugh. "How?"

He points to the wall behind him. "I think those could help."

Like I know how to use power tools. "Oh, I don't know how . . . ," I start.

"I *excelled* at workshop. Took it last semester. I got ya."

Did Brody Wells just say, "I got ya"? To me?

"What about the flowers?" I ask. "I don't think enough can be salvaged."

He scrunches up his face like he's thinking about it. "Wait . . . I think we can." He takes out his phone and starts typing. "Yeah, there's a grocery store nearby that's still open; we can go there. Let's do that first; it closes soon. Come on, I'll drive." He heads out of the workshop without another word.

I'm too stunned to protest. It's not like I've got a better idea anyway.

I follow Brody Wells to his car. I guess I'm getting grocery store flowers in the middle of Vermont with my after-school-club enemy. My life has already descended into chaos, might as well go for the full surreal experience.

⸻

Brody Wells has a lot of opinions about flowers. Far more than I ever would have expected from someone who carries a lacrosse stick around school like he might need it in the middle of science class.

"The dahlias in this arrangement would complement the white peonies. I think we can save some of those. How do we feel about roses though? Too cliché or just the right amount?"

"Um." I touch one of the stems on the nearest bouquets. "I like roses."

"We can go classic," he says, picking up a prearranged vase in front of him and putting it in our cart. He moves on to the next arrangement.

I wonder what other people in the store think of us, two over-dressed teenagers carefully looking over the floral department. Brody in his button-up and pressed slacks, me in my navy dress. We've looped the small section at least three times already, weighing our options. I tried subtly touching up my makeup in the car, but I don't think it worked. Fluorescent supermarket lighting probably isn't helping the matter.

"So," he continues, "what's the vibe of this wedding? What does your mom want?"

Isn't that the whole problem . . .

"Apparently she wants a completely different wedding than the one she's getting," I say.

"How'd that happen?" he asks. There's no judgment in his voice; he seems genuinely curious. He picks up a bouquet of white and blush roses, gathered together at the end by a pale green rubber band and wrapped in cellophane. He adds them to the collection in our cart.

I sigh. "She didn't say anything sooner. Or I wasn't listening. Not really sure which one." I pause. "I kind of took charge of the whole thing," I explain. "My grandma invited someone who could get me an internship at an event planning company, and I thought everything had to be perfect. And then tonight my mom was like, 'I would've been fine with going to a courthouse, who needs a fancy party, vintage china place settings are terrible, blah-blah-blah.'"

I can't believe I'm confiding in Brody Wells.

"That sucks," he says.

"It very much does," I agree. "The worst part is, I feel like it's too late to do anything about it. I mean, a bunch of the stuff is already booked and set up. The wedding is *tomorrow*. I just don't see a way to give her what she wants."

Brody stops pushing the shopping cart around the floral arrangements. "Idea alert," he announces. "We're in a grocery store."

"Thank you for telling me our location," I say. "Problem solved."

"No, come on, Felicity," Brody says. "We're in a *grocery store*. I'm sure they have some party supplies. You know, for like birthdays and stuff."

"So?"

"The problem is that things are too fancy, right?" He waves a hand at our surroundings. "I don't think we'll have a problem finding regular stuff here."

I look around. This place looks like any other grocery store I've ever been in: boring and standard. I doubt we'd find a single vintage china place setting or a shabby chic hanging lantern in one of these aisles. This might just work.

If I agree to this, I'm essentially sabotaging any chance at getting the Hartman and Co. internship. There's no way the senior director for a city-based event planning company would approve of buying supplies from a grocery store. I wonder if it'll disappoint the other guests too, like Eric's family or Mom's friends from college.

Still, it feels like the right move.

"Let's find the party aisle," I say.

Brody steers the cart, stopping to peer down each aisle as we go. "Oh, over here," he says. "They have streamers!"

We start throwing supplies into the cart, careful not to squash any of the flowers. First the streamers, two each in white and green and three in gold, then some paper cups with a faux firework design on them.

"How does your mom feel about superheroes?" Brody asks, holding up a stack of paper plates that I'm pretty sure is meant for a kid's birthday party.

"Loves them, actually," I say. "She's a writer. She's currently working on the novelization of a movie that may or may not star three out of five of those characters. But if my mom asks, I didn't say anything. She's all hush-hush about it."

Brody lets out a whistle. "Dude, that's awesome. Your mom is like super cool."

The way he says it reminds me of how Nancy reacted when she found out Mom created the *Sleepy Dog* game. I pick up another stack of plates. "Yeah, I guess she is."

We clear out as much as we can from the party supplies section. Then I remember Mom saying she'd be happy with an ice cream cake, so we grab one of those from the freezer aisle. As we're walking toward the register, Brody excitedly announces that there's a seasonal aisle and steers the cart down it.

"What about yard games?" he asks. His tone sounds giddy, like he just found out we could invite unicorns to the reception.

At this point, why not? "Add them to the cart," I say. "Actually, we have a mini golf course we could use. Do you think that would work?"

He nods as though I just asked if air was good for breathing.

We finish shopping just as the store starts to close. I can tell they want us out since the employees have already started turning off lights. The entire back of the store is dark.

We load everything into the back of Brody's SUV. It has a big trunk that opens up into the back seat. He moves a booster seat out of the way so I can put down the vase of flowers. "My sister's," he explains. "I do school drop-off. The elementary school starts before us."

I didn't even know he had a little sister. I guess I don't know a lot about Brody, period.

We get back into the car, and he starts driving. "All right, what do we have to do tonight, and what should we do tomorrow?" he asks. "'Cause I was thinking if we stay up, we could probably—"

I cut him off. "Why are you being so nice to me?" I ask. "You don't have to be."

He turns his head quickly to look at me, then back to the road. "Cool, I'll be real mean then," he jokes.

"It's just . . . okay, if our circumstances were swapped, I probably wouldn't help you. I'm kind of awful."

"What are you talking about? You're like one of the most supportive people I know," he says. "Like with the Social Friends Committee. You're always helping people out and asking what you can do. I don't think there's a single event that you haven't volunteered for; it's impressive."

That's a nice way of saying that I try to take control of everything, but sure.

"I swear, I'm a bad person," I continue. "I'm sure Roo's told you. He barely likes me anymore."

"Roo's been going through it this summer. Not my place to say anything, you know, but you should talk to him. He for sure misses you." Brody drums a finger on his steering wheel. "He talks about you a lot. You're in the *majority* of his stories. I couldn't believe he wanted me to come here for this at first; you're his person. I felt like I was being invited to a celebrity party or something."

I laugh. "Hardly. I mean this wedding is going to have superhero paper plates. I don't think a celebrity would abide by that."

"You know what I mean," he says.

We're quiet for a moment. I listen to the sounds of the car, the steady *shhh* of the air conditioner and the hum of other vehicles passing by.

I glance over at Brody, who is intently looking at the road. He seems different, nicer. Maybe he's been that way all along.

It's not exactly a great feeling—realizing the full extent of how I treated Brody. In my head, I had seen him as something flat. He's a jock, which obviously meant he was mean and entitled. He joked around, which proved he didn't take anything seriously. There was no way he might care about the same things I did. He would just ride that entitlement train in the sort of lazy way all athletes did, where they'd work hard on their sport and then just have everything else handed to them.

What am I, a filmmaker in the nineties? I should have known better than to turn him into an uninspired stereotype. Because here is this person next to me who would drop everything to help their boyfriend's jerk bestie, if that's what I even still am. Who has a little sister he brings to school and firm decorating opinions and knows how to rebuild a chuppah. A person—full and flawed and real.

Was I doing the same thing to Roo—jumping to assumptions and viewing him through a blatantly false lens? Maybe. I'm supposed to be the one person who knows him all the way, right to his core, but I didn't even know he had his first boyfriend. If I can't be trusted with things at the surface, what does that mean about us? About me?

"I'm sorry," I say. "I think I've been a jerk to you."

"You have?" He sounds surprised by this.

"There's a slight possibility I was jealous that you got the Junior Committee President position," I admit. "Basically miniscule. Don't ask Roo."

"You wanted that?" Brody does that thing again where he looks at me really quickly before he seems to remember he's driving, and he shouldn't do that.

"I super did," I confirm.

"Man, I had no idea." He pauses. "If it helps, you were never a jerk to my face."

"I said some really nasty things in private though, full disclosure."

He lets out a little snort. "You're funny; I like you."

"I guess you're not so bad either," I say. "I haven't decided if you're worthy of Roo though. Best friend code. I can't make a call on that too soon."

"Perfectly understandable," he says. "It would be a shame if you broke the code."

We fall into a comfortable silence.

I imagine next year playing out in a totally different way, with the two of us working together on the Social Friends Committee. I wonder if I should share my Pinterest board for the Halloween Haunted Hallway with him . . . He'd probably like that.

Weird. I guess I don't hate Brody Wells.

PAST MIDNIGHT, SO TECHNICALLY
THE WEDDING DAY

Roo's already in pajamas by the time Brody and I finish fixing the chuppah. It turns out Brody Wells really is good with power tools, though I think his real talent is flower placement. There's no way the chuppah would look as good as it does now without him.

We find Roo sitting at the kitchen island in the barn-cottage. He gives us a look like he's an exhausted parent whose kids just broke curfew and he had to stay up much later than he wanted to just to scold them.

"There you two are," Roo says. "Together?"

"I won over the best friend," Brody says proudly. "Through charm and brilliance."

"He helped me solve a crisis," I explain. "Long story."

Judging from Roo's quizzical expression, this doesn't clear up anything.

"I gotta go shower; I'm like *coated* in sawdust and pollen," Brody says. He gives Roo a quick kiss.

Before he leaves, he turns to me and whispers, "Talk, trust me."

"I will," I say, matching his volume. Then I add a bit louder, "Clean up, Wells. You're a walking allergen."

He smirks and leaves the room.

Which means Roo and I are alone in the living room. I don't even know where to start.

"So, um . . . ," I try. "Brody Wells, huh?"

"He's hot, right?"

"Gross," I say. "You know my brain doesn't work that way. Though I will admit from a purely aesthetic viewpoint, he's not awful-looking. And in a surprising twist, his personality isn't trash either."

"I think that might only be a surprise to you," he says.

I shrug. "Seems likely." Then I realize something. "Wait, are you two sharing a room? There's only one spare here."

"I'm bunking with you," Roo says. "Your mom was weirdly insistent about it. She legit called herself a 'responsible adult.'"

"First time for everything," I say.

I take a moment, trying to figure out what to say next. How do I go about fixing all the things I've broken between us? He wasn't even comfortable telling me this big thing about his life. "Tell me about Brody," I say. "Start from the beginning. Full details. I want to feel like I'm living through it all."

He rolls his eyes. "You don't have to prove anything," he says. "I was hiding things from you. It's okay if you're angry; I can admit *some* fault."

"I don't know, I kinda steamrolled," I say.

He takes a moment like he's mulling over my past pushy behavior. "True."

I nudge his arm. "So, we're both sucky friends?"

He shrugs. "At least we're compatible."

There's a beat before I reach over and give him a hug. "I missed this," I say.

"Making fun of each other?" he asks. "Or calling each other sucky?"

I nuzzle into his shoulder. He's the perfect amount of tall for me to rest my head against the crook of his neck. "Yeah, all of it."

I pull away. "Want me to make you anything? I don't know, tea? Lemonade?"

"Actually, there *is* something I'd like." He puts up a finger as if to signal that he'll be right back and heads down the stairs. He's barely gone a minute before I hear his footsteps coming up the steps. I look over and see that he's holding out a box in front of him.

Rupert Basra, my absolute hero, brought me matzo.

"Shut up," I say. "You didn't."

"It appears I did." He walks over into the kitchen and places the box on the counter.

I follow him over. "Matzo toffee, it is."

He tells me all about his relationship as I make the toffee. How he started dating Brody early in the summer. They'd already been friendly since they're teammates, but something changed hanging out at the store. Then that turned into spending time together after their shifts were over, which quickly became making out.

"I didn't even realize he's gay," I note as I take out the matzo and place it on the baking tray.

"Just because you're the *b* and the *a*, doesn't mean you can automatically detect the *g*," he says.

I raise an eyebrow.

"You know, in LGBTQIA," he clarifies.

"Wow," I say. "A big fail there." I lean over and check the toffee mixture boiling on the stovetop. "I meant he was never at a Queer Club meeting or anything."

He keeps going, telling me about everything that happened after they started dating. How fun work became anytime they shared a shift, their cute little outings. Apparently, they even went on a drive-in theater double date with these other boys from one of the neighboring teams who've been dating for like a year.

Roo sounds so happy.

When he gets to the part about his parents, he's less enthusiastic. "They've known I'm gay forever," he says. "But I feel like they weren't prepared to actually see me date. Dad isn't as bad. Mom started crying at the table over dinner when I brought Brody over, so there's that. Like thank goodness Amira's home, you know?"

"Ugh, I'm sorry," I say. I add in the butter and milk to the sugar mixture.

"I don't know," he continues. "It's a little better now. There were just parts of the summer where it wasn't great, and I guess I needed you, but I didn't even know what to say. I mean, you had other stuff going on and you made it pretty clear how you feel about my boyfriend."

"I've already admitted he's not terrible; don't make me say it again." I pour the toffee mixture over the matzo and put the tray in the oven. I turn to look at Roo. "I'm here, okay."

He nods. "So, am I going to hear anything about Nancy? Or perhaps find out why my boyfriend is covered in . . . what did he say? Pollen and sawdust?"

I set the timer, then grab a bag of chocolate chips from the pantry. "There's also a fight in there with my mom. It's a whole thing."

I tell him about my freak-out over Nancy's confession and her dinner talk. Then I move on to the fight with my mom and her

whole thing about not wanting a fancy wedding before ending with a dramatic retelling of my destruction of the chuppah and Brody's heroic save-the-day actions. By the time I'm done, I've already gotten the chocolate spread on top of the toffee and I pop it back in the oven one more time.

"So, wait, what does this mean for the wedding?" Roo asks.

"I'll probably stay up downgrading everything from elegant vintage chic to backyard family party," I say.

"No, we will downgrade the wedding. *Together*," a now-clean Brody says, walking over to join us.

"You really don't have to," I say. "Brody, you've done more than enough to help."

He waves this off. "Dude, this is going to be so much fun. It'll be like setting up the Arbor Day Dance all over again!"

"Yippee," Roo adds dryly. "But, like, yes, obviously we're going to help."

The oven beeps, signaling that the matzo toffee is ready for its sit-in-the-fridge-and-solidify phase. I pick up the red-and-white-striped oven mitt from the counter so I don't burn myself and take the tray out of the oven. Once they're chilling, I say, "Well, those have to cool. Might as well get to work."

"I call putting up the streamers!" Brody yells, as though this is a highly coveted task.

Roo makes a face like he's not sure what he's gotten into.

"Come on," I tell my best friend. "We left everything in the workshop."

I put out my arm like I'm ready to escort him to a ball. He takes it.

As we walk into the night to dismantle everything I worked so hard to put together this summer, I feel content. I have Roo and, in a surprise twist, Brody Wells. It's in no way what I pictured I'd be doing the night before my mom's wedding, but I don't know . . . I think it'll be fun.

THE MORNING OF

I cooked up a scheme for this morning, but because I am not good at literal cooking, I called in the expert to help.

Eric shows up at the door holding the groceries I asked him to get. He has a quizzical look on his face. "So are you going to tell me what's going on now, or . . . ?"

There's a chance I was vague earlier, but I had a good reason. I want this to be a surprise for him too.

"We're making breakfast. That's all I'm at liberty to say."

He smirks. "Well, let's get to it then."

We fall into a comfortable routine. Admittedly, Eric is doing most of the work, but I'm good at following directions.

We're working mostly in silence when Eric says, "Whatever this is about, I'm proud of you, kiddo. For all of this. I know you've been working hard."

I smile. There's something so comforting about the way Eric says it, like he knows exactly what I need to hear. I don't know if I'm proud of everything I did this summer, but I *am* proud of what I accomplished last night.

"How are you already so good at this?" I ask. "Being a dad," I clarify.

Should I have called him that? Would he prefer it if I say step-dad? Or should I just keep referring to him as Eric? Maybe I'll simply call him Mom's husband or That Guy Who Lives in the House and Married My Mother. Really rolls off the tongue.

He doesn't seem to mind the fact that I used the d-a-d word.

"The hard way: I was thrown into it." He doesn't look up from his current task chopping strawberries.

I think maybe he'll leave it at that, but he continues, "About seven years ago, my oldest sister got sick. It wasn't looking good for a while, treatment was rough, and there were all these appointments. I moved in to help out with the kids.

"I thought it was going to be a disaster. Maybe it was sometimes. I was in a relationship before, and it just didn't last when my nieces got involved. My ex, she never really understood kids.

"With my nieces, my whole life changed. It was like living in one of those old black-and-white movies, and then suddenly there was color."

Hearing this, I feel like I should have asked him sooner. I always kind of assumed he was born with all his sitcom dad tendencies, like he left the womb with wisdom and a sweater-vest. I knew he was close with his nieces, but I didn't realize he used to live with them. Maybe I just wasn't paying attention.

I'm about to say something about it when he adds, "Feels that way with you too." He glances up from the strawberries to give me one of those serious dad looks.

"Stop it, you'll give me a complex," I say.

He smirks. "Eh, well, after today, we're stuck with each other, complex or not."

Being stuck with Eric in the family doesn't seem like a problem at all.

———⚌ ———— ⚌———

I jump onto my mom's bed before her alarm goes off. She's spread out across the mattress like it's a challenge to see how much space she can take up. Poor Eric. He must be happy that he spent the night with his family if she's always like this.

"Happy wedding day!" I cheer.

She grumbles and pulls a pillow over her head.

"Rise and shine!" I continue, pushing away the pillow. "I will turn to tickling if I have to," I add as a warning.

She slowly sits up in bed. "Hm, we're talking again?" she asks sleepily.

"I could yell if you'd like," I offer. "The bride gets what she wants."

She cuddles up to me. "The bride wants to say that she's sorry."

"The daughter of the bride admits that there's a marginal chance she was at fault too," I say. "I should've listened to what you really wanted."

"Yeah, you should have," she says lightly. "No, I'm the mom; I should've said something. I was just so happy that you were . . . well, happy." She looks down at me and brushes a strand of hair off my face. It's one of those small moments I hope never ends.

"This has never been about me and Eric," she continues. "I never saw it that way. I saw it as something for all of us so we could come together as a new family. I thought this summer would be the perfect chance to do that. But then you were all stressed about the wedding stuff, and it all kind of got out of hand. So, yeah. I should've said something. I've never wanted anything traditional."

That used to be something that really bothered me. She was supposed to be traditional. There was something deeply wrong with her because she didn't follow the rules.

Except, are there really rules for any of this? I've watched enough wedding reality shows that I can list at least three different ways to arrange the order of events for a wedding, not even touching on the themes or venues or sizes of wedding parties. The list goes on. People have to make all different kinds of choices as it is. Who's to say that one way is better than another?

Really, who says there's one way to plan your wedding or have a family or live your life? Because even if my childhood was unconventional, it was filled with so much love. Still is, really. And what's so wrong with that?

"Get dressed, I have a surprise," I tell her.

She perks up. "A pony?"

"No," I say.

"Are you finally letting me get a dog?"

"You know I'd be the one taking care of it," I answer. "And, no, get dressed. It's a visual thing."

She climbs out of bed. "This better be good; I was going to sleep for another full seven minutes. Your surprise has to be seven-minutes-of-sleep good."

"It is," I promise.

Mom reaches over and grabs her robe, but I shake my head. "Real clothes," I say.

"A visual that requires real clothes? I don't know about this."
Still, she heads over to the closet.

"Oh, I forgot to tell you," Mom says, riffling through her options. "You missed quite the showdown yesterday." She pulls out a pair of shorts and a T-shirt. The outfit looks remarkably similar to her pajamas. "Your bubbe and I came to blows. Again."

Well, that's both surprising and extraordinarily typical. "In front of everyone?" I ask.

"Oh, come on. You know she wouldn't make a scene in public. She insisted I drive her back to her bed-and-breakfast so she could properly berate me for all the ways I've wronged her in the privacy of the car." Mom changes her shirt in front of me.

"What did you do this time?" I ask.

"I asked her to walk me down the aisle alone," Mom explains.

I cock my head, confused. "What about Zayde?"

"He's tied up with work. He's going to try to make it for the reception," she says like this isn't a big deal. "Honestly, I'm not even mad at him; he's always been like this. Bit mad at her, though."

"So she said no," I surmise.

"'Hannah, it's the parents of the bride's job. We'll do it together. There's a way this is supposed to be done.'" She does a really terrible Bubbe impression. "She said no," Mom confirms in her normal voice. "Sometimes I just wish the two of them would sort out their own problems. You know, you're lucky you have me," Mom continues. "Not as rigid."

I look over her graphic tee and shorts combo as she pulls her navy blue hair up into a messy bun. "Uh-huh."

She sticks out her tongue.

I guess she's right about Bubbe and Zayde. All Bubbe talks about are traditions, but it's not like her own life is that cookie-cutter. I mean, her husband isn't going to make it to their only child's wedding, and she didn't even know?

"I could do it," I offer. "Walk you down the aisle, I mean. If that's something you want."

Mom comes over to me, now fully dressed. "Child of mine, that's all I ever wanted." She kisses the top of my head.

The thing is, I think it's exactly what I want too.

I never pictured walking her down the aisle. It wasn't a part of my traditional plans. Most brides don't have daughters yet, let alone ones old enough to walk with them at their wedding. But it feels right that it'll be the two of us sharing this special moment. It's been us against the world for so long. I want to be there, to play this important part, as we officially welcome Eric into our family.

"All right, let's go see your visual," she says.

I lead her out toward the ceremony space, stopping at the end of the aisle.

"I couldn't get rid of everything," I explain. "I mean, people need a place to sit and stuff. But I can return the lanterns and some of the fairy lights and the lace. I'll admit I went a little overboard there. And Brody had way too much fun with the streamers, but, um." I look around at our work. Last night was mostly taking things down.

The new space doesn't look drastically different. There's still the mismatched armchairs and an aisle, leading up to the now-fixed chuppah. I guess the biggest thing is that it's simpler, more understated, which lets the space do most of the work. The view is already so beautiful; it didn't need all that clutter.

"The chuppah looks great," she says.

"Yeah? Grocery store flowers," I add, like I'm letting her in on a government secret.

"No way." She walks over to take a closer look. "*You* decorated this with flowers from a grocery store? I thought that would be against one of your moral codes."

"Some rules are meant to be broken," I joke. "They became necessary after an unfortunate smushing incident." Then something hits me. I let out a gasp. "Oh, no, I hope I don't offend the florist when she comes to drop off the bouquets."

"She might report you," she says with mock seriousness.

I roll my eyes. "Come on, there's more," I say. "We did the reception space too."

We head over to the area by the pond. I'm excited to show off the themed paper plates and yard games, but there's something else I think she'll like more.

I look around at the whole setup once Mom and I get there. My mini party committee ditched the too-fancy geometric terrarium centerpieces last night for disposable dinosaur-themed tablecloths. I even recycled the place cards. Getting rid of the seating chart was a rough one.

The most important surprise is Eric, who's waiting for us, standing by one of the tables.

"What are you doing here? I thought Felicity would murder us if we tried to see each other before the ceremony."

"That only counts for when you're all dressed up. I've decided you get a pass for this," I say.

"How kind." She walks over to the table. "Oh, wow, what are those?"

Eric smiles. "Breakfast empanadas. Those ones have a veggie scramble inside, and the ones on this plate are a take on French toast with a sweet cream cheese and mixed berry filling."

"Marry me," Mom says to Eric.

"That's the plan." He grins.

She pulls out a chair and sits down. "You guys did this?"

"It was all Lissy's idea. She called me up last night and begged for groceries. But, yeah, I mean, I did the cooking."

"Hey!" I say, pulling out my own chair. "I helped. I was in charge of sealing the empanadas, which is arguably the hardest task."

Eric chuckles. "She pressed a fork into those edges like a master chef."

We sit down to eat. There's enough food that I can definitely bring leftovers to Roo and Brody, but for now, it's just the three of us.

I think about what Mom said she wanted for this summer, for us to come together as a little family. I'm not sure when it happened, but I *do* think of us that way. Eric is one of us: I expect him to be home, cooking up something creative when I get back from school or knocking on my door to see if I have anything to throw in the laundry, mundane things I always expected a parent should do. I don't even have a problem with his sitcom dad heart-to-hearts.

As we sit there joking around and eating the absurdly delicious food, I get this overwhelming feeling of gratitude. I feel like I wasted so much of the summer running around and keeping busy with all the wedding stuff, when I should have been doing things like this, sitting down to meals or enjoying a movie night, just the three of us.

The summer isn't over, I remind myself. We still have time for more of this.

I watch as my mom creates a complicated ranking system to choose which of the breakfast empanadas she likes best as Eric seems to take the side of whichever one she isn't currently talking about so he can explain the merits of their ingredients.

What dorks.

I can't help but smile. I love this; I love them: *my* wacky, weird unconventional family.

⹀ ⸻ ⹀

I text Nancy after breakfast. If I can talk to Roo and my mom and even Brody Wells, I can definitely talk to her.

Felicity: hey nancy, this is fe

duh i'm texting obviously you know who this is

right well, i hope you can still make it to the wedding because i know i've been weird but like it's at your family's orchard, you're basically obligated to come

not that you have to but you're still invited you know

i hope i see you there

i miss you

THE WEDDING

I knock on the door to my mom's room. Despite my efforts to downgrade some of the more over-the-top wedding aspects, there were some things I couldn't change. It would be rude to cancel stuff last minute when small businesses are involved.

I haven't seen her with her hair and makeup professionally done yet. I don't even know what she told the stylists to do. I had some suggestions planned out, neatly printed, folded up in my wedding notebook, but in light of everything, I thought it would be best for her to choose what she wanted herself.

"Come in," she calls.

I open the door and walk over to her. She's sitting in a chair that we dragged down from the kitchen. The hair stylist and makeup artist must have just left, since we're alone in the room.

Her hair is in a loose chignon with some small crystal pins holding the bun in place. Just over the knot, there's a simple veil secured by a delicate floral clip. Her makeup is natural and understated, with a pop of color from her berry lipstick.

"That's kind of traditional," I say.

"I had to give you something." She looks me up and down like she's just realizing there's something different. "What happened to the prom dress?" she asks.

"Bridesmaid's dress," I correct. "With everything, I felt like it was too formal." I run a hand over my summer dress with its cream-and-rainbow-striped fabric and halter top and flowy skirt. I had my hair done too; it's braided in the back in a way I could never accomplish by myself.

"Save it, you can wear it to—"

"If you say prom . . . ," I cut her off.

"Something else," she finishes quickly.

She's insufferable.

She gets up out of her chair and does a little twirl. "What do you think?"

It's so weird seeing the final look, because my brain wants to hate it. I mean, she's in a blue cocktail dress and she dyed her hair navy. But everything together works, from the veil to her chunky powder blue heels.

"You look like a bride," I say.

"Weird, right?" She walks over to me. "I guess we should find me a spouse then."

"I think I know where we could find one," I say.

We're running a few minutes early, but I don't think it'll be a problem. I quickly text Roo that we're on our way. Another bonus of the simple dress—it has pockets, just the right size for my phone.

So we walk to the wedding. As we make our way to the ceremony space, I picture the whole event playing out the way I originally planned. It would've been pretty, but just not right for my mom. She's never been one to do what people expect.

I can't even picture her in the white dress anymore. She was always meant to wear blue.

We stop right before everyone can see her. I text Roo again, letting him know we're ready.

I hear the music start.

Mom lets out a little laugh. "You didn't," she says.

The music playing is a piano version of the *Star Wars* theme. "It appears I did," I say.

I put out my arm and she takes it.

We begin our way down the aisle created by armchairs. I see Eric waiting under the chuppah. He gives my mom this brilliant look, somehow surprised and delighted, like he can't believe she's here. Like he can't believe this is really happening.

There's someone else standing beside him.

"Did you ask Aunt Gwendoline to officiate?" I ask under my breath.

Aunt Gwendoline is, in fact, standing under the chuppah, right next to Eric. She's wearing a full tuxedo, her arm still in its blue sling.

"There might have been some hard ciders involved in that decision, but yes," Mom whispers back.

Well, I did tell her to find an officiant. If I was still throwing the traditional wedding, I'd be worried, but Aunt Gwendoline will be perfect for *this* wedding. She's as untraditional as they come.

There are a lot of wedding customs that, when you actually think about them, are pretty gross. Like how the bride's father is supposed to give away his daughter and hand her over to her new . . . what? Owner? I mean, I'm super at fault for romanticizing these objectively creepy traditions because they're just roped in with the whole experience, but come on. That one feels like a step too far.

As I walk her down the aisle, I don't think of it as giving her away. She's still my mom; it's not like I'm losing her.

I think about our breakfast this morning, sitting around the table and joking around.

I let go of her arm, and Eric takes her hand.

No, this isn't a loss. It's an addition.

———

I'm on the third hole of our homemade mini golf course when I finally meet Deborah Segal.

"Felicity?" she asks. "I'm Debbie, your grandmother invited me. I thought it was you; you look just like your mother."

I'm not sure that's true. Still, I smile. "Hi, it's so nice to meet you," I say. I mean it, too. Before, when I still thought I had a chance of getting the internship, this would've terrified me. Now she's just some nice woman Bubbe knows from temple. No harm there.

"This is great, by the way," she says, waving her golf club. "I've never seen anything like it before."

"Oh, um. Thanks," I say. "Can't really take all the credit; my friend Nancy designed this."

"Miniature golf at a wedding; I love it," she continues. "This whole thing, it's so much fun. I just lost a round of cornhole. It was exhilarating."

I let out a little laugh. "Thanks," I say.

"Your grandma did tell me you were the one in charge of all this. Very impressive."

Now she has to be joking. "Really?" I ask.

"Oh, definitely," she says. "One of the most important parts of planning any event is knowing what the client wants. I've known your mother since she was little. This is absolutely perfect."

I'm not sure I can hide the surprise from my face.

"Actually," she continues. "Your grandmother says you'd be interested in an internship this fall. After seeing all this, I think you'd be a perfect fit. I'd love to recommend you."

Yep, the surprise is definitely there.

This is everything I thought I wanted. Except now that I know Brody isn't an awful trash human, I'm going to keep working with the Social Friends Committee. Really, he should get credit for what we pulled off last night. With that and my schoolwork and Queer Club and even my minimal golf requirements, I don't know if it's the right time.

"Do you have a summer internship?" I ask. "I'd definitely be interested for next year."

She smiles. "We do. I'll keep you in mind; we'd love to have the genius behind the mini golf wedding on our team."

"Well," I continue. "If you still need an intern for the fall, I know just who you could talk to," I say. "He was the genius behind including cornhole."

"Oh, that seems like someone I want to meet," she says with a grin.

Brody isn't such a terrible person to meet, I think. In fact, he's really good at what he does. Even if his style of planning is nothing like mine.

I try to picture the next year playing out. Brody and I work together on school events like the Haunted Hallway and prom. He goes for the fall internship; I try for the summer one. Maybe I get it; maybe I don't.

Who knows what will actually happen, but I think all that potential is pretty wonderful.

———

I never pictured dancing with Brody Wells at my mom's wedding, but it turns out he's a decent dance partner. Maybe a little too enthusiastic when it comes to Taylor Swift and Whitney Houston, but I can't dock points for passion.

The song changes to something slow and gushy. Very *I'll love you forever* and *you're the only one for me.*

I feel a tap on my shoulder. "Mind if I cut in?"

I look over to see Nancy standing behind me. She looks stunning in her emerald-green jumpsuit.

"Is that . . . you know . . . *her?*" Brody asks in a not-so-subtle whisper.

"Brody Wells, this is Nancy Lim," I say. "Nancy, this is Roo's tactless boyfriend."

"Nice to meet you," she says.

"I have to go, you know, be not here," Brody says. Then he starts *moonwalking* away from us. It's hard to picture Brody as this evil club position stealer when he does things this goofy.

"Huh, he really is tactless," Nancy says, watching him leave. She turns her focus back to me and puts out her hand. "May I have this dance?"

I take a step forward.

I don't know the words to the song, but it's familiar. Something old my mom's probably played before. I like it. I try to pick out some of the lyrics; maybe I'll look it up later.

"So," Nancy starts. "This wedding looks a little different from what we had put together."

"Does it?" I joke, looking around like I'm just realizing the changes.

"And Brody Wells is here," she adds. "Is there a story?"

"Not one that makes me look particularly good," I say. "Highlights involve not listening to what my mom or Eric wanted and unnecessary stress."

"Oh, stop. You pulled it off in the end," she says.

I look around at the reception. Roo and Eric's brother Matty are in the middle of an intense game of cornhole against Eric's parents, while Brody, now off the dance floor, cheers them on. Bubbe is chatting with Eric's oldest niece and Tia, Matty's wife. No one seems miserable . . . I'd even venture to say that a good time is being had by all. Maybe I did pull it off.

"Want to go somewhere to talk?" I ask as the song changes.

It's not like the dance floor is crowded. There's a group of Mom's college friends who are chatting rather than dancing, Mom and Eric are swaying in the corner, and Eric's oldest sister, Francie, is dancing with her partner and their youngest two daughters near the center. It's just that I have so much to say.

"Come on," Nancy says.

We walk along the edge of the pond until we find a spot away from everyone else. We're not entirely removed from the party; I can still hear the music, an upbeat pop song Eric loves, but it's muffled.

We sit there for a moment before either of us talks.

"I'm sorry I shut down," I start. "I shouldn't have pushed you away."

She shakes her head. "Asking for space isn't a crime. I kind of sprang things on you when we were in Boston. I meant it though, when I said no pressure. The dinner thing wasn't about that. There's just been a lot on my mind." She pauses, looking out over the water. "You know, no matter what, you mean a lot to me."

I nod. "You mean a lot to me too. No matter what," I add. "Wait. What was the dinner about? What did you want to tell me?"

She glances over at me from the side of her eyes. "I don't even know why this makes me so nervous," she says. "It was just about applying to schools."

"Yeah, *just* your future. No biggie," I say.

"Well, I mean, everyone has to deal with this. I'm not the only almost-senior who's had to think about college." She takes a breath so deep I expect a yoga teacher to come over and congratulate her accomplishment. "I was probably about as subtle as your dance floor friend back there when we were at Northeastern, but I've been thinking about applying there. Specifically, to their architecture program."

"That's great," I say.

She nods, then does this little head bobble like she's not too sure.

"I always thought I'd stay near home. When I was really little, I was convinced I'd take over the orchard, maybe study business at a local school or something like that so I could help run the place. Part of it was that my parents gave up on Belmont Orchards,

315

so I felt like I couldn't do that too. But I never really stopped to think if it was what I actually wanted. It felt more like an obligation.

"Then I had soccer, and that was supposed to be it. I'd just go wherever I was recruited. Except that got taken off the table." She sighs. "Maybe that's not true anymore. If I threw myself into training, maybe I could still have that. I just don't know if it's what I want anymore.

"Plus, there's the fact that Aunt Gwendoline fell." She pauses. "That just seemed like confirmation to me. I couldn't go away for school; she needs me. Except then we went to Northeastern and the museum and I couldn't stop thinking about it all. Studying on that campus, having guaranteed work experience, maybe even building something like the MFA someday."

She looks directly at me. "It's scary," she says. "Having a new dream."

I can see Nancy becoming a master architect. I can see Nancy doing anything she sets her sights on.

"You should talk to your parents," I say. "I don't think anyone expects you to stay home and reopen the orchard or take care of Aunt Gwendoline. Though I'm not sure she needs taking care of."

"Quite the spirit in that one," Nancy says.

"Yeah, I couldn't believe someone could fit so many dirty jokes into a wedding ceremony. I thought my bubbe was going to faint like three times."

"And who knows; I could apply and not get in."

I make a face at her. "No disparaging talk like that. This is an optimism-only zone."

"Wow, I guess I just got accepted into college. Don't know what people complain about; I didn't even need to fill out an application," she says, playing along.

"You know," I say. "If you get into Northeastern, you won't be all that far from me."

"Is that a good thing?" she asks.

I nod. "I think it is."

"Oh, shoot, before I forget," Nancy says, starting to get up. "I got you something."

I raise an eyebrow. "Not sure that's customary."

She shakes her head. "It was supposed to arrive earlier, but it got delayed so . . ." She gets up. "I'll be right back."

It doesn't take her long to return, now holding a gift bag.

I clap my hands together. "Oh! This feels like my birthday," I say.

"You're ridiculous," she says, handing over the present.

I reach into the bag. Nancy included a serious amount of tissue paper. "You didn't," I say, pulling out the gift. Because there's no way Nancy got me my dream binder. Except, there is the proof right in my hands: a three-ring color-block binder with the words "Planning Perfect" embossed on the front.

"Found someone on Etsy who makes custom binders; it was supposed to arrive before the wedding, but . . ." She trails off. "Maybe you can use it for your next event."

As I stare at that binder, something clicks in my head. The moment is far from romantic; we're just sitting on the dirt, and she handed me stationery, and yet . . . I know. I know exactly how I feel and what I want to do.

"Nancy, I like you too," I blurt out. "*Like* like you. I'm sorry it took me so long to say anything."

"Really?" she asks softly. She looks unsure.

"Totally and completely," I say.

There's no swelling music or fireworks, just the two of us sitting on the ground with the sounds of the party going on in the distance.

I lean forward.

"You sure?" she asks. "I know we've talked about sexuality and our experiences and feelings before, and we can definitely talk more about it, so I just want you to know that I don't have any expectations and there's absolutely no pressure and—"

I cut her off with a kiss.

It's a risk, but it feels right.

It's my first kiss. I'm not sure I feel the way people say I'm supposed to feel, because it isn't like sparks or butterflies. I'm aware of the mechanics of all of it, the way her lip balm is a little slippery and the sounds of our mouths meeting. Not that it feels bad; the overwhelming feeling is comfort. I don't have to worry about doing it wrong and what everything means. Nancy makes me feel comfortable.

It's the best feeling in the world.

"Hey, what are you two doing over there? You're going to miss out on the hora," Roo yells from across the pond.

Nancy and I pull apart.

"We've been summoned," I say, getting up.

"Oh, I've never seen the hora," Nancy says, excited.

"I'll teach you to hava nagila with the best of them," I tell her.

We walk back to the reception hand in hand.

The rest of the night is a blur of dancing and food. I don't think I could have planned anything that happened, like when Zayde showed up after the caterers left, so we decided to order pizza, or the cutthroat round of horseshoes that ended with the bride victorious, or when Eric realized that the "guest book" I told everyone to sign was actually a Red Sox home plate. We stay up too late, and we're too loud.

To me, at least, it's perfect.

ONE HOUR AND TWENTY-TWO MINUTES UNTIL JUNIOR PROM

Nancy finds me flipping through my binder.

"There can't possibly be anything else you need to do," she says, standing in my doorway. "We're leaving soon."

I glance at her over my shoulder. "I didn't think I ordered enough props for the photo booth. I had to check." I point to a printed-out receipt she definitely can't see from where she's standing.

She lets out a small laugh. "Likely story. You're not bringing that with you," she adds.

"I don't know," I say, getting up from my desk chair. I move carefully so I don't wake Briar Rose, Mom's three-year-old dachshund mix we rescued a few months ago. "It matches." I tug at the skirt of my long eucalyptus green dress, the one that I was supposed to wear to Mom's wedding. I guess she was right; it does look great as a prom dress.

"Why am I dating you again?" Nancy asks.

"It's the charm," I say. "And overall demeanor."

She shakes her head. "That doesn't sound right."

There's a yell from downstairs, but I can't make it out.

"Come on," she says. "Brody's getting rowdy. He wants to do group pictures."

It *is* probably rude of me, being up here right now. We're hosting the pre-prom pictures, but it's not exactly a big gathering. It's just me and Nancy, Roo and Brody, and a couple of Brody's friends, Joshua and Gabriel. I mean, and their families.

I'm pretty sure checking on the prop purchases counts as a good enough reason to slip away.

"Brody's always rowdy," I say. "You'll get used to it next year."

It's strange knowing Brody Wells's quirks. Since he's been dating Roo, we've gotten the chance to spend a lot of time together. He even came with us when we went to visit Nancy over spring break. We're going to have a lot more time together next year, now that we've been named Senior Co-Presidents.

I think it'll be a good thing; we work really well together.

"I don't know about spending time with Brody, but I'm definitely looking forward to being close to you," Nancy says.

I smile. This is the first time we've been in the same place since she got accepted to Northeastern. If it wasn't already prom, I'd say we should throw a party.

"I'm looking forward to that too."

There's another yell from downstairs, but this time it's loud enough to hear. "Girls, we need pictures!" It's Eric. He did promise he'd go full dad-paparazzi-mode for this.

I laugh. "Be right down," I yell back.

I close the binder and walk over to Nancy; I've done enough planning. Now all I have left to do is enjoy the experience.

ACKNOWLEDGMENTS

It takes a village to raise a book, as the saying definitely goes. *Planning Perfect* exists because of so many brilliant minds, I'm truly in awe.

Thank you, thank you, thank you to Team Triada, with extra special love to Lauren Spieller, who took this idea from "What if *Under the Tuscan Sun* was gay?" and helped me turn it into an entirely different book. I still don't understand how you can respond to emails so fast, you might just be a superhero. Sending all my love to the Bloomsbury team, your continued support, savvy, and overall kindness is overwhelming in the best way. To my editor, Camille Kellogg, in particular, feeling grateful every day that we get to work together. Thank you to Ariana Abad, Erica Barmash, Donna Mark, Oona Patrick, Laura Phillips, Phoebe Dyer, Beth Eller, Kathleen Morandini, Jennifer Choi, Alona Fryman, Erica Chan, Sarah Shumway, Mary Kate Castellani, Valentina Rice, Nicholas Church, Britt Hopkins, and Daniel O'Connor. And thank you so much to Andi Porretta and Jeanette Levy for this GORGEOUS cover.

To my early readers, thank you a million times over. An extra special shoutout to Courtney, my always and forever first reader.

Thank you to everyone in the book community—from booksellers and librarians to reviewers. I wish you all the coziest reading spots for your hard work.

Thank you to my family and friends, always. If I even tried to list you all out, Mom would inevitably find someone I missed. That said, I made certain promises about thanking Suzy and Lindsay by name, so thank you to my two self-proclaimed biggest fans (though Safta, who informed me she needs a copy for every room at home, and Dad, who stayed up all night to read this once the advance copies arrived, might be fighting for that title). Special thanks to Rebecca and Josh, sorry I "stole" your apple orchard wedding. Boo, Felicity could only dream of pulling off your level of party planning prowess.

And finally to my readers. You can't plan perfect. There are so many unexpected moments of happiness ahead of you. I can't wait for you to be caught off guard by that joy.

ANTI-ACKNOWLEDGMENT

No thanks to Poppy, my mini bernedoodle rescue, who would rather I give her my undivided attention than write. If it were up to her, this book would not exist. Sorry, Popsy. Love you still.